We were all locked in. We were all prisoners. This was...

Officially Noted

7-7-14 Pen marks on
side edge. MKS

PRISON NATION

JENNI MERRITT

Paperback, first edition
December 2011

Merritt, Jenni, 1986-
Prison Nation: a novel/Jenni Merritt
JenniMerritt.blogspot.com

Summary: Freed from the prison Millie 942B was born and raised in, she finds the Nation she believed in to be the very enemy she feared.

ISBN-10: 146792928X
ISBN-13: 978-1467929288

Printed in the USA

For my **M**om, *for teaching me to create*

For my **D**ad, *for teaching me to dream*

"We hold these truths to be self-evident, that all men are created equal, that they are endowed by their Creator with certain unalienable Rights, that among these are Life, Liberty and the pursuit of Happiness."

The Declaration of Independence
July 4, 1776

Part One

1111

My name is Millie 942B.

Next week is my eighteenth birthday. And I dread it with every fiber of my body.

I guess my name might seem pretty strange to someone who doesn't know the world I live in. '942' is the cell number I was born and raised in. 'B' is the floor level of which my little cubicle resides. It is a symbol of my existence. I have no brothers. No sisters. Only a silent father and a state-proclaimed unstable mother. And it is because of them that I am here.

My handwriting darted across the yellowed page. Something about the words I had written seemed strange to me. Something I wanted to hide. Scanning over the writing again, my stomach twisted into a painful knot.

"Millie?"

The voice jarred me from my thoughts. Forcing my eyes to lift from the page, I looked up at the woman sitting across from me. Shadows cut long and harsh across her thin, pale face. My eyes trailed to her lips. They pursed tightly together, small wrinkles spraying out in every direction like an angry sun. With eyes bearing into me, she readjusted the glasses that sat perched on her nose.

"Millie, I asked you if you had finished your journal entry."

"Yes," I replied softly. I couldn't seem to tear my eyes off of her pursed lips.

"Are you going to share today?" she asked, impatience tugging at her voice.

Finally prying my eyes away, I glanced back down at the paper in my hands. The words still yelled at me, seeming to spring off the page in desperation. Something about them needed to be changed. The woman sitting across from me never let me make changes though. Whenever I would try to go back and scribble at something, she would stop me, reminding me that it was her job to correct, not mine.

She had been my psychiatrist since I was a small child. Something about this place that made the people in charge assume that, no matter who you were, you would eventually need help. In all honesty, I couldn't disagree.

I blinked my eyes, forcing my mind to focus. For a moment the name of the woman sitting in front of me became muddy in my memory. I blinked again, searching frantically in my mind until her name finally emerged, as if creeping out from a lost game of hide and seek. Marta Eriks. That was her name.

"Not today, Dr. Eriks."

It felt as if my mind had gone numb. At times a mental fog would envelope me, people who I saw daily disappearing into a thick haze that denied me all my senses. I would disappear into the fog, letting it carry me away from everything I knew. It was lonesome. It was freedom. Then suddenly, the fog would always lift, leaving me alone to recall everything around me in blinding light.

I relished my private release. Yet, at the same time, I feared it. I was not afraid of being alone in the fog. The momentary solitude was usually a sweet release from the world that surrounded me. The fear that gripped me was that someday I would be freed from one of my fogs and find that I was still utterly alone.

This was something I never told Dr. Eriks.

I blinked harder, fighting the fog at the corner of my vision as I forced myself to stay.

"Millie, your eighteenth birthday is just around the corner, isn't it?"

I nodded.

"How do you feel about it?"

I shrugged.

Dr. Eriks sighed, rubbing the bridge of her sharp nose as she let her eyes flutter shut. "Millie, you do realize that they require a recommendation from me before you can be discharged, don't you?"

I looked back down at the paper, now crumpled in my hands. "I know." My voice came out soft, submissive. I rubbed my eyes angrily, chasing away the last remnants of my fog that still fought to cloud my vision.

"Well then, Millie, you need to talk. I need to know that you will be an asset to the Nation."

Dr. Eriks' voice hissed out of her mouth, accusing me of things I could never imagine doing. There were times when I felt the urge to confess to anything, just to get the hiss to disappear. Then deeper, hidden underneath the hated hiss, I could hear the rhythmic strum of something else. Something that made me want to listen. Something that made me want to believe anything she said.

"The Nation needs you, Millie," she continued, the strum intensifying. I felt my mind softening, willing itself to listen to whatever the strum played next. "We need the strong, the good, to keep us going. This," she motioned with her hand, waving it in a loose circle, "this is not how we want our great Nation to be. We want everyone to be free and secure." Dr. Eriks leaned in, her bony elbows resting on her dull brown skirt. "It isn't your fault, Millie."

My eyes shot up to meet hers. "My fault?"

"It isn't your fault that you are here. In Spokane. Who's fault is it, Millie?"

I swallowed the dry lump that had suddenly grown in my throat. "My parents."

"Exactly. They are the criminals. You are not. You want your chance to prove that, don't you?"

I nodded, my throat too dry to allow my voice to break free.

A thin smile spread on Dr. Eriks' lips. "Very good, Millie. You can trust me. You know that right?"

"Of course, Dr. Eriks."

The smile widened, foreign and strange on her usually stern face. Whenever that smile cut across her face, my skin always went cold. Frozen goose bumps would spring up in quick lines along my flesh, a shiver taking me over as they spread. I could feel them beginning their rise on my arms as she watched me a moment longer. I waited. Letting out a sharp breath, Dr. Eriks finally broke her gaze and picked her notebook up from the small table next to her.

The room fell into an almost tangible silence. All I could hear was her pen as she scratched words onto the white pages. She seemed to cut into the paper, writing that I had never been given permission to read filling up the neat lines, permanently.

My stomach tightened. My tongue stuck to the roof of my

mouth and no matter how many times I swallowed, I couldn't chase away the dryness that had taken me over. Closing my eyes, I let my head hang slightly, the knots finally loosening their deathly grip in my stomach. Dr. Eriks' pen ticked like a pendant of a clock, scratching away the seconds as my mind wandered in the near silence.

Scratch. Scratch scratch. Scratch.

The clip of Dr. Eriks' notepad shutting made me jump. I snapped my eyes open, the sleep that had started to tug at my mind quickly chased away. Glancing down at my crumpled paper, I licked my lips. My throat was still too dry. I needed a drink. Squirming in my seat, I kept my head down and waited.

"Well, Millie." My head jerked up as her voice cut through the air once again. "It looks as if our time for today is over." The muscles in my tightened shoulders relaxed at her words. "I believe we made a small bit of progress, don't you?"

I nodded.

"I encourage you to write in your journal tonight. Finish what you started here today. We will talk again at your next meeting." I started to stand, but Dr. Eriks stopped me with a slight clearing of her throat.

She leaned forward, setting her notepad gingerly on the table as she pulled her glasses off her thin nose. Her eyes watched me, crinkling at the corners in thought.

"Millie, upon release – if you do get released – you will be free. Do you want to be free?"

I swallowed against the dry lump in my throat. I managed to nod, my eyes locked once again on her pursed lips. I knew if I spoke, my voice would come out raspy and harsh.

"Then I shouldn't have to remind you, Millie, that if you fail to follow our great Nation's laws once you are set free, you will be sent right back here. No trial, no pleas. And," she added, slipping her glasses back onto her face as she stood, "that would not be a good thing. At all."

Dr. Eriks watched me a moment, then turned and walked towards her desk. Keeping her back to me, she curtly tapped her wristwatch, her nails clicking on its glass face. "You can go now, Millie."

I stood, the ache from sitting for so long throbbing as I stretched my legs. Without another word I hurried out the door, shoving my journal page into the back pocket of my jeans. Dr. Eriks' receptionist didn't even look up as I passed her small desk. She had worked there for years now, and all I knew about her was the nasally drawl of her voice as she ushered me into my appointments.

The hallway echoed slightly as I made my way down it, away from Dr. Eriks. Made mostly of cement, the walls were a light gray, cracking in places from the years of wear and abuse. No color. A door occasionally appeared along its stretch, a black blip with unknown offices hidden behind. My footsteps were the only sound that echoed off the hallway's lonely walls.

I slowed as a couple appeared in front of me. They were meandering slowly down the hall, their hands loosely intertwined. Obviously, they were in no hurry.

I was about to duck around them when something crashed up ahead.

Stopping, I looked down the hall past the couple. We were almost to the entrance of the Commons, but I couldn't see the door. Any view of it was blocked by a mass of bodies, arms swinging and legs kicking as they pummeled into one another. People started shouting, a mix of angry growls and taunting jests. The two fighting inmates dove harder into each other. Spit and blood flew into the air. The blood splattered across the walls, its deep red an angry contrast to the dull gray cement.

I backed up as boots suddenly sounded down the hall behind me. Just as I pressed my back into the cool wall, three guards ran past, their batons already held in their meaty fists. The couple in front of me leaned against the wall a few feet away, watching the fight as they chatted casually with each other, as if nothing was wrong.

My mind raced. A few doorways back was a hallway that would lead around the fight. I could take that.

I took a step back toward the doorway, intent on avoiding the growing mass of cheering onlookers. Just as I started to turn away, something the man in the couple said stopped my feet mid-step. He had said Dr. Eriks' name. The tone of his voice, slightly shaking and tinged with anger, pulled me in. I clenched my eyes shut, his voice still ringing low under the rumbling fight.

Eavesdropping was something you did not do, especially here in the Prison. The secrets your ears might pick up were the kind that could haunt you for the rest of your life. I knew I should walk away, but I couldn't seem to move my feet. Letting out a sigh, I leaned back against the wall, shoving my hands in my pockets and trying to seem invisible as I resigned to my curiosity.

"...just another one of the stupid shrinks." The man grumbled.

Shrink? I had never heard that word used before when talking about another person. It was typically only associated with clothing that no longer fit properly, or gross anatomy. I turned my head ever so slightly toward the couple and held my breath.

"Dr. Eriks is the head psychiatrist here," the woman said, her head leaning back on the wall as she looked up toward the ceiling. "She is the queen of the damned."

The man chuckled. "Yeah well, lucky for me, I don't have to sit through her mind melting sessions anymore. Still..." he stood and stretched, watching the fight for a moment.

The guards had finally pried the two inmates apart, the men still fighting to get back to each other regardless of the guards' strong arms. Blood sprayed across everyone. Bruises, long and growing dark, stretched across the inmates' bodies where the guards had battered them.

The man let out a slow breath, his head shaking slightly. "I don't trust them. All they do is try to brain wash us. Every single session, it's just the same old brainwashing. The same hypnotic voices and indoctrinating crap." The man stared at the dying fight a few seconds longer before lowering his eyes to the ground, his face clouding over in sudden emotion. "I don't trust them," he repeated, his voice now soft and barely audible.

"I don't either," the woman said, her eyes still watching the ceiling above. "None of us do." She lifted a hand and softly stroked the man's arm. His jaw clenched a moment. Then his eyes flicked over to me.

I pretended to watch the fight, the inmates still yelling obscenities at each other as the guards struggled to keep them apart. The crowd that had gathered around the two inmates broke apart, leaving them with just the guards and the blood. I could feel the man's eyes look away from me.

Thinking back to the session I had just had with Dr. Eriks, I let an image of her fill my mind. As her smile flashed across my memory, I felt the same chilling goose bumps as before start to prickle along my arms and down my spine. I shifted my weight, pushing slightly away from the wall in anticipation. I wanted out of that hall.

The guards finally got cuffs on the two inmates and started to drag them down the hall away from us. I could hear the guards threatening the inmates. Their voices were harsh and angry, and loud. One of the inmates limped roughly, the other barely walking as he leaned heavily on the guard that shoved him into the shadows.

The couple watched the bloodied group walk away. Pushing from the wall, the woman pulled the man against her, giving him a small smile as she ran her fingers along his arm.

"Hey, no worries," she purred at him. "Never any worries. Remember?" The man watched her for a moment, then smiled back. Letting out a slow breath between her lips, the woman pulled him beside her as she started a slow walk down the hall. They barely glanced at the blood splattered walls as they passed.

The goose bumps were still thick on my arms, the knots tighter than ever in my stomach. I licked my lips, then carefully stood back up and followed the now disappearing couple.

I had always known there was something more to the goose bumps and dislike of Dr. Eriks' smile that left me so rattled after each session. I had thought it was just me, that I was reading into everything too much. Now I knew better.

Now I knew others felt it too.

There was something about Dr. Eriks that I could not trust.

2

Low voices rumbled ahead of me. Lifting my eyes, I saw three men leaning casually against a wall. Their arms and necks were covered in tattoos, rising above the matching white shirts like snakes trying to find their way out. One of the men saw me and nudged the other two, a crooked smile spreading on his unshaved face.

Lowering my eyes quickly, I scurried past, trying hard to block out their guttural laughter and disgusting remarks. One called out to me, but his words blurred in my mind. I could hear the rumble of laughter erupt again.

The laughter and taunts faded behind me as I rounded a corner and emerged into a room full of people.

The large Commons echoed with voices, bouncing off the high ceiling that always seemed to disappear in the floating dust. I didn't have to look up to know that the fist-dented walls were covered in plain white paper, the rules of the prison listed in solid black words on each flattened poster.

A few inmates grumbled angrily as I pushed my way past their small groups. In the middle of the day the Commons was always packed, leaving me with no other option but to push my way through the groups. I hated having to push, to touch, most of the people surrounding me. But stopping to ask them politely to let you pass usually got an answer you were not looking for. To get through the crowds, to live in Spokane, you had to be tough, even if it was just on the surface.

I placed my hand on someone's back, felt his low laugh as I shoved my way past. Hair pricked out of his worn white shirt and scratch against my palm. Everything about him ranked of musky sweat. Cringing, I scurried away. The man called to me, inviting me to join his group with another low laugh. I didn't even turn to respond, the feel of his scratchy hair still fresh on my sweating palm.

I hated this walk.

Emerging from the crowd, I glanced up to the wall in front of me. A new sign, still clean and smooth, hung carefully taped over a dent in the plastered wall. I moved closer, curiosity leading my feet.

In thick, black typeset, it read:

Spokane Prison

Plans to expand facilities

set for coming year.

Sign up now available

for labor workers.

Ask Warden

"Spokane Prison," a woman's voice huffed next to me.

I turned my head slightly to take in the owner of the voice. A woman, old and bent almost double, stood a few feet away, her eyes still riveted on the sign. Her hands shook slightly as they dangled limply at her side, her white shirt hanging off of her frail looking shoulders like wet laundry.

"I remember when this was a city. Just a city," she said, turning her eyes to me.

I cleared my still dry throat and looked back at the poster. "That was a long time ago," I replied, willing my voice to stay even.

I didn't want the sudden butterflies in my stomach to make themselves known. Though I would casually talk to others when the need arose, I preferred the mostly antisocial life. I had never been in any sort of fight or dispute, and I owed it all to my willingness to not make lasting friends. Or, most times, to even speak.

"Yes, well, if you can't tell, I am pretty old." Her voice cracked as she let out a snicker. "I barely remember that city. Only went there myself once. But it wasn't a bad one. Then they plowed it through and made this... prison." The old woman sighed and slowly shook her head. Her eyes, sunk under wrinkles, turned to look at me. "Are you a convict or a Jail Baby?"

I clenched my jaw at the name. Without answering, I turned my eyes back to the poster. It was hard to believe that Spokane was once a city. I tried to imagine it: skyscrapers touching the clouds, sunshine beating on tourists, sprawling parks full of green grass and laughter. I had seen the photos enough in my lesson books, snapped at their peak of majesty. It shouldn't have been that hard to picture one more city. As hard as I tried, all I could see was the endless gray walls.

The old woman cleared her throat.

"Been here forty years now myself. Ten more and I might finally be allowed that parole hearing of mine. If I am still breathing by then." She lightly chuckled. I could feel her eyes watching me. It took all my control to stay calm, breathing steady with my face slack.

Turning and running off now wouldn't look good.

"Not much of a talker, huh?" She asked, her voice slightly cracking. "Must be a Jail Baby then. We convicts, we're the criminals, the evil-doers. And boy do we know it. No need for us to keep all clammed up and goody-goody. We have already been screwed. Jail-babies are different. Born here and cursed with the unlucky sentence of being stuck with us until you turn eighteen. Unluckiest of all draws if you ask me. Though maybe..." The woman suddenly started to cough. I let my eyes glance over to watch her, her frail shoulders shaking as a thin hand reached up to pound on her nearly flat chest.

My hand twitched at my side. Something made me want to reach out and comfort this old woman. I could feel my fingers lifting, and forced them back down against my leg.

A moment of quiet passed. The old woman licked her lips, her eyes darting to the poster before glancing back to me. They were dull, swimming with a milky white that made me wonder exactly how much of me she actually saw.

"If this prison gets any bigger, there won't be anyone left out there for you to be released to, you know."

I couldn't break my gaze from hers. The milky clouds in her eyes drew me in, my eyes searching hers for any sign of actual sight.

"So?" she asked, her voice low and rough.

I blinked. "So?"

"Convict. Or Jail Baby?"

I looked away, my throat strangely tightening for a second.

"I was born here," I said curtly.

The woman went quiet, her eyes studying me. I felt my stomach tighten. Her eyes had turned sad, her lips twisting down at the corners slightly as she took me in. The moment passed. Shaking her head, the woman glanced at the wall once more.

"Pity. What a pity," she muttered, then limped away. Her left foot dragged slightly along the ground, her hands still hanging limply at her sides.

I stood frozen for a moment, watching the old woman walk into the Commons crowd. My eyes stared at the spot her bent back had disappeared into, my stomach still dancing with the angry butterflies that were desperately trying to break free.

Tearing my eyes away, I turned and ducked into the nearby door. The hallway beyond was long and dim. And empty. I hurried into the corridor, letting the noisy chatter of the Commons disappear behind me. My feet wobbled and my head spun as I tried to regain my bearings on the world around me.

There was no real reason for this uneasy feeling that had taken me over. She had just been a lonely old woman, looking for conversation. I kept repeating that to myself, willing the words to stop the jittery feel that radiated through my entire body.

The hallway opened up into a small enclave, a single metal door waiting on the opposite end of where I stood. A guard stood near the door, his arms crossed lazily over his chest and his face clearly bored. As he saw me approach, he grumbled something under his breath then pushed away from the wall to block my path.

Out of reflex, I lifted my left hand. The small bracelet I had worn my entire life dangled from my wrist, my name inscribed onto its dull metal surface. It was locked on, given just enough room to spin. Sometimes the metal dug into the skin around my bones, scraping it raw. I rarely noticed anymore.

The guard yawned, then pulled a small boxy device from his utility belt. Holding it up to my wrist, he pressed a button and waited. The enclave fell silent. I tried to swallow, but my throat was still dry. A beep finally cut through the air, a small green light flashing on the black box. The guard slid the device back into his belt and pushed open the door behind him. He didn't even glance at me again as he went back to his bored leaning, his eyes slightly drooping shut.

I stepped through and quickly turned to the left, making my way down the narrow, fenced in walkway. People moved about inside their cells, the doors still open for the daytime hours. The occasional shuffle of feet mixed with the low murmur of voices echoed down the stretch of floor B.

Most inmates preferred the Commons during day hours. Some had assigned work, others chose the fenced-in exercise yard. The rest packed inside the Commons, the only social place inside Spokane. Things were different on my floor. Inmates here, on floor B, tended to stay in their cells. Solitude had become the best companion for the convicted.

I had heard the stories, ever since I had started school and my teachers drilled the images into my head, of what these criminals were capable of. We were told of detailed, horrible crimes, the images from the stories frightening us awake at night. A few times I had tried to ask why those born inside, the Jail Babies, were kept in here if the people surrounding us were so dangerous. The teachers always would look at me the same way. Their face would go cold, lacking any sympathy, as if angry at me for even thinking the question. Then they would repeat the same reason: That it was our parents' faults. Their explanation always ended at that. Finally, I had stopped asking.

In their unspoken words, they told me this was something I just had to accept. And so, I had.

The old woman's parting words echoed in my mind. *Pity. What a pity.* I shook my head, chasing the words away, and pushed myself forward.

As I made my way to my cell, I barely had to look up. I had

made this walk my entire life. It was as trained into me as breathing or blinking. The voices of other inmates filled the air around me. I could feel it pulse. Beds rustled, pacing footsteps shuffled back and forth in cells as I passed. Someone called to me. The world seemed to swim around me, the sounds of life growing stronger in my ears until it dulled into an angry roar. I paused only a moment before moving on. I never looked up.

My feet finally stopped. I could see the open doorway out of the corner of my eye, the light of the walkway disappearing into the dimly lit cell within. I let my eyes trail up, locking them onto the number "942" that was painted above the cell door. Without another pause, I ducked inside.

Even though the cell door sat open during the day, allowing any one passing to easily look in, I always felt safe inside. I had been raised in this cell since the day my mother bore me into this condemned life. I knew every inch of it.

The same dull gray walls rose on all four sides, the only change in them being the open cell door on one end and the window on the other. During the day, a haze of sunlight would illuminate the thick plastic window, giving us our only sign it was no longer night. Daytime it glowed, nighttime it was dead black. If we wanted to actually see outside, we had to dare the exercise yard. Something that I rarely did. The yard was run by gangs and sweaty men, and always patrolled by heavily armored officers. It was better to avoid it.

The cell was just large enough for the bunk bed that was screwed against one wall, and the toilet and sink under the window. A small bookshelf that held our dismal stack of folded clothing and worn books was the only other furniture in the room.

This was home.

My mother sat quietly on the bottom bunk. She had cuffed up her jeans to her knees, her pale legs tucked up underneath her. Her white shirt was dirty from the lack of washing, creased and stained in spots as it draped across her thin frame. My eyes trailed down, landing on her shoes that had been kicked carelessly to the ground.

"Mom, you have to line them up," I said with a sigh.

My mother didn't respond. I sighed once more, then bent down and picked up her shoes. I tucked her dirty socks inside, then carefully lined the shoes along the bottom of the bunk. A stale scent of sweat wafted up from the socks. Sniffing, I realized the entire room smelled like dirty socks. The rumpled stack of clothes on the shelf behind me only added to the moldy reek. I noted in my head that I would need to do laundry duty. Again.

"Mom, if the guard comes in and sees your shoes like that, they will put you in solitary again." I looked up at her, my hands still resting on her old shoes.

She didn't return my glance. Her eyes were dancing around, loftily taking in the room around her. "They're just shoes, Mills."

"It's a tripping hazard. And against the rules. If something happened and we tripped and got hurt, they would have to hospitalize us. And that will cost us. Remember?"

"If, if, if. The rules are too strict here."

"It doesn't matter, Mom. They are the rules. The Prison's rules. Always have been. They will throw you in the Hole if you break the rules, just like last time. I don't want them to…" I rubbed my hand down my face. Standing up, I let a slow breath escape through my lips. "Please, just line your shoes up. Okay?"

My head still felt the remains of the fog. The fear of my mother disappearing again into the Hole threatened to bring the fog back in full force. She always came back worse. Blinking angrily, I turned away from her and walked toward the sink.

My mother finally looked up and met my eyes. Her brown eyes glittered. "Okay Mills. Okay." A smile spread on her face. "So, where have you been?"

I cranked on the faucet. Luke warm water drizzled out. Letting it run over my hands, I closed my eyes a moment in exasperation. "My bi-weekly meeting with Dr. Eriks, Mom." I splashed some water on my face, running my wet fingers back through my short hair.

A sheet of metal hung over the sink. It barely reflected anything, showing just enough to let you see a dented, dim reflection of your face. I had heard that they once had real mirrors in the cells. That was, until too many inmates smashed in the shiny glass to use as weapons. Against others. Or against themselves. After too many 'incidences,' the mirrors had been taken out. They were permanently replaced with the barely reflective sheets of metal that hung firmly mounted and screwed to the gray wall. I barely knew what I looked like.

Squinting my eyes, I tried to see the face that stared back at me. In the dim evening light of the cell I could barely make out my short, pale brown hair. It hung close to my chin. I ran my fingers through it again, hating the fact of how quickly they came to the cropped ends. Pursing my lips, I could feel the tight lines spray out across my face. I ran a finger along them, feeling their dips and rises crinkle along my lips. They were nothing compared to Dr. Eriks'.

"You are beautiful, Millie."

Startled out of my mindless staring contest with myself, I turned back to my mother. She still sat on the bed, legs crossed, hands resting on knees. A smile spread on her face as she watched me. Unlike Dr. Eriks' smile, my mother's smile always warmed me. Every time she smiled it was as if she had some secret brimming on her lips, wanting to explode out and be shared with the world.

"My pretty, pretty baby."

"Mom, I am turning eighteen in a week. I am far from a baby

now."

"Oh Millie-Millie, you are my pretty baby." My mother held out her arms, her fingers wiggling as she begged for me to come closer. I could hear her muttering 'pretty baby' over and over softly to herself.

The warm feeling that had just a moment ago flowed over me at the sight of her smile went suddenly cold.

She was lapsing again. My mother's psychiatrist had declared her as 'unstable.' She would be completely lucid one moment, then would suddenly disappear into some distant world of her own the next. I had been told that if we lived out in the Nation, I would have been taken from her long ago, but because we were in Spokane I was 'allowed' to stay in her 'care.'

Most times the lapses seemed to consist of me being a baby again. I used to love these moments, relishing in the deep hugs she would wrap around me. I could never seem to get enough. Until one day I realized the truth. That when these moments happened, she didn't seem to know it was me. She would call me by my name and talk to me, but her eyes were always glazed over by some hidden ghost. I didn't exist. Since then, I never let her hug me when she was 'gone.'

I watched her a moment. Her smile was contagious on her face. It must have been beautiful once. Under the wrinkles of prison-ran life and the dirt smudges that never seemed to wash off, she held a beauty that refused to disappear.

The strange glaze that now covered her eyes tried hard to chase the beauty away. It brought to light the stray hairs that stood on end, the greasy blonde twists that hung in clumps on her shoulders. I saw the shadows under her eyes. The deep gulps she took as she gasped in frenzied breaths and wiggled her fingers, begging to hold her baby.

Without a word, I darted out of the cell.

Choking back a sob, I leaned against the thin slice of wall that separated our door from our neighbor's. I let the weight of my body pull me down until I slid onto the floor. My hands shook as I ran them through my hair, still damp with the water I had just splashed onto my face. After eighteen years of living in the same cell with the same woman, I should have been used to those moments. But I hated them. I hated how I had to be the adult in this crazy, locked up world.

Lifting my chin I looked around. My father. He hadn't been in the cell.

Typically a silent shadow that followed my mother around wherever she went, I rarely even noticed him. He would mumble to me sometimes, asking how my day was and if I had any plans for tomorrow. I tried to answer and start a conversation, but it always failed and left us sitting in silence. What is there to talk about, when every day is the same?

To me, my father was only one thing: a silent reflection of my mother. I wanted to feel a connection to him, but it was impossible to feel connected to someone who barely seemed connected to life.

Looking down the walkway, I strained my eyes to see if I could spot his familiar stooped figure. A few other inmates leaned against the railing or sat on the ground outside their cell. I saw one man reading a tattered book, another man carelessly bouncing a ball over and over again on the ground. A girl walked past me, carrying a handful of papers. As she passed a pencil rolled off the stack and fell with a clatter to the ground.

It rolled and bumped into my foot. I reached out and picked it up, my fingers wrapping around its thin wooden surface. Before I even thought about it, I lifted my eyes to the girl and held the pencil out.

"Th-Thanks," she stuttered.

Squinting my eyes, I looked harder at her. She looked like she was just a year or two younger than me. I knew this girl. Fighting against the persistent fog in my mind, I tried to place her face and stutter. It slowly came to me. She had sat next to me in my classes, before I had opted out into independent study. She had always been mumbling to herself, her stutter causing her to slightly twitch when it got too intense. Her name was... I couldn't remember it.

"942B?" she asked.

"Uh, yeah. How are you?" The words felt thick in my mouth, obviously forced.

"G-Good." She forced a smile, one side of her mouth drooping slightly under a healing bruise. "H-How about you?"

I nodded, pulling my eyes away from the bruise. "Doing alright."

"Sh-shouldn't you have b-been let out b-b-by now?" the fellow Jail Baby asked.

"Next week. I turn eighteen next week."

"Oh. Well. G-Good luck th-then. I hope t-t-to never see you again."

I let a tiny smile spread on my face as I watched her shuffle away down the walk, her shoulder slightly twitching as she mumbled to herself. Her parting words weren't meant to be harsh. Everyone in Spokane hoped to never see each other again. It wasn't a hostile wish. It was the wish that you might never again be locked up inside these walls.

I banged my head softly against the wall, trying hard to remember the girl's name, but it never came to me. I could only remember the bruise on her drooping lip and the twitch of her thin shoulder.

My back started to ache. I must have been sitting for at least an hour. Losing track of time was too easy in a place where every day, every minute, everything was the same. Standing up, I rubbed my back, stretching my other arm up over my head.

The groan that escaped my lips came to a quick halt as I heard something echo down the walk. Footsteps. Heavy footsteps. They weren't the usual padding of worn out sneakers. These echoes were sharp, precise. Timed.

They were the echo of boots.

1 1 1 3

Pushing my back against the wall, I looked up to see two guards making their way slowly down the walk. They glanced into each cell as they passed, occasionally pausing a moment longer to stare inside before moving on.

Inspections.

I silently thanked myself that I had lined up my mother's shoes. Glancing inside, I saw she had fallen asleep on the bed, one hand hanging over the edge, her fingers occasionally twitching as she dreamed. I let myself relax a bit, my back leaning once more against the cool wall.

I had known the older of the two guards for most of my life. Saying that I knew him might have been an overstatement. He had patrolled this walk for as long as I could remember, yet I could never remember his name. Still, just the fact that I easily recognized his casual walk and drawling voice made me feel as if I did know him, in some small, pathetic way. His eyes were always hooded, a yawn always trying to break through on his chubby face. He was never angry or rough like the other guards. He just seemed… indifferent.

My eyes trailed to the second guard. He was new. Tall and lean, his muscular arms and shoulders were evident through his armored uniform. His short cropped hair shone in sandy blonde waves. I could smell his hair gel and the hint of cologne from where I stood. He looked as if he were made for the prison guard uniform. As the old guard waddled along, glancing inside each cell as he passed, the new one walked beside him, looking down the walkway instead.

Looking at me.

His blue eyes locked onto me, watching. As a slow grin spread on his chiseled face, I felt a lump form in my throat. It was never good when a guard noticed you. Noticing you meant that they had something on you. And having something was never good.

My mind reeled, retracing all of my steps. Appointments, exercise yard, laundry, schoolwork. I had done nothing out of the ordinary. I could feel the guard's locked gaze out of the corner of his eyes. Even though he glanced away to take in the rest of the walk, the guard watched me.

"Hello 942B," the chubby guard muttered.

He squeezed past me to lean into my family's cell. I watched as he stared a moment at my sleeping mother, then as his eyes swept down to scan the ground. They paused on the shoes a moment before I heard him let out his usual grunt of approval. He backed out of the cell, rubbing his eyes with his chubby hand.

The new guard gazed into my cell, occasionally letting his eyes flick back to look at me. I shifted my weight to my other foot, glancing at the new guard whenever he looked away.

"Good morning sirs," I said stiffly.

The chubby old guard stifled a yawn, his hooded eyes closing for a moment. Letting them droop back open, he caught me glancing tentatively at the new guard. "This is the new replacement day guard for Floor B," he offered, his voice sleepy.

"Replacement?" I asked quickly, my voice squeaking slightly. Embarrassed, I pursed my lips shut, feeling the Dr. Eriks lines spread out.

"The Nation is finally letting me retire. Got a notice saying that I successfully completed my service and am now allowed to relax." The chubby guard chuckled. "Relax meaning moving onto some desk job," he mumbled under his breath. Stretching his arms in front of him, he added, "It's alright though. I have had about enough of this walk."

"Oh. Okay," I replied softly, my eyes glancing over to the new guard.

He smiled at me, his arms folding across his solid chest as it rose and fell in perfect rhythmic breathing. The chubby guard motioned to the new one. "Carl GF4 gets to have this exciting job now."

"Oh yes, very exciting," the new guard, Carl, replied. He winked at me. I felt a chill go down my spine, but managed to keep my face calm as I looked back at him.

"Well, come on Carl. Gotta finish the line, then I can finally clock out for good." The chubby guard glanced at me. "Be good, 942B." With that, he moved on to the next cell, leaning his chubby frame inside. Carl watched me a moment longer, then silently followed.

Swallowing the lump that was still solid in my tight throat, I ducked back into my cell. I had suddenly remembered the dry thirst that had been growing and stretching through me all day. Cranking on the faucet, I grabbed my old metal cup from the shelf and filled it with the warm water that poured out, then tilted my head back and swallowed a large gulp. The water tasted like metal, stale and too warm to fully quench my thirst. I didn't care. It felt good to fill my stomach with something other than butterflies.

Something stirred behind me. I let my eyes lift to glance into the metal mirror. A dark figure was standing there, the familiar stoop of the shoulders relaxing my nerves. I didn't say anything. Turning away, I tilted the cup to take another mouthful of the metallic water.

"Hi Millie," he said, his voice slow and distant like always.

"Where have you been?" I asked, not bothering to reply to his greeting.

"Huh? Oh. My appointment."

"Your appointment?" I turned, my brow furrowing in confusion. "You didn't have an appointment today. Your appointment is always at the same time as Mom's."

My father sat gently on the edge of the lower bunk, barely squeezing on as he tried to not stir my mother. With a grunt he pulled off his shoes, carefully lining them alongside the bottom of the bunk. "They, uh, they changed it. They want to see us separate now."

For the last eighteen years my parents had been going to all of their appointments together. My mind reeled, wondering why they suddenly were being forced to be seen apart. Then something in my mind clicked. Moving toward my father, I waited until he looked up then locked my eyes onto his.

"It's because of me, isn't it?"

He offered a sleepy grin. "Of course it is, Millie. You are about to turn eighteen. Of course it is." His words faded out. Licking his dry lips, he laid down next to my mother. "They said dinner is in cell again tonight."

I nodded. I had heard that too. "Don't sleep too long then, okay? I don't want you missing dinner again."

"If I do, just have mine, Millie. No use letting it go to waste."

His eyes fluttered shut. I knew the conversation was over.

When I was younger, I would always jump at that offer. I would wait and see if he fell asleep early, then eagerly devour his small share of food. It wasn't until recently that I realized those nights that I ate his offered ration, he didn't eat at all. Once, while chomping down on a stale roll, I caught his eyes fluttering, watching me eat as he pretended to sleep. That had been the last night I let myself eat my father's food.

Letting out a slow breath between my teeth, I pulled the thin blanket over both of my parents. When they slept, they looked so happy and peaceful. My father always draped his arm over my mother, pulling her in protectively against his body, shielding her from any sleep demons that may have tried to snatch her away.

"Why can't you be that protective when you're awake?" I whispered, the words barely passing my lips before they disappeared.

The sound of metal grating across cement echoed in the cell. Turning, I saw the tray with three covered plates waiting in the doorway. Knowing that in a few minutes the inmate who was on food delivery duty would be back for the tray, I snatched the plates up and moved them to balance on top of the sink. I could smell the usual aroma of a tuna sandwich and a cup of some sort of sliced fruit. Variety wasn't something the prison cared much for.

Lifting the lid to one plate, I saw I was right. Apples, browned and wrinkling from the time they had sat in the open air before being delivered to our cell, filled a small bowl. Along with the sandwich and fruit, there was a small carton of milk. That was it. My stomach growled, hungrily reminding me that I hadn't eaten since breakfast.

Carefully stacking my parent's plates under the sink, I grabbed mine and climbed up to the top bunk. The pad was all but flat underneath me. My back already hurt at the idea of having to sleep on it tonight. We were already six months past due for new bedding, with no word about the hopeful change. I didn't even hold my breath anymore.

Picking up half of the sandwich, I tentatively took a bite. There was always too much mayonnaise, leaving the sandwich mushy and wet. Even though I didn't need to, I sat and chewed the mush, letting my eyes close as I leaned my head against the wall.

I felt something crinkle as I settled down. Reaching under my leg, I found the piece of yellow paper from my session, still wadded into a tight ball. It must have fallen out of my pocket when I climbed up. Sitting back again, I took another bite of my sandwich and flattened out the paper.

My name is Millie 942B.
Next week is my eighteenth birthday. And I dread it with every fiber in my body...

Something still nagged at me when I read it. I almost felt ashamed as the words sunk in. Like I should have never written them to begin with.

Shoving the last bite of the sandwich into my mouth, I pulled out my old notebook. Dr. Eriks had given it to me a year ago for my journaling assignments. I could tell it had already been used by someone before me. The cover was ragged. The pages hung limp, dog-eared, the spine giving away how many sheets were already missing. Still, it was mine. Few things in here actually belonged to me, so I couldn't complain about this one used notebook. It was mine.

Pulling my pencil out of the spine, I flipped it open to a new page. As soon as the pencil touched the paper though, my mind froze. I couldn't think of anything to write. For some reason, writing a journal entry about my mushy sandwich or my still unstable mother seemed useless. I had written about it all one too many times.

The face of the new guard, Carl, flashed in front of my eyes. I pushed the pencil against the paper, then stopped myself before the first word could form. My body started to shake. For some reason, I suddenly felt uneasy. The thought of writing my thoughts about him had stopped my pencil dead.

Giving up, I flipped the notebook shut and leaned back against the wall again. I looked over at the browned apples, my mouth twisting into a frown. I had never been a fan of apples. There was something about their texture that just bugged me. Seeing them sliced in the bowl, browning and already bad, didn't entice me to take a bite.

I pushed the tray aside, then swung my legs over the edge of the bunk and slid to the ground. My parents were fast asleep. My father softly snored, his mouth hanging open in his sleep, a thin line of saliva already trickling down his rough cheek. There was no doubt about whether or not he was faking. I quietly crept over and divided my apple slices into each of their bowls. Then I sat back on the ground, the coolness of the cement helping to keep me awake.

Something buzzed, loud and harsh. I barely twitched as the sound cut through the night. I could hear the sudden rush of feet hurrying down the walkway. The inmates were all returning to their cells for the night, the buzz warning them that it was five minutes until the doors shut and locked, leaving those locked out to be sent straight to the Hole.

The footsteps died down. I could hear the murmuring rise of the inmates as they crowded into their cells. The few that still passed were the older ones, unable to move as fast. On floor B, there were a lot of older inmates.

Floor B was the floor of Lifers.

The buzz cut through the air again. I could hear the familiar crank of gears rev up, then the slide of doors as they snapped shut, one after the other down the walk. Our cell's turn finally arrived. The door slid out from the wall, slow at first, then suddenly snapping shut tight as if it had been kicked awake. It was solid, with a small grating along the top and about three inches shy of meeting the ground. Just enough room was left along the bottom for the medicine that was slid in each night.

Right on time, I heard the matching footsteps of the two nurses as they made their way down the walk. They stopped before each cell, asked if everything was alright, then promptly passed along any prescribed medicine. Occasionally, during some nights, you would hear an inmate demand medicine that he wasn't prescribed. Usually a quick 'no' would suffice, but sometimes the inmate wouldn't let up. The quick, heavy footfalls of a guard as he approached the cell would echo down the walk to calm the situation. There had been a few times I had heard the door grate back open, then the demanding would abruptly be silenced. I hated those nights. Tonight, luckily, all was calm.

The nurses stopped in front of my cell.

"942B, is everything alright tonight?"

Not bothering to stand, I answered, "Everything is fine. My parents are asleep."

"Very well." With that, three small paper cups were slid under the door and the sound of the nurses moving on to the next cell disappeared into the night.

I picked up the cups and carefully lined them along the back of the sink. My mother's cup always had four pills in it. My father's held three. Mine held only one. They told me it was a vitamin supplement, something needed to keep me strong. I didn't really care what it was. Filling the cup with water, I threw the pill in my mouth and chased it down with the warm liquid.

The buzz sounded once more. This was the longest one. It cut through the prison for a good minute, making sure that every inmate had a chance to hear it. Then, as the last echoes of the buzz died out, the lights suddenly went dead. In each cell a small light glowed near the door along the floor. It cast eerie shadows along the walls of the cell that never moved or danced, the glow the only lighting we would have until five in the morning when they would snap all of the lights back on at once.

I blinked a few times, the darkness of the cell refusing to adjust to my eyes. Finally giving up, I forced them wider and leaned against the sink. My stomach still rolled with hunger. I thought for a moment about taking a half of my father's sandwich, but stopped myself as my hand hovered above the lid to his plate. I knew he would wake up hungry. I didn't want to be the one to cause that hunger to stay, again.

I slid my hand up onto the top bunk, feeling around until my fingers found the binding of my notebook. Pulling it down, I moved to sit near the glowing light on the floor. I quickly tore out a page, closed the book and laid the page down on the cover. Pulling my shoes off, I carefully unstrung the shoelaces, knotting them together to make one long rope.

What is blue?

I scribbled on the paper. Folding it until it wouldn't bend anymore, I tied the end of my shoelace rope around the paper ball and pulled it tight, then flattened myself to the ground. Sprawled out on my stomach, I laid my face close to the opening at the bottom of the door, and waited.

The sound of a night patrol's boots thumped past. I waited until it died into the distance, then slid my hand under the door. Holding tightly onto the end of the shoelace, I flicked my wrist, throwing the paper bundle far to the left. I could hear it as it hit the ground, barely audible above the rumble of whispers bouncing down the walk.

My eyes closed, enjoying the coolness of the floor against my cheek. Time passed. I could feel my fingers cramping as they held tightly onto my end of the shoelace. It was almost time to give up for the night. Just as I propped myself up onto my elbows, the shoelace suddenly tugged.

A smile spread on my lips. I yanked on the shoelace, reeling it back into my cell, then sat up. The note crinkled as I unfolded it. I glanced to my parents, but they hadn't even stirred. Smiling again, I leaned against the dim light and started to read.

Blue is water. Isn't it a bit early to be fishing?

My smile broadened.

Fishing was the one way to have hidden conversations with the other inmates, while never having to know exactly who you were writing to. Using my shoelace as the fishing line and the note as the bait, I had slowly captured and gotten to know the inmates along my walk. A few nights every week, I fished. In my own way I had found how to be the silent socialite of the prison.

Even in my extreme anti-social style, I couldn't resist fishing.

One night, about a year ago, I had tossed my note to the left and gotten a response almost immediately. His name was Orrin. I never asked for his state assigned last name, and he never had given it to me. The inmate directly to the left of our cell, along with the one just past him, were both male. I had no idea which one was Orrin. He said he was old enough to be my father, which didn't help slim down the choices. To be honest, I didn't even care. Orrin was good company to fish with.

Every time I threw a note his way, I would always start it with a simple question. One that any other inmate would either disregard or try too hard to answer. Orrin's answers were always obvious. I never doubted it was he who had answered.

Can't sleep. Have you met the new GF?

I tossed the note and waited. It didn't take long to feel the tug this time.

I have. He has worked here for some time. Don't know why he wanted to transfer to the day watch though. Used to be in charge higher up in Spokane.

I pursed my lips, then scribbled back.

He wanted to be here? Something must be wrong with him.

I could hear a low chuckle down the walk. Smiling to myself, I waited for the tug.

That's what I heard. Guessing they think the Lifers are more fun to annoy. Since we aren't going anywhere. Except up.

I never liked it when Orrin wrote like that. He was convinced that the only way out of floor B, out of Spokane, was death. I had tried a few times in the past to encourage him to file for parole. Orrin always said no, and left it simply at that.

Orrin, why are you here?

I paused a moment before tossing the note out the door.

There was an unspoken rule here. You didn't ask about the crimes that had locked the people in. Someone could seem like the world's most decent human being. You would sit there and wonder why they ever found themselves locked away inside this place. Then, when you found out the reason, you would want to smash their skulls in for the atrocities they had committed.

It was better to know the person that was locked in now, not the person they had been before. I had never even asked my own parents what their crime had been.

It was a long time before the shoelace tugged again.

Do you believe that not everyone in here is guilty, Millie?

I don't know, I wrote back.

I was living in a small town. Orrin wrote. *Had a beautiful wife and two little boys. Then some bad things started to happen in the town. People were being killed, brutally. There was one man who I had said some nasty stuff about, who later turned up dead. Everyone decided then and there that I was the murderer.*

I had no alibi, so they took me in. And that was the end of it. They stopped looking for the killer, decided it easier to declare that I was him because of some careless things I had said. I was sentenced, and locked away without a second glance. That is why I am here.

Do you believe me?

I read the note over again, taking in everything he had carefully written. His handwriting was perfect, curved and clear. Every "i" was dotted. Every single "t" perfectly crossed. Something in the back of my mind told me to not believe him. There had to be a reason why the Nation had sentenced him. They wouldn't have locked him away if he were innocent. There was always a reason.

I waited for the butterflies to take me over. For the fog to lick at my vision and dull my thoughts. Nothing happened. As I stared at his writing, I only felt my steady heart beat and heard my even breaths.

I believed him. I wanted to believe him. For some reason, I needed to.

Of course I do, Orrin. I wrote.

Remember that when you are out, Millie. Orrin wrote back. *Watch what you say. I never want to see you again.*

A small smile spread on my lips. Carefully, in the clearest handwriting I could muster, I wrote back.

I never want to see you again either.

The lights flashed on. I jerked my hand over my eyes, groaning at the pain of the sudden flood of light. Outside my cell I could hear similar responses as the declaration of day jostled everyone awake.

Rolling to my side, I looked down over the edge of the bunk. Both of my parents' plates were sitting on the floor, the lids pulled off and the food gone. Letting my head hang lower, I saw they had both already left for the day. My mother always had her appointments early in the morning. Usually the sound of the doors sliding open woke me up, but I must have slept deep enough to stay in my dead dreams, for once.

My body hurt. I could see the pad had completely flattened where my body had slept for the night. I stretched my stiff arms above my head and brushed my fingers against the low ceiling. Shaking my legs out, I dropped to the ground, landing hard on the cement. Pain shot up my legs, but I just shook it off.

Out of the corner of my eye I could see the pile of clothes folded messily on the shelf, the unmistakable smell of dirty socks and sweat saturating the air of the small cell. Sighing, I walked over to my parents' flat bed and pulled one of the pillowcases off the thin pillow. I quickly shoved all of the dirty clothes into the case then twisted it shut as I made my way out of the cell.

Others were walking down the walkway, obviously still half awake as their feet shuffled and dragged them along. I saw a few in the passing crowd carrying pillowcases heavy with clothes. I could smell their sweat, already permeating the morning air. At the last minute, I remembered my towel. Ducking back into the cell, I snatched it from the shelf, then joined the crowd as it moved toward the single doorway at the end of the walkway. Below and above me I could hear the same hustle of sleepy footsteps.

The prison was awake.

I made my way to the women's showers. It was still early enough that the line hadn't grown too long. I quickly walked in, making my way back to one of the changing stations closest to the shower stalls. Shoving the pillowcase into the cubby hole, I peeled off my clothes and folded them neatly then placed them on top of my little pile. They smelled of sweat and dirt, but would have to wait to be washed until the next laundry day.

I grabbed my towel and wrapped it around my naked body, shivering in the morning air. They never seemed to keep any room warm enough here. Even in the dead of summer, a strange chill hung in every corner of the prison.

A female guard waited at the entrance to the showers. Opening my towel, I spun in a circle. She half watched, obviously not wanting to be on naked shower duty. After proving that I hadn't tried to sneak anything in with me, she let me pass. I hurried to the back stall and hung my towel on the small hook. It always ended up damp by the end of the shower. At least in the very back of the shower room the towel avoided most of the water as it danced off of the bodies and walls.

I cranked on the water then braced myself. The water gushed out. It hit my skin hard, already warm as it beat into my tightened muscles. Most times the water shot out so hot it felt as if it had come straight from the boiler, heated in Hell. Other times it was ice cold, instantly locking your body up as it froze every inch of your exposed flesh. It was rare to have it come out warm in the shower. Just warm. Relaxing, I let a smile spread on my face as the water covered me.

The guard impatiently cleared her throat. Cracking my eyes open, I saw she was looking directly at me, a scowl on her thin face. I snapped out of it, grabbing the soap and quickly rubbing it all over my body and through my short hair. I hated my hair. Most women in here kept their hair short. It was easier to manage and harder to pull. Even though it seemed practical, I hated how short the barber always cropped it. It barely reached my chin, and rarely stayed when I tucked it behind my ears.

I rinsed off, then wrapped the damp towel around myself and scurried back to my cubby. Modesty wasn't a luxury. Naked women stood around me, some waiting in line, others drying themselves off. A few younger girls stood nervously away from the others, casting their eyes down as they tried to avoid the crowd of nakedness that pressed around them.

I toweled off, then threw my dirty clothes back on and shoved the towel inside the bag. Without pausing a moment longer, I made my way through the crowd and out the door.

The Commons already teemed with inmates, most leaning against walls or slumped in chairs as they waited for their assignments for the day. There had once been a time when there were limits on how large a gathering could get before a guard rushed in to break it up, or site them for an unauthorized assembly. In the last few years, crowds had been getting larger, and the guards rarely broke them up. It was pointless. There were too many people. The doorway across the room finally came into view, and I ducked inside.

Just past the door a narrow staircase shot down into the shadows below. Its steps were cracked from years of disrepair. The handrail, always grimy from the hundreds of unwashed hands that grasped it each day, hung from the dark wall. I carefully positioned myself in the middle of the stairs and made my way down.

Nearing the bottom, I could hear the bustle of the laundry room. I pulled open the door and was instantly overcome with the distinct smell of soap and wet clothes. The room was already packed with people, most of them women, casually talking as they scrubbed clothes in the large bins full of water or waited in line to use the worn-out drying machines that always left your garments damp.

Nodding politely at the few women who smiled limply at me, I pushed through to a free spot along one of the bins. Here in the washroom, women who would usually glare and yell always seemed to mellow down. It was as if the act of scrubbing and washing the dirty clothes brought back traditions of old, and the women escaped into those adopted memories. The laundry room was one of the only places inside Spokane where you could hear women laugh and sing, with no intermission of anger.

A woman, her face blank as if lost in another dream, mindlessly passed me a bar of soap then went back to her slow rhythmic scrubbing. I watched a moment as she scrubbed over and over at a spot on the white shirt in her hands. I couldn't see anything on it, but she didn't seem to notice as she bore her weight into scrubbing.

Pulling a shirt out of my pillowcase, I dunked it in the warm water and quickly rubbed the soap through it. I hated this soap. The smell stung my nose, and it always left my hands red and chapped. Over the years I had become the only one in my family who remembered to wash our laundry. Occasionally my mother would seem to snap out of her strange world, gather everything, and wash it until it shone. But those days were getting fewer and fewer. If it weren't for me, our clothes would be stiff with stink. Gritting my teeth, I rubbed the soap harder into the dirty shirt.

I let my mind relax, settling into the mindless task of dunking the clothes: rubbing the rank soap across their surface, scrubbing, then squeezing out as much of the soap as I could manage before draping them in a pile on the edge of the bin. If I made it a point to not think, this chore didn't seem too tedious. I had heard there were worse assignments out there. I never bothered to ask what they might be. I didn't want to find out what could be worse than soap that rubbed your flesh off and burned your sense of smell until tears stung your eyes.

Finally ringing out the last sock, I quickly dunked the pillowcase into the sudsy water, scrubbed it, then gathered the soaking pile in my arms and hurried to join the line for the drying machines.

The machines were ancient. A single row of them lined one wall, their circular metal doors rusted and cracking. As they spun, they banged against each other and the wall, giving the laundry room a steady washing rhythm that would continue the entire day. The beat of the machines sounded like the heart of the prison, steadily keeping it alive with every thud.

The line inched forward, one inmate at a time being allowed to find a free machine and throw their contents inside to hopefully dry. My pile of wet clothes pressed against my body. I could feel the dampness saturating my still dirty set of clothes that I wore. A shiver ran down my body, the air suddenly feeling even colder as I wrapped my arms around my wet load of worn laundry.

My turn finally came. A guard standing near the front of the line pulled out the small device and scanned my bracelet. After it lightly beeped, he waved his hand, motioning me forward. I ducked my head and scurried to a machine, its rusted door still swinging from the last load that had been pulled out.

Throwing my armload in, I slammed the door shut and pressed my thumb down hard on the button. The machine seemed to gag, then slowly spun up until it joined the others in beating itself against the wall. I watched intently as my load of clothes began its spin behind the thick glass.

The smell of smoke drifted into my nose. Startled, I jerked my eyes from the load and looked around. Down the row, a line of smoke flowed out of a machine. The inmate standing in front of it started to panic, her eyes wide as she watched more and more smoke billow out. Desperately she yanked on the handle of the door, but it didn't even budge, locked shut in mid-cycle.

The guard who had scanned my bracelet just a moment before pushed his way through the stunned crowd, shoving the woman aside to jam a key into a small hole hidden near the top of the drying machine. The machine came to a dead halt. Smoke streamed out of the cracks and joints, its mass seeming to groan in pain. The guard yanked the door open. As it swung on its rusty hinge, a large cloud of black smoke rolled out.

The guard reached in with one hand and shoveled out the contents of the dryer. Everything was burned; the shirts a dark brown, the jeans patchy with ash. The woman started to bawl as she watched all of her clothing hit the ground, completely useless.

"Another machine backfire," the guard said into a small mouthpiece positioned on his shoulder.

"My... my clothes!" the woman sobbed.

The guard quickly scanned the woman's bracelet, then checked the device. "821A, you will be charged for a new reimbursement set of clothes and partial fixture of machine."

"What?!" The woman's eyes filled with more tears. "It wasn't my fault. These machines break all the time. You should be reimbursing *me!*" Her head whipped around, taking in everyone who had frozen to watch. "It wasn't my fault!"

The guard let out a low chuckle. "Nothing is ever anyone's fault it seems. But I guess you're wrong, huh? Otherwise you wouldn't be here, Inmate." He spat out the last word as if disgusted, then uttered a 'clean this up' and made his way back to the start of the line.

The woman, still sobbing, gathered her ruined clothes in her arms and backed away from the machine. Smoke leaked out of it, curling into thin tendrils as it snaked its way toward the ceiling. As the woman walked slowly past me, I could hear her mumbling incoherently under her shuddering breath.

My fingers twitched at my side. I felt the urge to reach up and stroke her arm, to pat her back as she hurried past, anything. Just like with the old woman the day before. I lifted my hand. Just as I moved to place it on the woman's shoulder, a series of grumbled curse words escaped her mouth. My hand fell to my side, my mouth slightly agape at the angry words that fell from her lips in a manic rush.

The woman disappeared into the crowd, a hiccup of a cry echoing behind her.

I turned back and intently watched my machine, terrified that I would see smoke pouring out. My load still tumbled over and over, flecks of water splashing against the glass door. I refused to pull my eyes off of the machine.

More and more machines had been breaking down lately. Instead of ordering new ones, a mechanic would occasionally come down and slap the broken machine back together. It always broke again. I heard people muttering about where the replacement money was going, but I didn't care. All I cared about was that my clothing came out mostly dry and still intact.

The machine chirped once, then shut itself off. I pulled the door open, relieved to smell the familiar aroma of dried soap. Shoving the clothes into the still damp pillowcase, I threw it over my shoulder and hurried to the stairs. Behind me I could still hear the sobbing of the destitute woman.

▯ ▯ ▯

The cell was still empty when I got back. Normally my parents were back, casually talking or napping the day away. My father had a job in the mailroom, but it had been decreased to only two days a week. It was strange to see the cell completely empty.

I dumped out the clothes onto the bottom bunk and loosely folded them, leaving out a clean set of clothing for myself. Even though I had taken a shower that morning, I felt sticky and dirty. Peeling the clothes off that I had been wearing for the last week didn't help. I wished I could go back and wash them. But we were only allowed two laundry days a week. The clothes would have to wait.

I shivered as I tugged the clean shirt on over my head. It was still damp, the drying machine obviously petering on its last leg. I silently thanked it for not burning my clothing. The crying of the woman still rang painfully in my head. Pulling on my worn jeans, stiff with dried soap, I wadded my dirty clothes into a tight ball and tucked them onto the bottom shelf.

Finally feeling clean, or as clean as I could ever feel, I climbed up onto my bunk and pulled out my notebook, flipping to the back.

Conversations with varying inmates were stacked in a pile, the pages crumpled from the many times they had been folded and unfolded. I pulled out the most recent page, looking at the careful curves of Orrin's writing. Whenever he wanted me to pay more attention to something he wrote, he wrote in perfect penmanship. The letters arched and curved at just the right places. My writing next to his was ugly, a foreign language.

I found the yellow paper from my last visit with Dr. Eriks and carefully tucked it in behind my conversation with Orrin. My eyes grazed the words, still trying to find what seemed wrong with them. Shaking my head, I closed the notebook and sat back against the wall.

The prison was fully awake now.

I could hear the nonstop chatter of inmates. The shuffle of worn out shoes. The occasional angry shout. I let my eyes shut, the sounds enveloping me. Someone shouted louder, their voice full of anger. I could hear a body slam into something solid. The gasps of people standing by. Then, right on cue, the heavy thump of boots as the guards ran to join the fight. Inmates shouted, some cheering on the fighters, some scared and trying to get away from the crowd. Then suddenly it fell quiet, everything quieting back to the shuffle and murmur of the usual rhythm.

This was the music my life consisted of. The beat of the laundry room, the strum of the shuffling feet, the occasional solo of a frenzied fight, always ending with the finale buzz declaring lights out. I had only heard true music a handful of times in my life. It was beautiful. Every note was clear and lacking chaos.

I longed to hear it more, but in Spokane, only the privileged got any kind of actual music. I didn't have a job, and my parents rarely worked. This meant we had no points, and no special treatment. The only music I was allowed were the daily songs of the prison walk.

My mind drifted more.

I felt my lips vibrating as they hummed an uneven rhythm that swayed and moved with the sounds of the prison. Occasionally a small snatch of one of the unnamed random songs I had heard before mixed in, giving my melody a strange, haunting sound. I let a small smile spread on my lips. It felt good to be alone in the cell. No chattering. No need to check in and make sure my mother was clean or my father awake.

In my mind I watched as a green field took form. I let myself fall into the daydream. The field was one I had seen many times in my schoolbooks. Rolling hills, green with occasional patches of white flowers. The sky blue with light fluffy clouds floating by. I could hear the songs of the birds in the distance. The lap of unseen water.

Laying down in the grass, I let the sun bake my soft skin. My clothes were clean, smelling of flowers instead of the usual stink of rank soap and dirty sweat. No one was around. Aside from the crash of the waters and the singing of the birds, I was completely alone. My smile grew wider.

The sound of someone clearing their throat snapped me from my day-dreaming. Blinking my eyes open, I leaned forward and looked down at the open cell door. Carl GF4 leaned in the opening, his arms folded across his uniform chest, a sly grin smugly spread on his face. From how settled he looked against the door frame, he must have been standing there for longer than I dared to think.

"Nice humming," he said, his voice low and smooth.

I licked my lips, the heated flush of embarrassment racing to my face.

"What song was it?" he asked, taking a step inside.

"It was... it was nothing. I didn't know I was humming."

Carl chuckled, his eyes sweeping the cell. "Nice and tidy in here. Good to see."

"Uh… thanks." My mind reeled, wondering why he was here. Wondering, more so, why he was talking to me.

"I hear you turn eighteen in a few days." Carl stepped back to lean in the doorway again. "How does it feel?"

"Feel?"

"You know. Finally getting away from the crazies." He swept his eyes around the cell. "Your parents."

A sudden flush of anger swelled in my chest. Forcing it down, I licked my lips again and looked away. "I haven't thought much about it."

"Hm," Carl said, humor hinting his voice. Lifting my eyes, I saw him taking me in. He smiled as my eyes met his, a silent chuckle evident on his lips. "I came to get you. Dr. Eriks says you have a meeting."

I knew I didn't. My meeting wasn't for another two days. Worried I had noted it wrong, I grabbed my notebook and flipped it open to the page where I jotted my daily schedules.

"It's not in there," he said. "She is changing some of the releasing policies. Guess you are one of the lucky first for her new interviews."

"Oh," I said softly.

Climbing down from the bunk, I swept my hands over my jeans, flattening out the wrinkles. I walked out of the cell, pushing quickly past Carl. His body remained firm and unmoving.

"I will escort you," he said in a matter-of-fact tone.

Something fluttered angrily in my stomach.

"No." Catching myself, I softened my tone. "I go there every week. I know the way. It's… it's ok. Thank you for getting me, sir."

Carl opened his mouth as if ready to say something, then slowly pulled it closed. He was close enough that I could hear the clink of his teeth as they met. He let his eyes flick down me again, then nodded. "Alright, Millie." His voice came out low, almost seductive. "Have a good day then."

Turning, he walked away, occasionally glancing into an open cell as he passed. I watched him a moment, my mouth dry and my stomach nervously flipping. Fog threatened my mind. Blinking madly, I forced it away, then turned and hurried down the hall.

I didn't like how Carl had looked at me. Each time his eyes scanned my body, I felt naked and vulnerable. I didn't like the sly smile that crossed his face, covering whatever thoughts were hidden behind it. This new guard was strange, different from all the others I had known my entire life.

Guards were paid to watch us. Their job was to keep us in check and to keep order. I had never second-guessed their gazes or questions. For eighteen years, I had never felt my stomach tighten and body jitter the way it did when Carl watched me. I felt as if I should have ducked into my bunk and hid under my blanket like I used to when I was little and a fight broke out in the dark night.

There was something else.

Something my mind fought to place as I made my way down the hallways towards Dr. Eriks' office. I barely noticed when I had to pause to let a guard scan my bracelet, or when I had to skirt around the random groupings of inmates. There was something more than how Carl had looked at me, or how he had taken the time to talk to me, that made me this jumpy and nervous.

As I rounded the last corner and approached the desk of Dr. Eriks' secretary, it finally hit me. Guards always addressed us by our cell number. That was all we were to them: inmates. Numbers.

It wasn't strange that Carl knew my name. It was printed on all my paperwork, even on my bracelet that I now nervously spun around my wrist. But guards rarely remembered more than our numbered last names. Carl knew my first name. And he had used it without hesitation. That was what sent the shivers racing one after another down my back.

He had spoken to me like an old friend. As if he knew me.

And something inside me did not like that. At all.

5

The secretary glanced up at me. Her dull hair was pulled into a loose bun, a few stray strands curling around her lean face. Nodding toward a chair, she let her eyes drift back to the old book propped up in front of her on the worn wooden desk.

I moved toward the chair, letting my weight drag me down onto its cold metal seat. The realization that Carl GF4 had called me by my name really shook me. I couldn't stop the nauseous twist of my stomach, the shake that had taken over my usually steady hands. Something about me felt invaded. Most things were not private here. We showered together. Ate together. Died together. But few things, like our names, were rarely shared.

Why did he even bother with knowing mine?

My thoughts stopped as I saw the door crack open. The secretary glanced up, then lazily said the standard "Dr. Eriks is ready to see you now" before gluing her eyes back to the book in front of her nose.

Standing, I brushed my jeans smooth again, then moved to push the door open. The room sat dim and cold, as usual. One wall held a wooden bookshelf, full of books I had never been allowed to look at. There was no window. Just a framed painting of dull swirled colors hanging alone on the gray wall. A desk rested against the last wall, everything on it neatly organized in perfect stacks. Even the pens were laid in order, perfectly lined and ready to grab at any needed time.

Dr. Eriks sat in her usual chair, her legs neatly crossed. Her hair was in a perfect bun as always, her glasses perched carefully on her nose. I could see the lines spraying out around her pursed lips from across the room.

There were three chairs lined up in front of her. To my shock, I saw the backs of two other people sitting nervously in the chairs. As I stepped closer, I felt my breath catch in my throat. I knew the balding patch on the back of the man's head. The messy, unwashed mane of hair on the fidgeting woman.

Snapping my eyes up to Dr. Eriks, I let my voice shoot out, more forceful than I had ever let it be in this office. "What are my parent's doing here?" I demanded.

Dr. Eriks barely reacted to my question. Motioning one hand toward the empty chair, she said evenly, "Have a seat, Millie."

I sat down, looking over at my parents. They both sat with their hands clenched tightly in their laps. I could see my mother's leg shaking. My father kept his eyes glued to his worn sneakers. Looking up, my mother offered me a weak smile.

"As you can see, Millie, we are changing some procedures. We have found that," Dr. Eriks paused to clear her throat, "that those born in the incarcerated world, have an unusually harder time adjusting to true life. I am attempting to weed out those issues. We want you to be an asset to the Nation. You are the good, the strong."

I silently recited the last sentence with her. Dr. Eriks repeated it often to me I had memorized it. Nodding slightly, I felt my eyes fasten themselves to the lines around her mouth.

"Part of the change is doing one of your last sessions with the parental units present. I would like to better know your relationship with them. Ask them some questions. I need to observe items that, well, I was never able to get you to open up about before. We need to be fully honest to make our Nation strong, Millie." Dr. Eriks settled back in her seat, opening the notepad and setting it neatly on her lap. "Shall we begin?"

I nodded.

"Millie, have you been keeping up your journal?"

I thought back to the pages still to be written in. The moments that my pencil froze as it hit paper. I hadn't written a word in the journal for months now, aside from my daily schedules. I was about to admit to that, when the image of the small stack of fishing papers appeared in my head.

"I have," I said.

Dr. Eriks watched me a moment, then forced a small nod. "Very good. It is important to never keep your issues locked inside. Unaddressed problems can lead to undesired outcomes. Isn't that right, Leann?"

The sound of my mother's name shocked me. I had rarely heard her first name used. Even my father addressed her simply as 'Mom.' Letting my eyes trail over to her now, I could see her nodding.

"Tell me, Millie, are you looking forward to your release?" Dr. Eriks asked.

My tongue suddenly felt thick and dry. "I… I don't know."

"Why are you unsure?"

The words of my journal entry appeared in my mind. I had read them over and over, trying to find what was wrong. Trying to find what I was afraid to admit. The words seemed to slow, allowing me finally to see what they were actually saying.

And I dread it with every fiber in my body.

I looked over at my huddled parents, then in a weak voice answered, "There will be no one left to take care of my parents." I could feel the choke of a sob softly escape my mother's lips. "If I am not here —"

"The Nation takes care of all of its convicts, Millie." Dr. Eriks voice cut into me.

"I know. But... my parents... they need me. For all the small things, you know? I just, I don't know, I just don't want them to..."

I didn't add the other reason. The fear that I knew nothing outside these walls. I had learned the history, I knew the laws. I knew the prison rules. Outside these walls though, I didn't know that life. I didn't know its rules.

Dr. Eriks leaned back, locking her fingers together in front of her almost flat chest. I felt my voice trail out as I watched her. A strange expression crossed her face. It almost seemed... smug.

"Leann," she said, her voice clipped and clear, "I think it is time you tell your daughter why you are here."

My heart felt as if it had stopped. I had never been able to bring myself to ask my parents what crime had sentenced them to life in Spokane. Every time I let the question form on my lips, I found myself fearing I would hate them after the truth was finally told. That I would see the true monsters they were, the true criminals who deserved this punishment. I knew my parents were odd. But in my own strange way, I did love them. Would that love leave once I knew the truth?

My mother nodded again, then in a soft voice, barely audible, started. "There were three men. I didn't like them. So, I jumped them. Knocked one out. The second I stabbed with a knife. Over. And over." My mother's eyes were glued to her shaking hands. "It… it felt so good. Over. And over."

I could hear the crack in her voice. She paused a moment, then went on. "I couldn't stop stabbing. I wanted to keep stabbing."

"And the third man?" Dr. Eriks asked, her voice cool and expecting.

My mother glanced at my father, then looked back to her hands. "The third man… the third died. Your father killed him. With his hands."

She started to rock back and forth, muttering unknown words under her breath. I couldn't breathe. The words sat on the surface, trying hard to sink in as I battled to fight them away. I let my dry eyes trail over to my father. I searched his face for some hint of denial. There was only pain. A tear trailed down his unshaved face.

Dr. Eriks bore her dull eyes into my mother, the hint of a satisfied grin on her tight face. "And do you regret it at all, Leann? Would you take it back?"

My mother shook her head, her hands shaking in her lap. Though her body shook, her voice came out firm and angry. "No."

I took a deep breath, trying to steady the shake that started to grow inside. Dr. Eriks had always taught me that I needed to be the good and the strong. The Nation needed me. Criminals were what destroyed it, criminals like my parents, and it needed the good to make it strong once again.

At that moment, I didn't feel strong at all.

My mother's words still repeated over and over in my mind. I didn't want to believe them. I couldn't see my gentle mother stabbing a man until he was dead. I couldn't let myself accept that she enjoyed it. I couldn't picture my shadow of a father strangling a man with his own hands. But now, as I let my eyes settle on my parents, that was the only picture that formed in my racing mind. My parents were gone.

I felt Dr. Eriks watching me, a small smile spread on her thin lips. She looked almost amused. At that moment, I hated her.

"Is it true?" I begged, hoping it was a lie, a test of some twisted sort.

Lifting her chin, my mother tightened her jaw and fastened her eyes to the ceiling. I could see the glaze threatening to engulf her. Reaching over, my father laid a hand gently on her shoulder. In a soft voice, cracking with tears, he answered with the two words I did not want to hear. "It is."

"Why?" I whispered.

My mother let her eyes finally meet mine. I could see the glaze taking her over. "Because," she said, her voice slightly shaking. "I wanted to. I needed to. I didn't like them. I would have killed the third man too, if he hadn't woken back up and ran away." A small smile curled on her lips a moment, then disappeared as she tore her eyes from mine and leaned her head back again, staring intently at the ceiling.

Nausea boiled through me. The taste of bile rose in my throat and my vision started to blur. I suddenly felt hot. As if someone had lit me on fire then sat back to laugh as I flailed, trying to survive the murderous heat.

"Millie, why do you look angry?"

I slowly rolled my eyes to Dr. Eriks, the hint of a smile still present on her ugly face. I couldn't form words. For some reason, I had always hoped that my parents were here by mistake. Like Orrin. I had hoped they had been wrongly charged and convicted and someday the truth would let out. Then we would all be set free, finally given the chance to live a normal life for the Nation.

That day disappeared before my eyes.

"Millie, do you feel prepared to be released?" Dr. Eriks voice grated at me. It cut through me, the bile still rising in my dry throat.

I let my eyes look back at my parents. My father's eyes were red, his cheeks shining from the tears that now dried in the graying stubble. My mother still had her eyes glued to the ceiling, her body rocking back and forth. I could see her lips moving, muttering something over and over. In the silence of the room, the words floated towards me.

"My baby. My little baby."

Feeling the heat rise, I turned back to Dr. Eriks. "I am ready."

"Very good," she clipped, then let the room fall back to silence as she scribbled notes into her book.

I could see the fog drifting into my vision. My mind started to feel heavy and thick. Instead of fighting it, I welcomed it. I let the fog cover the images that still re-enacted before my tired eyes. The final glimpse of my mother stabbing the man, a smile on her face, faded to nothing as the fog took over. I knew I still sat in the chair. I could feel it firmly holding me to my existence. But my mind, my memories, were now filled with my only release.

I slowly became aware of the creak of my parent's chairs as they rose to leave. I could hear their footsteps as they moved toward the door, the creak as the door opened, the pause as they both waited for something, then reluctantly disappeared.

"...you can leave now." Dr. Eriks' voice bled into my head, nagging and bored.

Without looking at her, I stood and made my way to the door. I felt strange. As if I had no true tie to this place I had called home my entire life. I floated in a numbing limbo, hiding from the hate and questions that hid in the dark corners of my mind.

As soon as I reached the door, I could feel my stomach twist sharply, bile suddenly shooting into my mouth. Gagging, I ran for the small trashcan that the secretary always kept empty next to her desk. My body heaved, emptying the scarce contents of what they called a breakfast into the bottom of the can.

I could hear the protest of the secretary, but ignored it. I didn't care. Heaving again, I fell on my knees and watched the swirls of liquid in the bottom of the now soiled can. I could feel the heat from the vomit drift up to my face, carrying the strong reek of bile and regurgitated food.

Before I could heave again, I pulled my head back and wiped the corner of my mouth with a shaking finger. The secretary stared at me in sheer disgust. I tried to utter an apology, but my throat was too raw.

Please, I thought, *please stop looking at me like I am a monster too.* I could feel my face burning in embarrassment, the smell inside the can reminding me of what I had just done.

The secretary's face strangely softened. Spinning in her chair, she grabbed something, then stood and moved around the desk to bend down next to me.

I realized she was holding out a thin paper tissue and a small cup of water. My hands shook as I took them from her, gratefully swishing my mouth with the cool water.

"Don't worry about it," she said in a hushed voice. "Not the first or the last time that will happen. Dr. Eriks has… she has a way with people."

I wiped my mouth with the tissue, then let it drop into the trash can. Drinking the last gulp of water, I placed the plastic cup back into the secretary's waiting hand. "Thank you," I managed, my voice coming out tired and rough.

"Here's a mint. Don't want to smell like puke all day." I could feel one hand softly rest on my back. The other held out a small mint, its surface white and speckled with blue. Placing it in my mouth, I felt the rush of spearmint spread over my tongue. "You will be alright. I'm sure of it."

Someone approached from down the hall. The secretary glanced up for a moment before turning back to me. "Here, I called someone to escort you back." The secretary held out a hand and helped me back up to me feet. I wobbled slightly, her hand on my back holding me upright until I had control of my balance again. "You know. Until you are steady. Take it easy, okay?"

I nodded, confused at the sudden kindness of this secretary who had all but ignored me for years. I self-consciously brushed my jeans smooth as I watched her return to her seat. She didn't look at me. She only sighed, then picked up the used book and flipped it back open. It was as if she had never moved.

As I turned, I saw Carl standing in the center of the hallway, a small smile on his face. "Intense session?" he asked.

"You could say that." I started to walk, careful to not bump into him. He quickly spun and joined me. I could feel his body a mere inch away, the heat threatening to brush against me at any moment. "I'm okay. You don't need to escort me."

"I think I do," he said, his voice closer to me than I liked.

The hallway had more people in it than before. It had to be almost noon now. It was the time of day when inmates flooded the offices for their appointments and treatments. They walked in both directions, some disappearing into random doors while others appeared and joined the lines of white t-shirts. I melted into the line, Carl still close to my side.

"Three more days I hear."

"Yeah."

"Excited?"

The image of my mother briefly flashed before my eyes. Blinking it away, I quickly answered, "More like ready."

Carl chuckled. Something in me flared. I didn't like how he kept staring at me. How he seemed to know too much about me. How he kept grinning and chuckling, as if I were some cute form of entertainment for him. I tried to speed up my pace, but the crowd in front of me blocked my path, keeping Carl glued to my side.

"You know, you can get a job in here."

I almost laughed. "Why would I want to work in here?"

"Oh trust me, there are perks." Carl scanned the crowd around him, his hand resting lightly on the holstered gun. "You don't have to work in the blocks. There are office jobs. Higher up."

"Isn't that where you worked?"

Carl turned his eyes to me, the hint of alarm flashing on his face before it was covered with his usual coolness. "I got bored. There is more incentive down here. For me. But for you..." He scanned me again with those eyes. I suddenly felt naked and vulnerable. "There are many positions that would work for you."

Wrapping my arms tightly around myself, I turned my head forward, focusing on the crowd ahead. I wished it would move faster. It seemed like the harder I wished, the more it slowed. I could feel Carl watching me, his eyes searing me with their mocking stare.

"I think it would be good for you," he said. I didn't answer, keeping my eyes fastened ahead. "I think you should take a job here."

We finally got to the walkway for my block. The crowd dissipated enough to let me quicken my step. Carl sped up, keeping up in stride with me. He waved his hand slightly at the guard waiting by the door. The guard, his hand gripping the scanning device, slowly nodded as we passed.

I began to count the cells, my eyes glued to the ground as I pushed toward to my cell. I felt Carl's hand grip my elbow, holding it in a firm clamp. The urge to shake him off grew. I tensed my arm, ready to pull it away from his grasp. Then I remembered: Carl was a guard. If I shook him off, he could take that as resistance to authority. I couldn't risk that.

Carl pulled me to a stop. He stepped behind me, leaning his face close. Keeping my eyes on my cell, now in view, I tried to ignore the feel of his breath on my neck. "Why don't you like me, Millie?"

"What?" I turned my face slightly to look at him. He was leaning close, too close, his breath now on my cheek. "You're a GF. A Guard. I —"

"And?" His voice was soft and low, rolling into my ear. I locked eyes with him a moment, his blue eyes chilling my soul. They cut into me, demanding an answer.

I shrugged.

Carl glanced behind us a moment. There were no other people on the walk, the path oddly empty. Moving closer, I felt his body brush mine. "I'm not all that bad, Millie. You just need to let me show you that." Lifting a finger, he tucked a loose strand of hair behind my ear.

I sucked in a deep breath and turned my head back toward my cell. It called to me, offering me a momentary escape from Carl's warm breath and piercing eyes. I inched forward. A couple, their chatter low and casual, passed on the walk. Carl moved away a few feet, standing behind me where I couldn't see him.

"I want to get to know you better," Carl said, his voice rumbling in his throat.

It felt as if the very blood in my veins ran cold. Even those passing nearby wouldn't be able to hear him. To them, he was just a guard assisting me into my cell.

Without lifting my eyes, I muttered a quick "Thank you" and

stepped inside. I didn't want him to see the terror in my eyes or the sudden paleness of my face.

"Just think about it, Millie," he said to my back. I didn't move. After a time, I dared a glance over my shoulder. I slowly turned my chin, my back still rigid, my feet still cemented to the ground.

Carl was gone.

6

I couldn't sleep.

Every time I closed my eyes, I saw my mother. Blood dripped down her arms, her eyes strangely sharp and focused as the blade glinted in her trembling hands. My eyes would snap open, then slowly drift back shut, only to see Carl's grinning face, his focused eyes as they watched me.

I had already been lying in my bunk when my parents finally crept back into the cell that night. Turning my head slightly, I saw my mother glance up at my bunk. My father moved a step closer, his mouth opening as if he had something to say. Then they both looked away together, my father's shoulders sinking.

Dinner slid under the door. I still didn't move. I listened as my parent's ate in silence. The crunch of the stale bread and slurp of applesauce didn't entice me to ask for my plate. After they rinsed the plates they crawled onto their thin mattress. No one spoke the entire night. Time passed and I could hear the light snore of my father as he finally drifted into sleep. A soft, stifled sob escaped my mother, then she too fell silent as night claimed her.

The darkness of the cell didn't help to ease my tense body. As I lay on my back, staring into the dark ceiling above me, I felt completely alone. It wasn't the alone I longed for, the alone that I relished as I dreamed of the open field and blue skies. I felt betrayed. Forgotten. All the years of my parents acting meek and gentle were washed away as I realized, somewhere inside of each of them, they truly were the monsters I had been in denial of. They had killed people, and didn't even regret it.

My eyes burned from staring at the ceiling. I felt as if I were searching for a hole to suck me in and let my disappearance become complete. It never happened. I could still feel the hard bunk beneath me. I could still hear the murmur of the block settling down for another night in this hell.

The final buzz of the night cut through the air and the door to the cell quickly snapped shut.

I gave up.

Quietly, I climbed down from the bunk. I knew my parents were asleep, but I didn't want to chance accidentally waking one up. The idea of facing them right now made my stomach churn.

"942, is everything alright?"

I didn't answer. I could hear the shift of feet outside the cell door as the nurses moved closer. Someone wrapped their knuckles on the metal.

"942B?"

"Yeah, we are fine." I glanced at my parents, their snores already rolling from their parted lips. "Just tired."

The pills, nestled in their small cups, were pushed under the door. I could hear the nurses hurry away without another word.

Lying down next to the door, I let the soft glow of the light envelope me. The coolness of the ground felt good on my almost fevered body. I pushed the pill cups away, watching as one tipped over and spilled its two pills across the ground. I didn't move to clean it up. Opening my notebook to a blank page, I froze, staring at its empty lines. The idea of fishing tonight suddenly drained me of any energy I had thought I had.

Footsteps sounded down the walk. I listened to the boots click on the ground, gradually growing louder as they neared my cell. Then the footsteps stopped. I froze, holding my breath. It wasn't against the rules to be out of bed after lights out. That didn't stop the guards from insisting though.

"Millie?"

Letting out my breath in a gush, I felt a smile spread on my face for the first time in hours. "Jude GF4, is that you?" I whispered.

Out of the slit at the bottom of the door I saw a shadow move, then suddenly a face appeared. He smiled at me, his white teeth glowing in the dim light. "Hey there, jail-bird."

Jude was a few years older than me. He had been working night shift at the jail three years now, ever since they had allowed him to don the vest and boots. I had never seen him work day. And to be honest, I was happy about it. Jude didn't seem like a guard to me. He always stopped near the cells where people cried inside, and asked if everything was alright. His smile was real, never full of a hidden agenda.

He was, in my own twisted, strange way, a friend.

"Where have you been?" I asked.

He settled himself on the ground outside my cell, looking in both directions first to make sure no one was approaching. "Vacation." He smiled and winked. "Just wait 'till you get to discover that perk."

I felt a laugh escape my lips. It felt good to feel it tickle my throat and chest. "Where did you go?"

"Absolutely nowhere. I sat in my house, slept when I wanted to, ate when I wanted to, and read way too many books. It was awesome." I didn't admit it to Jude, but that sounded too much like heaven to me to believe it could be real. "So, you ready for the big day?"

I rolled my eyes. "I am ready for everyone to stop asking me that."

"Well, you better bite the bullet and stay good. I want to see you outside these walls, not locked in a cell of your own."

I chuckled again. "Hey, Jude..." I stopped when I heard him laugh. "Okay, really, why do you laugh every time I say that?"

"Right, I guess you don't get the joke. Here." I could hear Jude roll to his side for a moment, wrestling something from a pocket. Flipping on his flashlight, I could suddenly see his face clearly. His eyes were big, always seeming to smile, his face smooth and clean. Shaggy light brown hair hung on his forehead, moving back and forth as he fidgeted with something in his hands. With a smile on his face, he held a small ball out to me, a thin spike of metal sticking from its side.

I looked at it doubtfully.

"You put it in your ear, Millie. It's called a headphone." Taking it delicately between my thumb and index finger, I pulled it up and placed it in my ear. It felt strange to lie so close to the opening of the door, the earphone in my ear, Jude's face only inches away. I watched as he shoved the other small headphone into his ear, then fiddled with a little box that he held in his hands. I started to giggle at the sight of the metal spike sticking out from his ear, but stopped as my own ear suddenly vibrated.

Something crackled in my ear. I heard Jude mumble something, the crackling getting louder as he fiddled with the small box. "Scoot closer, Millie. Reception in here sucks."

I inched forward, my head pressing against the bottom of the door.

Snips of music suddenly vibrated in my ear. A few seconds of a song played, then Jude hit a button and it skipped to another melody. My eyes shot open, my mouth watering for the music to continue. Finally a song started and Jude smiled, letting his thumb rest on the side of the little box.

"Hey Jude, don't make it bad. Sing this sad song and make it better..."

I could hear the sound of a man's voice softly singing. About Jude. Amazed, I shoved the headphone deeper into my ear, taking in the words, the strum of music, the gentle rolling rhythms. Rolling onto my back, I let the music envelope me and carry me away. It was beautiful.

Jude didn't move. I could see him smiling, his eyes closed as he listened to the song. It finally came to an end, the music fading out into nothingness. Jude hit a button on the box and let his eyes open to look at me.

"The group is called The Beatles. They were real big, popular, way back in the day. My mom still loves them. I guess her mom listened to them a whole heck of ton. So when I was born... she named me Jude."

I smiled. "I like it." Catching myself, I licked my lips. "The song. I like the song."

"Me too." Jude rolled to his side, part of his face disappearing into the walkway's shadows. "Listening to it makes me think of her. I miss her."

"Where is she?" I asked tentatively.

"My mom? Last I heard, it was Canada."

I could feel my body stiffen. "Canada?"

Jude let out a chuckle, his face still hidden in the shadows. I could see his eyes, the smile still glittering on their surface. "A few years back, just before I joined up in the Guard Force, my family decided to leave. They didn't agree with the Nation. With the Wall.

"I grew up in a beach house." Jude rolled back toward me. His face lit up in the dim light. "Well, it was supposed to be a beach house. It was big, with a wrap-around porch, even a whale that spun up on the roof with the wind. The Wall though... they had to build it right behind the house. I could hear the beach every day, but I never saw it. My mom said we had a door we could use to go to the beach... but it just seemed useless. I guess it got useless enough that they decided to leave."

Jude fiddled with the little music box, spinning it between his fingers. I inched closer to the door again, the cool metal pressing against my forehead. "Why didn't you go with them? Why didn't you leave the Nation?"

"Couldn't." Jude smiled at me. "My family definitely had the money to get anywhere they wanted. There was never an issue there. But I have always had this feeling that I needed to do something. I know I can do some good, I just need the chance."

"So you became a GF?"

Jude chuckled. I could see the shadow of his hand sweep across his face, as if painting his words in the air. "Guard Force, prison number 4. A permanent name change and a high risk job, with all the perks that low pay can offer you." I heard his hand drop back to his chest. He let out a soft sigh. "Can you believe that there are three more prisons out there in the Nation, just like this one?"

I didn't answer. Spokane was huge, with its constantly expanding walls and packed cells. It was too hard to believe that there were three other prisons just like it. Each corner of the Nation, stamped with a prison. I slowly shook my head, trying to chase the thought away. Something about it caused my stomach to tighten.

We lay on the ground in silence for a moment. I could hear Jude's steady breathing, his finger as it aimlessly tapped against his armored vest.

"Do you hear from them? From your family?" I finally asked.

Jude didn't respond right away. I thought I could see a shadow pass over his face. His lips seemed to tighten, his eyes blinking faster. Then it passed as quickly as it had come. "No."

"What is the Wall like?"

Jude chuckled. "It's a wall, Millie. A very large, very cold wall. You can see it stretch into the distance in both directions, and you never see the beach. You just hear it." Jude let out a sigh, rolling onto his back. His face disappeared into shadows. "But it protects us. Our great Nation built it to keep the good in and the evil out. We are in our sanctuary."

I recognized the words. They were the exact words that were printed in all of my school books. Dr. Eriks repeated those words to me in almost every session. I felt my lips moving along with his, silently reciting them.

"We are the good," Jude said softly.

"And the strong," I whispered back, tears trying to sting my eyes.

Jude let out a sharp breath of air, then rolled back to face me. "What were you going to ask me? Before I interrupted you and corrupted you with music?"

I didn't respond.

Jude spun the music player in his fingers again, then waved it at me. He smiled. "Want to hear more?"

"Really?" My voice came out too loud and I quickly glanced up to my parents. My mother stirred, then settled back into sleep.

Jude glanced at a watch on his wrist. "Yeah, I have some time. Think of it as an early birthday present." With that, he hit the button. Music flooded into my ears again. I laid my cheek on the ground, letting the sounds envelope me as my eyes closed. I was floating, carried away once more by the music.

I could hear Jude humming along, and I let my voice quietly join his. My smile felt warm and welcome. I couldn't imagine it leaving my face in that moment, even if I wanted it to. My eyes grew heavy, my breathing calming as the songs lulled me to sleep. I didn't feel it as Jude tugged the piece out of my ear and disappeared to rejoin his shift. I didn't notice the cold floor or the dim light. In my head, I listened to the endless music as sleep finally claimed me and whisked me away into empty dreams.

▯ ▯ ▯

The pool of drool under my cheek woke me up. Blinking my eyes, I lifted my head and looked around. Every inch of my body hurt. Pulling myself up, I felt the pain in my hips flare from sleeping on the hard ground. My hand wiped the drool off my cheek as I moved to stand in front of the metal mirror.

The music still played in my head. I could see Jude smiling as his song played over and over. I found myself wishing that more people could be like Jude. Somehow, even though we hadn't seen each other for weeks, he knew the exact gift to give me to chase away the nightmares that had stayed fastened before my eyes.

Shaking my head, I turned on the water and splashed my face. The air was warm, leaving a sheen of sweat on my body regardless of the fact that I had been sleeping on the always cold ground. The heat would be dying out soon, quickly erasing into a chill that blankets and jackets would never chase away as autumn crept in. Wiping the water from my face, I crawled up onto my bunk and slumped against the wall.

The buzz cut through the air, announcing morning. The doors suddenly clicked, then slid open. I could hear my parents stirring in their bunk below me. Before they stood, I quickly curled onto my side and closed my eyes into slits. I could see my father stand and look at me, his shoulders sagging. He moved to the sink and let the water run over his hands before splashing it on his scruffy face.

My mother stood, moved to the center of the room, then suddenly spun and looked straight at me. I was sure she knew that I was awake. I didn't move. I slowed my breathing to even, long draws and stared at her out of the slits of my eyelids. She just stood and watched me, a strange mix of confusion and pain painted across her tired face.

"942B," a voice suddenly cut into the air.

Both of my parents jumped in fright, then quickly spun to face the guard who stood in the door. I didn't need to sit up to know who it was. I could hear the smirk in his voice. The pierce of his gaze sent strange shivers down my entire body.

"Alan 942B," Carl continued. "As of today, you have been reassigned to Assembly. You will be expected to work five days per week. If you accomplish this, your points will be increased per week as well. You begin today."

I could see my father nod, trying to mask the sudden confusion that flooded his face. "Leann 942B, when not in your therapy course, classes, or on assigned cell rest, you have been assigned laundry room duty. You begin today as well."

My mother started to stammer, the words mixing together in confused chaos under her suddenly thick tongue. My father stepped forward and placed a hand on her shoulder. As if drawing peace from his touch, my mother calmed and nodded. "Thank you, GF," she said, her voice lacking any of its often distant loftiness. "It will be grand to work again."

Carl chuckled. "We must make sure that all of our inmates are properly taken care of. As you both are." I could feel him look at me, his words slow and meaningful. I swallowed the lump in my throat. Clenching my eyes shut, I tried to keep my breathing even. Dr. Eriks must have done this. She was telling me that my parents weren't my responsibility anymore.

I should have been relieved. Instead, I suddenly felt sick.

I could hear the rustle of paper. "Alan 942B, when your daughter wakes up from her sleep, would you please make sure she gets her agenda. It is needed to prepare for the Finals."

My father must have nodded his acknowledgement. I could hear Carl's clipped boot falls as he left the cell, joining with the morning flow. Creeping my eyes open just enough to see my parents again through my hooded eyelashes, I watched as my father glanced over the paper then softly laid it on my bunk next to me. His hand lingered a moment, then he curled his fingers up and pulled them away.

"Alan, Alan! You got a new job!" my mother chirped happily. In a very dramatic voice, her hand painting the word out in front of her in the air, she proudly announced, "Assembly."

My father just nodded again, falling back into his usual shadow existence. Smiling, my mother bounced past him and turned on the sink, splashing the water on her face and into her hair. She paused to look at her face in the mirror, pulling back the wrinkles in her forehead with a finger. "And it is about time they gave me a job. I am just stir crazy!"

You are something crazy, I thought.

My mother tried to run her fingers through her matted hair. Disgruntled, she let out a huff, her face wrinkling up like a child's. "I think I will go take a shower before my new day begins!" she chirped.

Grabbing her rarely used towel and a stack of clean clothing, which I had washed and folded and never been thanked for, she bounced toward the cell door. Just before she passed through the door I saw her pause, her chin turning slightly towards me, her back stiff in anticipation. I didn't move. Her shoulders sagged, a heavy sigh escaping through her lips. She paused a moment longer, then suddenly perked up again and bounced away down the walk towards the showers. My father grabbed his own stack of clothing and quickly followed, not even bothering to pause.

As soon as I was sure they were gone, I sat up and snatched the paper. I wished that I didn't feel so secluded from them. I could feel myself longing for the ability to let the fog permanently take away the newfound memory of my mother's unremorseful words. But I couldn't. When I saw her face, I saw a murderer.

I blinked my eyes then looked down, forcing them to focus on the white page in my hands.

Discharge Procedures

Spokane

Nation Prison No.4

0500 – Lights on

0530 – Breakfast

0800 – Report to Exam Room

0830 – Begin Exam

0930 – End Exam, Dismiss

1300 – Report for Parole Board

TBD

Reminder: Exam will be delivered orally and
before the five listed parole board members.
Be prompt and prepared.

Warden Frank Binns
Honorable Judge Albert Wood
Reverend Rolan Smitson
Dr. Marta Eriks
Oscar Ramos

I read the list again. I hated seeing Dr. Eriks' listed, but I knew there was no way they wouldn't include her in this decision. The Judge and Reverend meant nothing to me, and the Warden was to be expected. I had no idea who Oscar Ramos was.

I had heard that many times they would pull in a random citizen from one of the nearby farms to sit in. They thought it helped the inmate feel like the decision was fair, being as one of the five was of no power. That must be who Oscar was. A powerless nobody.

I laid the paper aside and pulled out my textbook. With nothing better to do for the next two days, I figured I might as well brush up on the material that my brain needed to remember in order to pass. Before standing in front of the parole board, it was required for all Jail Babies to take an oral exam. I would need to prove that I had the history of our Nation drilled so well into my head that I could recite it in my sleep.

Which I could.

I cracked the book open and began to read the same pages I had been reading my entire life.

I knew every word before I even read it. When I had turned six, this exact book had been assigned to me. Ever since then, I had read it, cover to cover, at least twice a week. The pages were full of the history of the great Nation. Why the Nation had to do what it did to save itself. How we needed to be the good, the strong, to bring the Nation back to its greatness. I hated reading it. The words were dull and boring, often repeating themselves every few pages. But twice a week, while I still attended school, we had to sit quietly in the cold schoolroom and read the book cover to cover.

No one ever failed the exam. And no Jail Baby was ever denied parole.

That knowledge only made me even more nervous.

The nerves I felt twisting in my stomach at the thought of the coming Exam wasn't only fear of the test itself. It was of the results. How I did on the test would put a stamp on me. It would decide where I would be placed after my release. It decided who I would become.

If they liked me, and if I proved to be a promising citizen, then my life outside would be easy. But if I got a bad label, one bad note, I would be watched. I would be doubted. And, as many of the younger convicts here, I would finally wind right back up where I did not want to be. I had seen it happen, too many times. I needed to prove that I was the good, the strong.

Realizing my mind had drifted, yet again, I slammed the book open until the spine cracked and started reading from the beginning.

I finished reading my textbook, then flipped it back to the first page and began again. By now I wasn't actually reading. My mind had become a thick mess of solid fog. I could feel my eyes swimming uselessly, barely focused on the pages. They seemed to be moving more out of memorized motion than out of actual need.

Every time I heard someone pass outside my cell, my entire body tensed. Their shuffled steps, soft from the same worn sneakers that we all wore, would finally calm me. Then I would hear movement again, and tense back up. I felt completely ridiculous. I hadn't been this uneasy since I was little.

I felt on edge, and no matter what I tried, I couldn't seem to calm myself down.

A few times I heard the clipped, heavy steps of boots as the patrolling guards passed. They wouldn't even pause as they walked past my quiet cell. As the day wore on, that changed. Every time I heard the heavy boot falls, I would glance out of the corner of my eye at the open door. The boots would slow as they approached my cell, pausing a fraction of a second in the light of the opening before moving on down the walk.

Each time, I could see Carl's darkly smiling face take me in.

The boots approached again. Even though I already knew who I would see, I still found my eyes trailing over to the door, my breath freezing in my lungs.

Carl stood in the door, grinning at me.

"Good day, Millie," he said coolly. "Studying hard?"

I didn't answer. Carl chuckled to himself, eyeing my entire cell before taking me in once more. Nodding his head, he disappeared back to his patrol.

I licked my lips, forcing myself to take a deep breath. My fingers shook as they turned the page of my worn book. The next time the heavy sound of boots approached, I didn't look up.

My parents didn't reappear all day. The glow of our window started to dim, and they still didn't return. I should have felt worried. I knew I should have been peeking outside the cell, looking for their familiar faces. Instead, in my mind, I found myself hoping that they had done something wrong and were sitting alone in the Hole. I didn't want to face them.

My internal clock told me that lights out was only minutes away. I finally gave in and sat up, leaning over the edge of the bunk to peer out the door. Inmates were shuffling by, pushing to get to their cells before the series of buzzers screamed at them.

The first buzz sounded. Just as it died into the static noise, I saw my mother duck into the doorway, my father close behind her. They walked straight to the shelf, jamming their dirty clothes onto the bottom shelf next to mine. My father washed his hands, running one over his tired face. I could see his hands shaking.

I stayed hanging over the edge of the bunk, carefully watching them. They always wound down the same way. Aside from the days where they just gave up and crashed into bed, there was a routine my parents did that never changed.

After turning off the water, my father drank a sip out of the metal cup, swishing it in his mouth and spitting it into the sink. Then he backed out of the way, hand coming to rest on the small of my mother's back as he beckoned her forward. She repeated exactly what he had done, first rinsing her hands, then her face, then swishing the water and spitting it back out.

My father followed my mother to the bed. The bunk underneath creaked as they both sank their weight into it. I could barely see them from where I leaned over the edge. They slowly untied their shoes and pulled them off, my father letting out a soft grunt. Tucking their socks deep down into the toes, they carefully lined the shoes along the bottom of the bunk. I could hear my father groan as they laid down, side by side, on the flat mat. Without having to look, I knew he had his arm draped over my mother, her body nestled against him.

The only thing different today was the silence. Usually my mother would chatter about trees or dinner or, when the moments took over, her swaying repetition of 'baby.' It was a wind-down noise I had grown used to. I had heard it my entire life. My father would grunt and mutter single words occasionally as my mother went on and on. Then they would fall silent together, drifting into sleep.

I don't know if it was because of work, or because of me, but tonight the cell was silent.

I sat back, realizing for the first time that my father wasn't as inexistent as I always had seen him to be. He rarely spoke. His body was always stooped and I had seen one too many guards and inmates push him around. Those were the only things I had ever noticed before.

Tonight I saw what I had always missed. His constant following of my mother wasn't because he was a shadow. He was a guard. His hand rested on the small of her back, calmed her shoulder, held her close against the nightmares I never knew. He let her talk instead of shutting her up, as much as that would have been appreciated.

There wasn't a doubt in my mind that my father loved my mother.

And, I suppose, he was the perfect one to love her. For he was just as much of a murderer as she was.

The strange softness for my father that had overcome me quickly disappeared as I remembered the truth about him. I could see him, his large hands clamped around a defenseless man's throat, squeezing tighter and tighter. The man fought, then finally slowed as his lips turned blue and his eyes bulged. Did my father ever think of stopping? Did he hate the feeling of draining life one second at a time from another living, struggling to breathe human being?

Or had he been like my mother, enjoying every second of it.

I slammed my head back against my pillow, trying to chase away the thoughts. I hated the anger that boiled inside. I wanted to hurt them. I wanted them to stop pretending. I wanted to see the true monsters they were.

Was I a monster too, for wanting that?

I could hear the snoring of my father rise up from the bunk beneath. Climbing down, I silently paced the floor. My bare feet softly slapped the concrete, becoming more ice-cold with every step.

They created me. I was a part of them. Was I doomed to the same insanity I saw engulf my mother and shroud my father? The thoughts hurt my head. I could feel the headache grow, banging angrily on the inside of my throbbing head. Laying down flat on my back, I let the coolness of the floor chill me. I welcomed the shivers that fought against the always present sweat.

"942B, is everything alright?"

I blinked my eyes. The nurse's voice sounded harsh and loud, causing me to crinkle my face up in pain.

"Uh, headache," I said, barely loud enough.

I heard the nurse shuffle some papers. Her foot tapped the ground impatiently as the papers flipped. "I'm sorry 942B, but you are not approved for any sort of pain medication."

"It's just a headache, can't you just −"

"I am sorry 942B, but you are not −"

"Okay, I get it." I wiped my hand over my face, my headache flaring.

I heard the nurse shuffle outside. "Is everything else alright tonight?"

"Yeah," I mumbled. "It's just great."

The three cups were shoved under the door. Before I could even look, the nurse hurried away, her shadow disappearing down the walk. Angry, I swiped at the cups, spilling all three across the ground. The pills rolled into the shadows, scattering across the cell floor. Laying one hand across my eyes, I let the darkness engulf me.

"Millie? You awake?"

Without moving, I reached and wiggled my fingers underneath the door. I could hear Jude crouch down outside. The light of his flashlight shot into my cell.

"Is everything alright?" he asked, his voice suddenly panicked.

Rolling onto my side, I looked through the opening. Jude's face was lit by the light, his eyes searching and worried.

"I'm fine," I said, trying to smile. "Killer headache."

"Here," Jude said, fishing into his pocket. He pulled out a little plastic container, dumping a white pill into the palm of his hand. I reached out and took it. Without asking, I threw it into my mouth and swallowed.

"Jude." My voice came out even and solid. "My parents are criminals."

I could hear Jude laugh. "And you just realized this?"

"No, Jude, really. They are crazy. They should be in here, and they should never leave." I swallowed hard. "They are monsters."

No response. I could hear Jude breathing, so I knew he was still there. I let the silence grow between us. I wanted so badly to voice the fears that now ran rampant in my mind. I wanted to scream out my anger. I wanted to cry in heavy tears my utter disappointment.

Instead, I just lay there.

Jude finally cleared his throat. In a weak voice, he tentatively asked, "So... have you been studying?"

I nodded, then realized that he couldn't see me. "Yes," I said simply.

"Good." I could hear him squirm in his spot. Something was wrong. He cleared his throat again. "Millie, they changed my schedule. This is my last night on night patrol. I had been hoping... you know... to catch up a bit before you disappear into the Nation. But, well, it looks like tonight is it."

"Oh." I suddenly felt empty again. My headache was disappearing thanks to the pill Jude had given me. Now I just felt numb.

"You be good, okay?"

"I will."

"And you better pass that test with some crazy flying colors."

I felt a chuckle tickle my lips. "You know I will."

Jude took in a deep breath, leaning his head against the door. "I'm going to miss you, Millie. You're a good friend you know... Jail Baby and all."

"I'll miss you too, Jude. GF and all."

In the distance I could hear the sound of boots. Jude sighed, then sat up. I could hear him part his lips to say something, then snap them back shut. Without another word, he stood and began to walk away. I pushed up against the door, trying to catch a glimpse of him through the small opening along the bottom. I only saw the beam of his flashlight as he swung it back and forth, pausing at each cell to shine it in.

Just as he disappeared from sight, I faintly heard his voice, lightly humming.

I crawled back into my bunk, my eyes suddenly heavy and burning.

I begged for the fog to take me. As if to spite me, it hid out of my reach. Everything was messed up now. I should be feeling elated to be so close to my release day. Instead, I had found that my entire life I had been sleeping above monsters. I would never talk to Jude again. Orrin was only a cell or two away, but always unreachable. Every one of the people I had let in as friends I had always kept at an untouchable distance, and now they were about to disappear.

Tears stung my eyes and I angrily wiped them away, turning on my side to face the dark wall. Crying wouldn't get to get me anywhere. Letting out a shuddering sigh, I felt the words of Jude's song form on my lips.

"And any time you feel the pain, hey Jude, refrain. Don't carry the world upon your shoulders..." I softly sang into the wall. I could feel my voice crack, but kept going, the words burned into my head from the time Jude and I had laid on the ground just the other night and played it over and over.

Before I knew it, I was asleep.

◧ ◧ ◧

I wish I could say I was strong. In the world I grew up in, a person had to know how to act strong. I knew how to throw on the tough face, how to push through the crowds, how to put the glare in my eyes that warned others to leave me alone. But inside, every time I found myself forced to act strong, I shook in utter fright. My heart sped and my eyes threatened at any moment to leak the tears that built so strong behind them. I could only act for so long.

The next day, I decided that acting strong was the last thing I wanted to do.

I could see the worried looks on my parent's faces as they got ready for their new jobs that morning. I still hadn't spoken a word to them. As they dressed and prepared to go, I just laid in my bed and stared at the ceiling. They kept glancing at me, obviously trying to decide if talking was even worth the try. I hoped that my cold presence gave them the answer.

Maybe I was acting immature. I was sure that is what Dr. Eriks would have said. She would say that even though they were convicted criminals, they were my parents, and blocking them out mere days before I would leave was causing more damage than good. I didn't care about damage. At that moment, as I lay frozen on my bunk, I didn't care about anything.

That was my day. I didn't bother to eat. Or even stand. I just laid on my bed and listened to the prison. Everything was ticking, every footstep and thud another second gone. There was no music. Just the clock of prison life ticking slowly until I was finally gone.

I fell back asleep before my parents even returned. No dreams came to me, nothing but blackness and silence. When I woke up again, the prison was already awake and moving. My body hurt worse than ever before, the entire day spent laying on my back on the cement bunk causing my muscles to lock up in pain.

I slowly climbed down off the bunk, willing my knees to bend and my back to straighten. Standing in the center of my cell, I squatted up and down a few times, feeling the joints pop and protest with every bend. My neck felt stiff, my eyes suddenly throbbing.

Realizing that my only other set of clothing was still dirty, I pulled on my old sneakers and bent down to the bottom of the bookshelf with a groan. All of the dirty clothes were gone. My mother hadn't done the laundry at all for the last year, if not longer. My breath caught in my throat. I knew I should have felt relieved. The woman really didn't need me. Instead, I felt a sudden sting of tears threaten my eyes.

My notebook sat near the edge of my bunk, its worn pages hanging over, threatening to fall out and scatter across the cell floor. I grabbed it and flipped it open to my schedule.

"Crap," I hissed, looking at the scribble of writing telling me that today was my last appointment with Dr. Eriks. And it was about to begin.

I shoved my journal under my pillow, ran my fingers quickly through my mess of hair, then booked it down the walkway. A few inmates, lounging along the walls or in their open cells, glanced up at me as I hurried past. No one ever hurried here. There was nothing ever worth hurrying for, aside from the lock of your cell door at lights out.

Luckily the hallway was empty as I ran toward Dr. Eriks' office. I paused just long enough for the guard at the hallway door to scan my bracelet. It felt like it took forever for the little device to beep.

I had no idea what time it actually was. I usually timed my day mentally from the moment the lights flashed on. When I missed that one event, I always felt off for the rest of the day. I silently begged that I wasn't late this time. Nothing would look worse than showing up late for the last appointment.

I should have known better.

I abruptly drew to a stop in front of the secretary's desk. She didn't even bother to look up at me, just waved her hand to motion me to go ahead in. I thought I could see her glance briefly out of the corner of her eye at me as I passed, but I never looked back to see.

"You are late, Millie."

My heart sank. I could feel my pulse racing, throbbing in my head and chest. Every muscle in my body screamed in protest at the sudden burst of movement and I could hear a distant ringing in the back of my head. Clenching my eyes shut a moment, I nodded. "I'm sorry Dr. Eriks. I overslept."

I slowly peeked my eyes back open. Dr. Eriks was eyeing me. "I told you to bring your journal today. Where is it?"

"I…uh…" It was my last session, and I was already messing up. I bit the inside of my cheek before looking down to the ground. "I forgot it."

"Sit down."

I ducked into my usual seat, thankful to see that there were no added chairs today. Dr. Eriks deftly picked up her notepad then took her usual seat across from me, crossing her legs under her stiff brown skirt. I found myself wondering if she owned anything else in her wardrobe other than that brown skirt. In every meeting I had with her, she always wore the same type of dull brown skirt that fit just tight enough to show her lack of hips. Looking down at my own clothes, I took in my worn jeans and crumpled white shirt, dirty from wear. They were the same items of clothing I wore every single day, without choice. I suddenly longed for the choice, the feeling sweeping over me in a way I had never felt before. As I looked back up at her skirt, I made a mental note to never buy a white t-shirt for myself again.

"How are you doing today, Millie?"

I shrugged. "Alright I guess."

"I see that you failed to attend any meals yesterday."

My mouth went dry. "I... I wasn't hungry." As if denying my statement, my stomach growled loudly. Dr. Eriks raised an eyebrow, watching me closely with her lips pursed. I lowered my head. "I wasn't hungry," I repeated softly.

"Millie, are you angry at your parents?"

I stared at my hands. I already knew what she would say. I had already repeated it over and over to myself the last day, and it still didn't make any difference. Without saying anything, I let my head slowly nod.

"Good. You should be."

I wondered if I had heard her correctly. Lifting my eyes, I saw no humor on her face. Just a perfect mask of stern seriousness.

"Your parents are criminals, Millie. They killed two men and attempted to murder the last. If he hadn't been able to get away and find authorities, they may have gotten away with it. You have watched your parents. You know they are... strange." Dr. Eriks flipped open her notepad. "You have told me that you are the only one who does the laundry; that you must remind your own mother to bathe herself. Your father rarely speaks. At our last meeting, you stated you were 'needed here.' Do you still feel this way?"

I couldn't answer. I could sense the fog creeping in, and I wanted so badly to dive into it and disappear from this sudden interrogation. Dr. Eriks watched me a moment, then picked up a slim folder that sat on the table next to her. She pulled out a paper, skimming it for a moment with her eyes before looking back at me. With one hand, her eyes still locked on me, she pulled the table around, setting it between us.

"Your mother is unstable. She suffers from self-imposed 'amnesia,' psychosis, and bi-polar disorder. I am sure that you have seen the moments, where her reality slips." She paused. When her voice spoke again, it came out gentle, almost soothing. "This is the only safe place for her, Millie. Spokane sees to all her needs, while guaranteeing that her crimes cannot be repeated out in the Nation."

Dr. Eriks reached into the folder and pulled out a small stack of photos. She laid them out in front of me on the small table, one at a time. The first was my father's mug shot. His hair looked as disheveled as ever, but his face was young and barely hinted with stubble. His eyes were bloodshot, heavy with dark bags. The next was my mother's mug shot. She was beautiful. Her skin glowed. Even though it was knotted with twigs, her hair somehow managed to still flow in honey waves around her slim face. Her eyes, though focused and intense, were blood shot, the stain of tears still evident on her cheeks.

Dr. Eriks watched me carefully as she laid down the next photo. A shot of a knife laying on the ground, a number propped next to it. Dark blood covered the dirty knife. I could feel my stomach twist, but I couldn't close my eyes.

Another photo. This one of a man, his face a chalky blue, bruises dark and painful around his swollen throat. Dr. Eriks carefully laid down the last photo, her hand resting on it a moment before uncovering it for my eyes to see.

A man lay sprawled on the ground, dirt smudged over his body, twigs stuck in his hair. His face was frozen in a grimace, his eyes wide open. The rest of his body was red. Dark, blood red. I tore my eyes away, biting hard against the nausea that fought to take me over.

"Your parents are criminals, Millie," Dr. Eriks said slowly, carefully emphasizing each word. "But you are not. You owe these criminals nothing. You owe the Nation everything. The Nation needs you. You are good and strong and loyal. Aren't you, Millie?"

I still clenched my eyes shut. My lips pressed harder together, biting back the waves of nausea that beat against every inch of my body. I barely managed a nod. The soft shuffle of papers let me know that Dr. Eriks had put away the photos. I found myself silently grateful that I hadn't eaten for the last day. I inched my eyes open.

"I hope you have studied hard for the Exam tomorrow, Millie. It would be a shame to find my assessment of you has been wrong." Dr. Eriks sat back and watched me, the smile growing on her face. She looked so smug, so strangely content.

"Is there anything you would like to discuss, Millie?"

I shook my head.

"Anything about the fogs?"

My eyes shot up to meet hers. I had never told her about the moments the fog took me over.

Dr. Eriks leaned forward in her chair, her thin wrists dangling loosely off her knees. "Your mother experiences moments where, as she says, a 'fog' takes over and sets her free. It would be natural for you to notice. Maybe even experience them yourself. It is simply your subconscious, in its untrained way, trying to 'protect' you. But you know you need no protection, from us, don't you Millie?"

Her eyes pierced into me, as if daring me to argue.

I nodded.

Fogs. My mother had fogs. My crazy mother, who murdered a man with her own hands and now escaped into her own world in a snap, had fogs. And so did I. My mouth went dry.

Dr. Eriks grinned once more, then settled back in her chair. "You may go, Millie."

Without a pause, I stood and hurried out the door. I could feel those photos behind me. They taunted me, screaming at me to look them in the face. I needed to get as far away from them as possible. As I walked through the door, I looked up to see Carl standing in my path.

"What…" I could feel my tongue freeze stupidly in my mouth.

The secretary glanced up at me, then over to Carl. "I called for escort again. The last session is always the hardest." Her voice sounded doubtful. I could see her watching Carl, her brows slowly knitting together. "But maybe —"

"No," Carl cut off her. "Procedure is procedure. Besides, I'm already here." He grinned at me, then moved aside and beckoned me forward. "Well, let's get going."

The secretary watched me walk past her desk, her face still knotted in sudden anxiety. I looked away from her, walking quickly past and headed down the hall without pausing. I had always thought that walking away from this office for the last time would be liberating. But now as I moved down the hall I felt thicker and slower than ever before.

Carl hurried to walk next to me. As we rounded a corner and finally disappeared from the secretary's stare, Carl grabbed my arm and slammed me hard into the nearest doorway.

My faced smacked hard into the metal door before I even had time to throw my hands up. I blinked. A small grunt escaped my lips as my head spun madly, my cheek already throbbing in instant pain. Carl grabbed me by the shoulders and spun me around, driving my back into the wall of the doorway.

"So," he hissed in a low voice, "this is what I am thinking. I think you should apply for a job here. I think it would be a very good choice on your part."

He held me tight by my shoulders. I cringed in pain as his fingers clamped harder into my flesh. I could feel the wall behind me, grinding against my spine as he shoved me harder against its cold surface.

A few inmates walked by, glancing a moment into the doorway. As soon as they saw us, they quickly lowered their eyes and scurried away. To them it looked like a guard punishing a fellow inmate who had acted up, nothing more. They didn't want to chance their own actions becoming noticed as well.

"Wh-why?" I forced out, my lungs still gasping for breath. I could feel the headache throbbing behind my eyes and the burn of pain flaring on my cheek.

Carl chuckled. He leaned in closer. I could feel his hot touch as it grazed my flesh. He rose up slowly, his breath on my neck, my cheek, my ear. Stopping at my hair, he slowly drew a breath in. I could see his lips part in a grin.

"I like you, Millie."

My body tightened, chills running down my raked spine.

"Carl…"

Carl slammed me again against the wall. I couldn't breathe. My head threw back, the back of it smacking dully against the wall. Foggy patches swam in front of my eyes. Trying to blink them away, I felt the sting of painful tears. Carl's eyes bore into mine, something unstable and dangerous floating across their icy blue.

"Don't. Interrupt. Me." he said, his voice low and growling. I could see the anger in his eyes flare. Then, as quickly as it grew, it disappeared. He smiled again, so close I could see the hint of stubble on his upper lip. "I said I like you. I have for some time. Why the hell else would I volunteer to come work down here? I needed to be near you, Millie. I needed to make sure that you…" He breathed me in again. "I needed to guarantee I would get you. I get what I want Millie. And I like you."

He pressed harder against me. "Please, Carl, you're hurting me," I managed to force out.

He just ignored me. "So, I think you need to ask for a job here. In the upper blocks, where I will be transferring back to very soon. I have tried to suggest it nicely. But obviously nice just didn't get my point across." He pushed harder against me. "If you don't accept…

well... I really, really think you should accept." He looked into my eyes, his eyes dark and icy.

"Carl GF4, what is the issue here?" The sound of another man's voice startled both of us. Carl loosened his iron grip as he backed away a few inches. Another guard stood in the center of the hall, watching us.

"Inmate was being resistant," Carl said coolly. "I was just reminding her to stay in place."

The other guard watched him a moment, then let his eyes slide over to me. I knew my cheek was red and I couldn't calm my gasps for air. "Well, it looks like she got it. Cool it a bit, GF."

"Yes sir," Carl said, his voice oddly submissive.

"Well, come on then. You can help me with patrols." The guard glanced at me again, his face bored. "I recommend you find your way to your cell, Inmate."

I couldn't even bring myself to nod.

Carl looked at me once more. His eyes screamed a million words to me, all of which managed to only make me shake worse. Then the grin spread on his lips again. A second later he turned away, joining the guard as they made their way down the hall.

I couldn't move. I sucked in air in ragged gasps, colors swimming before my eyes. A few inmates walked by. I could see them glance at me, taking me in. My face must have been white. I could feel the cool perspiration on my cheeks, contrasting the hot pain that throbbed in my tender cheek.

Finally shaking away the shock enough to shuffle my feet, I made my way back to my cell. Crawling into my bunk, I pulled my thin blanket over my shoulders. I would have given anything at that moment to see the door slam shut, locking me safely inside my cell. Alone. I had never been handled that way in my life. The sight of the wall flying at my face made me flinch again, even as I huddled under my blanket in the dark cell.

I didn't realize I was crying until a sudden shuddering gasp wretched out of my throat. Tears streamed down my face. Carl's words replayed in my head. He liked me. I had always thought that someone liking you would make you feel warm, comfortable. Happy. But the low rumble of his voice, the grasp he had as he clenched my shoulders tight against the wall, I knew this wasn't right. I wasn't liked. He didn't want me for who I was.

He wanted me for something else. Something I couldn't fathom.

▯ ▯ ▯

My parents returned to the cell just before the buzz of lights out. I stared numbly at the ceiling, my face still throbbing. A few times I had thought to climb down and look to see if there was a bruise, but the thought of standing in the open doorway where anyone could see me glued me immediately back onto the bunk.

There was no talking, again. Along the walk the mumble of the Lifers echoed as they prepared for yet another night in the prison that had claimed them. But here, in my family's cell, it was silent.

My parents looked exhausted. My mother's eyes were glazed, giving away that she was already lost in a distant trance. Her hair stood in every direction, parts still sudsy from the vile laundry room soap. I could see her hands as she shakily took off her shoes. They were red and raw, small cracks in the worn flesh still lightly bleeding.

My father barely moved. He came into the cell far enough to pull off his shoes and line them along the bunk. Then I heard the thud and gush of breath as he landed hard onto the bunk. Everything fell completely silent. I almost leaned over to check on him, wondering if he still was still breathing, but stopped myself.

My mother stood in the center of the cell, swaying back and

forth. I could see the side of her face, the exhausted droop of her lips tugging her face down. With my father asleep, no one would guide to her to bed now. When I was young, I would sometimes wake in the night to her standing just as she was now, mechanically swaying back and forth, for hours. I would lay and watch her, mesmerized by the clockwork of her movement. I thought it was beautiful. Like a dance to hidden music I had never been allowed to hear.

This time I could only see one thing: Insanity.

I felt oddly awake, as if someone had finally opened my eyes to the nut job my mother truly was. Her hands were gripped in tight fists at her side, nails digging into the soft flesh of her palms. A drop of blood, squeezed out from one of the open cracks on her hand, dropped with a tiny splash to the ground. As I watched, I realized that she wasn't just swaying. She was moving. Her hands would slightly lift, then drop. Her head would lean to one side, turn to the other. Her eyes widened, then drooped.

Even though I knew better, I let my eyes glance to look at the space in front of her. Something in me expected to see another person standing there, silently joining her in this strange, silent conversation. Only the cold wall stood in front of her.

An hour passed. I couldn't take my eyes off of her. She looked exhausted. Even in the darkness of the cell I could see the bags grow darker under her eyes. Her shoulders slumped, her wrists heavy at her sides as if weights had been tied to them and forgotten. Her lips quivered as she mouthed words. She whispered the hushed words over and over, sound never escaping her dry lips.

A sob suddenly escaped her throat. It was barely audible, easily missed if I hadn't been watching her so intently. A choked cry of utter pain. Loss. Agony. It ended in a low growl of deep anger that continued for a solid minute. Then she stopped. Stopped moving, stopping talking, even stopped breathing as her entire body seemed to freeze into dead stone.

As if someone had slapped her across the face, my mother suddenly came to. Turning her head sharply, her eyes met mine. I could see the shine of tears in her tired eyes, glowing in the dim light of the cell. We didn't speak. I just watched as she finally up-rooted her bare feet from the cold ground and crawled into bed next to my father.

Snatching up my notebook, I crawled down as soon as I heard her breathing even out into the slow, long draws of sleep. I crept across to the door then flopped down on my stomach. My shoe laces were already knotted together, the note already tied securely to the end. Without waiting, I threw the note out the door.

A minute later I felt the tug.

Reeling it in, I nearly ripped the paper as I pulled the note open, barely scanning my question that I had scribbled on the page.

What is a bird?

In careful curves, the returned note simply read:

Free.

I read the word again. I let myself whisper it, carefully pronounce it. It rolled off of my tongue, tickling my lips and disappearing into the murmur of the prison night. Something inside me longed for that word. I had never felt this way before. Now I couldn't seem to feel anything else.

Orrin, what if I inherit this madness? They are both mad. Will I be too?

Orrin wrote back quickly, his hand-writing slurred as if he too felt the need for the answer that was pounding inside of me.

You are who you are, Millie. No one decides who you are but yourself. If you want to be mad like them, then be mad. But if you want to be different, please, be different.

But what will I become? I wrote. *What is going to happen to me?*

I swore I could hear the sigh of someone just down the walk. Then the echo of a light chuckle. The shoelace tugged.

Dear, that is a question every child your age has asked since the dawn of time. Life is ahead of you. What this Nation is doing... Something was scribbled out, impossible to read past the angry dark slashes. *They lock away the people and make them become the criminals they so fear. I do not know what you will become. But I pray to God that you don't allow them to decide your fate.*

I felt confused suddenly. *What do you mean? What is the Nation doing?*

There is a lot you don't know yet, Millie. Orrin's handwriting slowed, curving carefully as he emphasized his words. *There is a lot to learn. Remember everything your schooling has taught you. But remember: To every truth, there are a million untold truths.*

Do I get to meet you before I leave? I wrote it carefully, trying to copy his perfect curving letters. I hoped that he understood the emphasis, the meaningful question of my words.

It took longer this time to feel the tug. Pulling it in, I carefully opened the note, my breath held.

Millie, believe me, I would love to meet you. You have become like a daughter to me in here. I lost my boys, and now I am losing you. But I would rather you leave with the memory of me as this fishing pseudo father of yours than the balding old man with nothing memorable about him. Can you do that?

I could feel sudden tears of disappointment sting my eyes. I had hoped that Orrin would instantly say yes. I could see us in my mind, finally meeting just as I left to take my Exam, his eyes proud, his smile broad and reassuring. It was true what he had written. Orrin truly had become like a father to me in this prison.

I could look. I could find him. He was only a cell or two away. It wouldn't be hard to discover which man he was. I just needed to see him, to know he was real. To know that even after I left, Orrin would exist. I knew though, even as the desperate thoughts flooded my mind, that it wouldn't happen.

His words, speaking in my mind, repeated over and over. Was his sentencing all truly just a big mistake? Or was he lying, knowing that the truth of him also being a monster would only chase away this young girl he had mentally adopted as his own? I forced the thoughts away. Orrin had never written anything to me that seemed like a lie. I believed him.

I needed to believe him.

I had to.

Orrin, I wrote carefully, *Why don't you fight it? Why don't you try to prove your innocence?*

I tried, once. He wrote back. *I had found out that after my sentencing, there were more murders in the town.* The handwriting suddenly smudged. I stared at it a moment, confused at the strange spray of wet pencil scratch. My finger lightly touched it, its surface still warm. It was a tear. *My wife had been killed. My older son too. They had been killed the same way as all the other murders and I was miles away, locked in this cell, unable to protect them. I tried to use it as evidence that I was innocent. But the authorities didn't care. They deemed it as a copy-cat killing, and denied my appeal request. I search the archives but I never could find my youngest boy who had survived. He had vanished. He was gone. I had to give up.*

Seeing that Orrin had given up felt like a slap across my face. My cheek began to throb, suddenly reminding me of Carl.

But it is the truth. They have to listen to the truth. I wrote back. I felt feverish, my hand pressing the pencil so hard into the page that it tore through and scratched loudly against the ground. Glancing up to my parents, I caught my breath. They didn't even stir.

Orrin seemed to tug on the shoelace as soon as it landed. I pulled it back in and read the scribbled words, spotted with more tears.

I had no truth to return to. Here is your first lesson outside of the books, Millie: In Prison Nation, the truth can't set you free.

░ ░ ░

Orrin hadn't responded any more to me that night. I tried. I threw the note out and waited, but no tug responded. I read his last message over and over, after finally climbing into my bunk. My eyes ached from squinting in the dark. Whether it was the intense slant of his painful writing, the splattering of tears, or something else, I couldn't bring myself to stop reading.

I must have fallen asleep. When I woke up, my hands still painfully clutched the paper. The doors hadn't opened yet. Grateful that my inner clock was finally working again, I tucked the note tightly into my notebook then climbed down, stretching my fingers out painfully. Stepping in front of the mirror, I threw on my clean clothes, breathing in the smell of the soap I hated so much. I finally stopped to look at my cheek.

It was still red, but luckily had not bruised. I raised a fingertip to lightly touch it and winced as a sharp bolt of pain shot through my cheek and down my jaw. Cranking on the water, I felt the sudden sting of ice cold water pelt out of the tap. I bent down and splashed it over and over on my face, grateful for the coldness that shocked me awake. Before long, my face was numb. My entire face was red as I looked back into the mirror, the sting on my cheek masked by the cold shock of water.

I felt fully awake for the first time in days. Moving to stand near the door, I let my body lean against the wall as I waited for the buzz and the door to slide open. It seemed to take forever. I could see the glow of morning light shining in the thick window. Inmates in cells nearby moved around, prepping themselves for the day ahead.

My parents were still asleep. Frozen in time, always in the same position, they looked like stone etched statues. Monuments left to lie forever in that small bunk as a cold reminder that they did, in fact, exist. I turned away, focusing my eyes on the door.

It finally slid open.

As I hurried down the walk, I could feel my stomach growl in hunger. I couldn't remember the last time I had eaten. I didn't have time to go to the cafeteria though. Luckily, most days a cart was left along the wall in the Commons, equipped with a small pile of old fruit and stale rolls. Someone would roll it in before lights on, and its stale stockpile quickly disappeared before the first rush of inmates emptied the Commons.

Pushing my way toward the cart, I grabbed a crusty roll and ducked away as those behind me reached for their share. The roll was stale, obviously left over from some meal the day before. I forced myself to swallow it, feeling it stick in my throat. After a few hard swallows, I finally felt it move down.

As I hurried away, angry voices started to rise behind me. Someone shouted something about the food. Followed quickly with the dull thud as a fist made contact with a body. Before I knew it, more voices rose, screaming at each other as the sound of bodies slamming into each other grew louder. The pound of heavy boots was the last thing I heard as I ducked into the doorway and disappeared down the hall.

I didn't pause to look back.

I had only been down this hall one other time in my life. One year ago, almost exactly to the date. I had requested to pull out of the schooling program and continue as an independent study. Before they could grant me the request though, I had to meet with the Warden.

His office tucked neatly away at the end of this hall. My parents had come with me that time. Sitting before the man, his large body barely tucked behind the small wooden desk, had been intimidating. I had been grateful that my parents sat on either side of me, feeling as if their presence had been some sort of protection against the unknown.

It seemed that most of the citizens who worked in this prison were bored, their eyes almost always hooded, a yawn always present on their face. That was the Warden. I had heard he was once a Marine. Special Ops. Whatever that meant. Once the Nation had built the Wall, the push for Marines diminished. The rest of the world had decided to leave the Nation alone. The need for armored grunt men became almost inexistent. I had always wondered if the bored look on the Warden's chiseled face was regret.

He had carelessly warned me that if I failed to accomplish the schooling, I might not be allowed out on my eighteenth birthday. Then, without waiting for a promise or any questions, he had stamped my request and sent me away.

My eyes trailed down the hall into the darkness, knowing his office waited beyond. That day, a year ago, I had walked away with my parents on either side. My mother had jabbered excitedly about my future, my father silently smiling as he kept his eyes glued ahead.

No one else stood in the hall today.

I finally reached the door.

As I stood in front of it, I felt my stomach tangle up. This was the test that would help decide the rest of my life. Would I go free? Would I fail and be labeled? My hand hovered over the metal handle, suddenly scared to twist it and walk in. My confidence had fled me, hiding away in a place I knew I would never dare to go and retrieve it.

A feeling rose inside me, longing for my mother's laughter and my father's presence. It had always been there. Gritting my teeth, I shook my head. The feeling disappeared, escaping into the fog hiding in the corners of my mind until it was gone.

Knees shaking, throat tight, I finally twisted the handle.

"Millicent 942B?"

I stood in the doorway, my hands clasped tightly together. "Yes."
My voice shook. I cleared my throat, trying to chase away the shake
that spread like fire over my entire body. It wouldn't leave.

"Come in and stand on the line."

I watched my feet as I quickly walked in and made my way to the
yellow line painted on the cement floor. The door swung shut
behind me, clicking loudly. With my toes carefully touching the line,
I finally dared to look up.

In front of me, sitting in a row behind a simple metal table, five
people stared back. A single light hung from the center of the
ceiling, casting strange shadows across the room and darkening the
faces of the panel. Letting my eyes adjust, I watched them nervously
as they took me in.

Reverend Smitson sat at the left end of the table. My family never attended church, but I had seen him before when I walked down the prison hallways. He had his own small chapel near the psychiatric wing. Sometimes I would slow as I passed, listening to his booming voice as he preached about God's love and mercy to his small congregation. Barely anyone, it seemed, bothered to publicly practice religion in here anymore. The few who chose to attend always had to travel in tight groups, protecting themselves from the many inmates who were intolerant of faith.

Faith, it seemed, was a dying trend.

Reverend Smitson watched me, his brow knitted and his lips parted as if ready to launch into another 'Praise the Lord and God's great Nation' tirade. His skin was dark, nearly black in the dim light of the exam room. It shone as if polished. He was dressed in his usual black, a strip of white tightly wrapped around his slim neck.

Next to the Reverend sat Dr. Eriks. Her lips were pursed, the spray of lines drawing my eyes in. Even though I hated seeing her sit there, her dull eyes smugly watching my every move, I felt a strange comfort in seeing those lines.

Warden Binns sat in the center. His stomach had loosened since the last time I had seen him and his dark hair, neatly cropped, had new sprinkles of gray. The Warden's hat sat neatly on the table, his fingers occasionally reaching out to lightly stroke its worn rim. Crammed awkwardly in his chair, his face echoed the angst of being forced to sit.

To his right sat Judge Wood. I had never seen him before. I only knew it was him because of his nose.

A few years back there had been a large commotion in the Commons. It was so loud, roaring so thoroughly through the cement walls and closed doors of the prison, that I had heard it clear in my cell. Out of dumb curiosity I had crept down the hall and peeked into the crowded Commons. Inmates were standing around, laughing and cheering as they happily clapped one another on the shoulder. It was a strange sight to see.

One standing near the door was talking rather loudly. I barely had to lean in to hear what had happened. A man had been in court, fighting against a charge of Arson 1. Even though he had evidence proving his non-guilty plea, there had been one small stipulation that had managed to sentence him. Judge Wood had slapped him with a fifteen year sentence.

In rage, the man had jumped the table and reached the Judge before the guards had a chance to react. In one swift swing, his fist made contact with the Judge's nose. It had shattered instantly. Everyone in the Commons cheered on the man, who was now sentenced to life with no parole.

Judge Wood's nose now sat severely crooked on his chubby face. I could hear the soft wheeze of breath as he sucked air in and out. Everything about him was chubby. His sausage fingers tapped the table mindlessly, dimpled knuckles bending and popping. He licked his bloated lips, his bulging eyes blinking slowly.

The last person at the table had to be Oscar Ramos. He was small, his shaggy brown hair oiled down in an obvious attempt to better his dirty appearance. Everything about him seemed oddly dusty. Even though his clothes were cleaned and pressed, they still held the worn look of a farmer. One hand nervously brushed across his mouth, his knuckles pressing hard into his thin lips.

The Warden cleared his throat. "942B, are you ready?"

Licking my lips, I forced myself to nod. The Warden glanced at the others, then looked back to me. "Begin."

I shut my eyes a moment, focusing on the memorized words I had practiced over and over the last few days. Looking them in the face was too intimidating. I could feel their focus on me, waiting. Flicking my eyes back open, I focused on the table. I hoped they would accept this as a fair trade.

"In the late 20th century, the United States of America stood as a strong force in the modern world. With allies scattered across the globe, the U.S. held a power that other nations could only dream of. But within the country, they were weak. National debt was rising. The very citizens tore at each other worse than any war ever could." I took a deep breath. My voice was coming out strong, clear and sure of its words. Inside, I shook harder than ever.

"Crime rates were rising on a crazy upward climb. Law offices sprouted up, taking advantage of the accused to rake in money that should have been going back to the government. By the dawn of the 21st century, it became the norm to sue instead of settle. And crimes still kept climbing. The country was bankrupt.

"The U.S. government finally realized that their nation was crumbling. They formed a plan to save it. Discarding the cursed name, our country renamed itself the Nation. A strong, powerful name, lacking any shame of the past.

"Changes began with simple measures: guaranteeing harsher punishment for crime. The Nation hoped this would deter potential criminals. It worked for a short time, but soon that plan showed its weakness. Lawyers and juries still leant a soft ear to the lies of the criminals. Twisting the truth and playing on the selected jurors' weaknesses still enabled the criminals to go free.

"That was when the final laws were put into motion. The Nation discarded the practice of law offices. Along with that, all trials were only conducted as bench trials, leaving the well-trained and fair Judge to determine the sentence without having to deal with simple-minded jury members and lawyers."

I paused. My eyes flicked up to the panel. Their gazes were locked on me, waiting for me to continue. Judge Wood had straightened in his chair, a proud look crossing his chubby face at the mention of his job.

"Twenty-five years ago, the UN accused our great Nation of crimes against its people." I went on, steadying my breath. "The Nation realized it no longer required the allies of the world. All it required was itself. Our Nation withdrew from the UN. And the UN threatened war.

"That was when our great Nation built the Wall. It stretches along each coast, and through the land that borders between Mexico, and Canada. No one without clearance is allowed in, or out. It is our protection. Within our Wall, we can now keep in our justice, and shut out the world's threats.

"We are safe now. We are secure now. The good, the strong, walk free in our great land. And those who commit crimes are justly punished. We need not fear evil, for the only evil is that which we lock away."

I stopped. Something inside me twisted. I could see my mother's face, looking at me with the glazed look of insanity. My father leaving his dinner out for me to eat. The fishing paper, with Orrin's perfect handwriting carefully lined across it. The memorized textbook words twisted in my mind. My head started to spin.

I could hear someone clear their throat. Looking up, I saw all five were staring intently at me, leaned forward slightly in their chairs as if waiting for something. I mentally shook my head, forcing the twisted knot to hide away.

"I... I am proud to be part of our great Nation." I said. "I look forward to my release, where I can prove that I am good and strong. I will work for our Nation to keep it strong. Those in the Prisons deserve their sentences. Criminals are liars, and we cannot trust them. I hope to be trusted, as I prove that I have been cleansed of the evil that brought me into this world."

For some reason, I felt the sting of tears behind my eyes. I tried desperately to push it away. To show weakness now, at the end of my exam, would be a catastrophe.

The panel was quiet, watching me. I could see Oscar running his clenched hand across his lips, glancing occasionally at the others who sat down the table from him. Dr. Eriks had the smug smile spread on her lips. The Reverend was nodding, the Judge bearing into me with his disheartening gaze.

The Warden stifled a yawn. "Thank you, 942B. You may be excused."

That was it. The Exam was over. I realized I had finished it too soon. I had heard that the Exam could take hours. Mine took mere minutes. Panic raced in my mind, worrying that I had left out something. Replaying my words in my head, they all seemed perfect. But why had I finished so early?

I didn't realize that I was walking down the hall until I hit the Commons. Inmates sat in small groups, barely noticing me as I passed. I could only see the tattooed bodies, the angry faces, the shaded eyes, the occasional flitting eyes of a hiding Jail Baby. I could only see danger. I couldn't wait to get away from this place.

With hours to kill, I did the only thing I could think of. I crawled into my bunk, and fell asleep.

☐ ☐ ☐

The sound of someone washing their hands pulled me from my empty dreams. My father leaned at the sink, scrubbing at his hands vigorously. I could see a stream of red mixing with the water that flushed away down the rusted drain.

"What happened?" I asked before I could stop myself.

My father jumped at the sound of my voice. I could see his shoulders sag as he let out a heavy sigh. "Just a cut. At work. They said I don't even need stitches." I saw him wince in pain as he scrubbed at it again. "Don't worry." Still wincing, my father pulled a small sliver of metal out of the cut on his hand, dropping it to wash away down the drain.

I climbed down from my bunk and crossed over to him. Unrolling some of the rough toilet paper, I waited for him to turn off the water, then handed him the wad. "Thanks," he muttered, taking it carefully from me and pressing it to the cut. I could see dark red already soaking through the thick paper.

"You should go to the Infirmary. You need to get that checked again."

My father stared at his hand, pressing harder against the bleeding. "No, they said I'm fine. Don't worry, Millie." He looked up at me, forcing a small smile to pass on his face before he winced again in pain.

Moving past me, he sat heavily on the edge of the bunk. Unrolling more toilet paper, I walked over to his side and waited. He kept his head down, carefully pulling the now blood saturated ball of toilet paper off his hand. As he moved to cover it with the new bundle, I caught a glimpse of the wound.

The side of his left hand, right along his thumb, was sliced cleanly open. I could see the bulge of white fat and gleam of bone clearly, all covered in the thick red of flowing blood. It clearly needed stitches.

My father pressed the clean ball of toilet paper to the wound, shamefully handing me the dirty one. Without pausing, I moved over to the toilet and dropped it in. I watched as the red toilet paper soaked up the water, already tearing apart and disintegrating. I hit the flush handle and the red mess disappeared.

He didn't need me. He was my father, but he was also an adult. I had been told that the prison would take care of him. I almost turned to walk away, to let him lie down and rest. They had told him he would be fine, so who was I to argue?

I looked back to my father's face. It was losing color fast, his lip quivering as he pressed harder on his bloody hand. His eyes were focused on the ground beneath him, drops of blood splattering onto the cold cement.

"Dad..."

I stepped closer, my hand rising to softly touch his shoulder. He lifted his eyes too look at me. They were watery, floating in the pain he tried so hard to bite back. My fingers snagged on the rough fabric of his shirt. I felt something in my chest heave.

I parted my lips. I wanted to say I forgave him. I wanted to feel him cradle me in his arms like he had when I was small, chasing away the shadows of this world. I wanted him to protect me like he protected my mother.

As if hearing my thoughts, my father tore his eyes away, glancing out the cell door. "Where is your mother?" he asked, his voice suddenly anxious.

"What..." I felt the heave in my chest snap. Jerking my hand off his shoulder, I took a step back. My father was still staring out the door. His hand shook, blood dripping into the deep red pool on the ground. "Who cares. You need to take care of yourself right now, Dad."

He shook his head, his eyes swimming dangerously in his head. I could see his cheeks losing color. "No, they said I am fine. Where is your..." His voice slurred. Licking his lips, he forced his eyes to the ground. His face paled even more.

"I'm getting a Medic," I announced.

"Millie, I said that I'm —"

"I said, I'm getting a Medic."

With that, I stormed out of the cell. The Medic room was just down the walk, positioned to be nearby for a reason. There were a lot of injuries here. I banged roughly on the door then waited. After some time a woman finally peeked out. I could tell she wasn't a convict. The scared look on her face, the long wavy hair pulled back into a clean pony tail, the neatly trimmed nails with white tips only served to give her away. There was no way she had ever served time.

"My father is injured."

"Name?" she asked, pulling out a small plastic box that fit into the palm of her hand.

"Alan 942B."

She typed in the name then waited. The machine sat silent a moment, then beeped. "It says he was examined at the site and deemed fit to return to cell for rest."

"I can see fat," I snarled through clenched teeth. "And bone. He won't stop bleeding. Does that sound 'fit' to you?"

The nurse's eyes widened for a moment at the hiss of my voice. Checking the device again, she added nervously, "And his points amount only allows —"

"Take it from my points." As she opened her mouth to protest, I cut her off again. "Yes, you can. I am given points as an allowance until I leave. Take the amount you need and fix his damn hand."

The nurse looked at me a moment, her eyes wide in fear. Then she nodded once, picked up a small bag, and pushed past me. I watched as she made her way toward my block, then I let my body slump heavily against the now closed door.

I felt strangely exhausted. Even though I had just woken up, my eyes were now heavy, my body laboring for breath. I didn't know what had come over me. The sudden rage that had driven me was something I had never felt before. It scared me. Yet, at the same time, I felt oddly powerful. The look the nurse had given me as I hissed my words at her seemed oddly fulfilling. And that feeling, the feeling of enjoying the innocent woman's fear, was what scared me the most.

A clock hung on the wall above the nurse's station, covered in strips of metal. Looking up at it, I saw that it was almost 1300. I had just enough time to make it to the Parole room. Cursing at myself for pushing time again, I started to run.

My toes lined along the yellow line once again. The Parole room looked nearly identical to the Exam room. The only change was the small desk set up in the corner, an old typewriter waiting on its worn surface. I was alone in the room. In my rush, I had arrived there early and was told by the guard in the hall to go in and wait.

So I waited.

I heard the door swing open. Keeping my eyes glued to my toes, I could hear the shuffle of feet as the Panel made their way to their seats. I could hear Dr. Eriks sigh, the groan of Judge Wood as he lowered himself into his seat. Another light shuffle of feet sounded as the typist made her way to the waiting typewriter.

Someone cleared his throat, loud and demanding. I jerked my eyes up.

There, sitting in the Warden's spot, was Carl.

"Hello 942B," he said, his voice cool and relaxed. I could see the hint of a grin on his lips. My whole body went ice cold. "Warden Binns was unexpectedly called away to other duties. I have been asked to sit in for him at this hearing." He bore his eyes into me. "Are there any objections to this decision?"

I could hear the quick typing as the woman in the corner recorded every word he said. I licked my lips, feeling their sudden dryness crack under my quivering tongue. "No." I barely managed to speak.

Carl smiled, leaning back in his chair. "Then let it be on record that the release hearing for Millicent 942B has begun." He turned slightly to Dr. Eriks. "Doctor, would you care to begin?"

Dr. Eriks flipped open a folder that laid on the metal table. I could see my photo taped to the inside, my black and white face staring intently out. Swallowing hard, I tried to calm the shaking that threatened to take over my body.

"Patient, casually addressed as 'Millie,' has been seeing me weekly for the past fifteen years. Her mother has been incarcerated for life, Murder 1 and Assault 1. Her father has been incarcerated for life, Murder 1 and Aiding. Medical evaluations have found Millie's mother, Leann 942B, suffers from self-imposed amnesia, psychosis, and bi-polar disorder. Medications have worked to an extent to calm violent episodes."

Violent episodes? In my entire life, I had never seen my mother lift a finger to any person. When stress or fear or anger came up, she would just disappear into her strange trance. I found myself wondering suddenly if those trances were just drug-induced controls. My mind started to swim in questions, and I tried desperately to suppress them as Dr. Eriks went on.

"Neither parent shows remorse for their crimes. They have insisted that the men 'deserved it.' Upon their entry into Spokane Prison, inmates Alan and Leann found that they were pregnant.

Abortion was strongly urged, but they refused."

I couldn't understand why Dr. Eriks was talking about my parents. I had come in there expecting a review on myself, on who I was. Instead, she sat stiffly in her chair, her dull eyes reading the words printed permanently in my folder. Words about my parents.

Something she said slowly sank in. I had always thought I was conceived and born inside this prison. That wasn't true. My parents were already pregnant with me before they were committed. And they had refused to abort me when urged to. Something tugged at my mind, but I forced it away, realizing that Dr. Eriks still had not stopped.

"...always seemed indifferent to parents' crimes. In most sessions, has been calm, aloof, and quiet. Millie has stepped up to her parents' responsibilities. Millie withdrew from school a year early to proceed in independent study."

Pausing a moment, Dr. Eriks dug through the folder, finally finding a sheet of paper. She took a moment to read it, then proceeded. "Her final exam showed extreme knowledge in the greatness of our Nation. Millie has been awarded an A, thus securely passing."

I felt my shoulders relax slightly. Moving my eyes from Dr. Eriks, I took in the rest of the room. The others at the table were all watching me. Reverend Smitson had a soft look on his dark-skinned face, as if ready to offer me the salvation of the Lord at any moment. Judge Woods looked bored. Oscar still had a fist up to his lips, his eyes watching me almost in fear. I lingered on him a moment, confused. Then I finally let my eyes trail to Carl.

He was smiling.

Dr. Eriks closed the folder, knitting her fingers and resting them neatly on top. "Millie has never proclaimed any affiliation to any gang, group, religion, or faction. She has proven her loyalty to the

Nation. She has never been in any confrontation and has never been accused of any crime. Her submissiveness and humbleness are appreciated by the Nation. I -"

"Yes, but do you recommend release?" Carl asked, leaning toward the doctor.

Dr. Eriks' eyes widened for a moment. Turning her face towards Carl, she stared at him as if in disbelief. "Excuse me, GF?"

Carl leaned back, knitting his fingers across his chest as he glanced at me. "You say she is an asset, you tell us about her parents and her exam results. But we already know all of this." Carl looked back toward Dr. Eriks. His eyes were squinted, bearing into her.

Her lips parted a moment. I could see her brow knit together, anger flaring behind her narrowed eyes. Dr. Eriks was not a person accustomed to being interrupted. "I was getting there, GF." She spat out the last word, her lips tightening into angry lines. "I was —"

Carl looked away from Dr. Eriks. His eyes locked back onto me, a smirk passing his lips before he cut her off again. "Then I suggest you get there already."

Dr. Eriks paused, her eyes locking onto mine for a moment. I could have sworn I saw contempt flash across them, but it vanished as fast as it had appeared. "I give my approval for release."

I couldn't speak. It seemed so sudden, so simple. I had expected Dr. Eriks to tear me apart. I had thought she would reveal all the secrets she must have discovered and written in that notepad of hers. Instead, I had just been awarded her approval without hesitation.

Looking over to her, I saw the hate radiating from her eyes. Then, slowly, a thin smile spread on her pale face. I felt sick.

Carl leaned forward. "Millie 942B, due to your shining report and passing grade, you will be given the option to accept a job for the great Nation and work here in Spokane. All your needs will be taken care of as you work to better our Nation as we reform its criminals. You must announce your decision now. Have you decided?"

His eyes suddenly turned cold. I felt them bear into me, cutting through my very being like jagged knives. No one else seemed to notice his intense stare. The slight parting of his lips. His fists as he clenched them tight. I could feel his hot breath on my neck as he had pressed me against the wall. His words echoed suddenly in my head, angry and distant.

"So, I think you need to ask for a job here. In the upper blocks, where I will be transferring back to very soon. I have tried to suggest it nicely. But obviously nice just didn't get my point across."

"I —"

"Might I remind you, 942B," Carl interrupted, his voice coming out business-like and indifferent. As if he had never spoken to me before. "Accepting a job within the Prison is a great honor. You will be compensated well, and offered the ultimate protection from the… unjust." His eyes scanned me a moment, so quick I knew no one else could have caught it. "Have you decided?"

I knew then, as sure as my blood now ran like ice through my body, that I did not want to be anywhere near this man.

"I have," I said, my voice obviously shaking.

Carl let out an exasperated sigh, his lips slightly smiling as he awaited his expected answer. "What is your decision?"

I swallowed hard. When I finally spoke, my voice surprised me by coming out clear and strong. "I wish to be released. To work and earn my freedom within the Nation as I better the land and people around me."

Carl's face turned dark. I could see his muscles tighten as he clenched his jaw in anger. Dr. Eriks' eyes flicked to look at him, her lips tightening into a thin line before looking back to me. Her eyes focused on my shirt, refusing to look me in the face. In a level voice, his eyes still bearing into me, Carl coolly asked, "All in favor of Millicent 942B's release?"

The four others raised their hands, muttering "Aye." Carl watched me a moment. The vote had to be unanimous. If it failed, I would be detained until a consensus was decided. I suddenly realized that Carl could make that indefinite.

In a low voice, he finally answered, "Aye."

Judge Wood cleared his throat. His bored eyes rose to look at me, barely taking me in. "Millicent 942B, by permission from our great Nation, I am proud to be the first to announce your release from Spokane Prison. As is practiced, you will be on watch for the first month. Your job will be assigned, and you will be expected to earn your living. Spokane will release you come midnight of your birthday, with any points earned and any belongings thus acquired. Are there any questions?"

I shook my head.

Judge Wood nodded. Without another word, he pushed himself up from his seat, breathing hard against the weight that tried to keep him down. Oscar rose, his eyes nervously watching me. I could hear the paper shuffle as the typist gathered the records and left the room. The others followed close behind.

Carl stayed in his seat, watching me. He looked about ready to launch himself over the table at me. Then he suddenly smiled, standing smoothly.

"Remember, Millie," he said, his voice an unsettling calm. He smoothed his hands over his vest, glancing coolly at the empty doorway. "I get what I want. Enjoy your release. I will see you around."

With that, he excused himself from the room.

⧫ ⧫ ⧫

That was it. I was going to be released. Even though I always knew I would be, it still felt strange to stand there, knowing that tomorrow I would leave the only place I had ever known. I was finally going to be set free.

When I got back to my cell, both my parents were standing near the bunk. I could tell they were nervous. My mother kept trying to flatten her knotted hair. My father shifted from foot to foot, watching her every move, one hand resting lightly on her back. He cradled his other hand across his stomach, the bright white gauze that covered it a stark contrast against his dirty shirt. As I walked in, my mother saw me and jumped, clapping her hands together.

"So? So, so, so?" She sounded like a young child, bouncing up and down and repeatedly clamping and unclamping her hands.

"I passed," I said simply.

"Oh, Millie! I am so proud of you! I am so, so, so proud!" My mother moved to wrap her arms around me. I threw my hands up, stopping her mid-step.

"Thanks," I mumbled.

My father sat down on the edge of the bed, his tired eyes watching my mother. Wondering what he was looking at, I turned my eyes to her. She stood where I had stopped her, her hands hanging limp at her sides. Tears were flooding down her face, her lower lip quivering as she sucked in a sharp breath.

"M-Millie. I just wanted to hug you. Can't I just hug my baby?"

The thought of her wrapping her arms around me caused my stomach to tighten. I could see her, covered in blood. I could see the photo of the man lying dead on the ground. I didn't want to be touched anymore, by her, by anyone.

"Is it true?" I blurted out, my voice suddenly full of anger. "Is it true that you don't even regret it?"

"It?" she asked innocently, genuinely confused.

"The men you killed! Remember that! The whole reason our family has been locked in this God awful place instead of living a normal life, free in the Nation! God Mom! You killed someone! Don't you regret it?"

My mother watched me, the tears still streaming down her face. Regardless of her quivering lip and sniffing nose, her voice came out strong and sure. "I don't regret a single stab."

I wanted to scream. I wanted to shake her until her stupid crying stopped and she finally admitted that what she had done was wrong. My nails dug into my palms, the pain a welcome release from the thoughts that ran like angry fire through my mind.

"You have to understand, Millie. Those men, they needed to die."

"Why, Mom? Why did they need to die?"

She snapped her mouth shut, her eyes widening as she stared at me.

"Because," her voice was low, trembling slightly. "Because I didn't like them."

"Mom," I said, my voice barely audible. "My entire life I have known you were strange. But I loved you. I believed you were normal, somewhere deep down inside. But now I know." I took a deep breath. "You really are the crazy monster everyone in here sees."

My mother choked on her tears. I could see my father lower his head, his hand rising to wipe at his face. He should have yelled at me. He should have leapt forward and slapped his insolent daughter who stood there and insulted his wife. But I knew he wouldn't. He was just her shadow, her silent watch dog.

My mother raised her arms, her fingers reaching for me as a strangled squeak escaped her lips. I could see her retreating into her own world, the glaze taking over her tear-filled eyes. "Oh, my baby... my baby..." she took a step for me, her fingers pleading to let her hold me one last time.

I looked straight into her eyes. She stopped talking, her glazed eyes watching mine.

"I never want to see you again." My voice was barely audible. It held no humor, no side smile at the irony of the statement. I meant it with every inch of who I was.

My mother began to shake, raking sobs taking over her entire body as she started to crumple to the ground. Darting forward, my father wrapped his arms around her and dragged her back to the bunk, laying her gently down. He cooed softly to her, whispering things I could not hear. She finally calmed, passing into a dead sleep.

I just stood there and watched. I wanted my last sight of my parents to be one of who they truly were. I felt like I didn't know them. They were just a pair of crazy, random inmates who I had been forced to live with for the last eighteen years.

My father glanced at me, his eyes full of pain. I felt something in me reach for him, hating the look of betrayal in those tired eyes. But I forced it away, locking it behind a door deep inside of me. Without a word, he laid down next to my mother and closed his eyes, his bandaged arm wrapped tighter around her than usual.

The buzz cut through the air. I hadn't even heard the first two warning buzzes. Behind me I could hear the door slide shut, locking me in for my last night.

I didn't climb into my bunk. I walked just close enough to inch my notebook out from under my pillow, then settled down next to the door. Guards walked by, their boots pounding the ground as they checked each cell. The med cart rolled by, pushing the three cups under our door as soon as I answered their usual question. I stared at the cups, frozen in time, waiting for the walk to die down into night. Before long it fell into the usual nighttime murmur.

What is life? I scribbled. Tying it to my shoelace, I threw it out from under the door and waited. As soon as I felt the tug, I reeled it back in.

It isn't death. Did you pass?

I did. I wrote. *This is my last night.*

I am so proud of you, Millie. Orrin wrote, his handwriting clean and smooth. *You better be careful out there. I really mean it. I don't want to see you rot away in a place like this.*

You haven't ever seen me. I wrote back.

As soon as I threw it, I regretted the words. They were harsh. Orrin didn't deserve my hostility. He had always been open with me. He had listened to me like a father should have, and had given me advice when I needed it the most.

Yet he had still refused to ever meet me.

I have. It's hard to miss one of the only young women in this block, Millie. You stand out. I read the words over again. Orrin knew who I was. He had seen me. And still he never had stopped to introduce himself.

Why haven't you told me that before?

Because you would ask why I didn't say hello. I smiled. He did know me. *You are magnetizing, Millie. A true beauty. Somehow this ruined life hasn't affected you. I fear that others will see that, and try to ruin you. Please. Protect yourself.*

I remembered Carl. His broad grin, his hungry eyes. My pencil hovered above the paper, ready to tell Orrin about my encounters. But then I stopped myself. There was something about Carl. Something that made me scared to even mention him to Orrin. I didn't want to put him at a risk that he could otherwise avoid. My throbbing cheek agreed.

I know. I will. I finally wrote. *Tell me about the world. Where is your favorite place? Maybe I can go there?*

It took a while to feel the tug on the shoelace again. It was slow, meaningful.

It was the beach. I had a home on the beach, with my wife and boys. At night we would sit out on our porch and listen to the waves crash against the sandy shore. My sons would cuddle on my lap, their heads on my shoulders as they fell asleep, safe in my arms. I remember the smile on my wife's face as she sat curled up in a blanket, hot cocoa in a warm mug in her delicate hands. She was beautiful.

When you walk along the beach, you feel a strange peace with the world. The ocean waves wash away your thoughts, letting you feel the sun on your back and the sand between your toes. It is truly a beautiful, breathtaking sight. I could sit for hours on the beach, watching the world disappear over the watery horizon, and never regret a single moment of the wasted time.

It sounds amazing. I wrote.

I already knew though. I knew I would never get to see that sight. The Wall stretched along both coasts, blocking out the beach from everyone but the guards who patrolled. And the wealthy privileged with beach access. I felt a pang of sadness for Orrin. He knew this too. Even though he would spend the rest of his life behind these locked doors, the knowledge that the beauty of the beach was locked away even from the free must kill him.

I felt a tug on the shoelace. When I started to pull it back toward my cell, it felt oddly heavier than usual. As I pulled it into the dim light, I saw a strange lump in the folded paper.

I carefully lifted the edges of the note. There, sitting on top of Orrin's neat handwriting, was a piece of glass. It was a soft green, looking almost frosted. Its edges were worn smooth, its surface almost sandy to the touch. I held it in the palm of my hand and stared at it. I had never seen anything like it. It was beautiful.

This is sea glass. Orrin wrote. *When glass falls into the ocean, it gets tossed and beaten by the waves. After some time, all of the rolling and roughing smooths its surface. It loses its sharp, deadly edges, and becomes a thing of beauty. I used to spend hours scouring the beach for sea glass. I would bring it home to my wife, who would turn it into jewelry and centerpieces on tables. Her face lit up every time I would come in the door with my small handful of sea glass.*

This was the last piece I found. The day they locked me away. I never even had time to give it to her, to my wife. I have held onto it since. It has been my only connection back to the life I lost. And now, Millie, I want you to have it. Think of it as my birthday present for you.

I can't take this, Orrin. I wrote.

I waited for his agreement, the glass now held softly in my hand. I couldn't stop looking at it. It was so beautiful. It looked almost like a small rock, except for its clear green surface that glowed in the light.

You can't give back presents, Millie. I want you to remember what I said about that glass. Can you do that? The world has a way of making even the most deadly, jagged shards into something beautiful. Let's hope that someday it may do it to this Nation.

I could hear footsteps sounding down the walk. Tears stung my eyes as I realized I didn't have time to send him one last note. Sitting back against the wall, I let the tears hit my cheek. The footsteps slowed, checking every cell as they passed. It almost felt as if they were taunting me, reminding me that I would never speak to Orrin again.

I was about to leave everything I ever knew. Everyone I knew. My life would be wiped clean and I would start new, in a world I didn't know. I would never meet Orrin now. I might never see Jude again. I found myself weakly questioning my decision to leave.

Down the walk, in a loud whisper, I heard someone say my name. I crushed my face against the opening of the door, holding my breath.

"Happy birthday, Millie," the voice roughly whispered. The words carried down the quieting walk to my anxiously waiting ears. "I hope I never see you again."

Then it fell silent. I stood up, wiping the tears off my face with a shaking hand.

"Goodbye Orrin," I whispered.

Part Two

 LIBERTY

I finally stopped the tears.

Climbing up onto my bunk, my head hit the pillow, hard. I could hear my parents breathing below me, soft and even. Outside the cell, the murmur of the block nightlife continued. Occasionally the heavy stomp of guards passing in the dark echoed down the walk, only to disappear once again into the dull murmur. I held the sea glass firmly in my fist, letting it press hard against my palm. Every so often I would creep my fingers open, gently rubbing a fingertip along its smoothed surface. I could almost feel the sand and waves as they rolled over the glass. Then I would snap my fingers back shut, locking it away in the safety of my palm.

I heard the clink of the door unlocking. Sitting up, I turned and watched as the door slid all the way open. Light from a flashlight flooded the cell.

"Millicent 942B?"

I nodded, feeling the bright flashlight flood my face.

"It is ten minutes until midnight. Midnight marks the start of your eighteenth birthday. You have been cleared for release. Please gather your belongings and come with us." I squinted, barely making out the silhouette of the deep-voiced guard. He tapped his foot.

I had thought I would leave when the lights came on. I had always assumed I would get one last glimpse of the prison waking up before I escaped to my freedom. But here they were, whisking me away in the dead of the night. I climbed down, pulling my notebook with me. As I reached up to grab my blanket and pillow, the hand of the officer firmly stopped me.

"Those are prison property, 942B."

"But, they have been mine since —"

"Those items are prison property," he repeated. Motioning behind him, another officer stepped forward. The second officer stepped held out a small canvas bag. The first officer turned back to me as he grabbed the bag from his comrade and put it in my hands.

"You are to only gather your clothing and personal items." He watched me a moment as I stared dumbly at him. In exasperation, he tapped his wrist, his short nail clicking on his metal watch.

I spun and faced our small shelf. Pulling open the bag, I shoved my small pile of clothes inside. I glanced over my shoulder at the guards standing behind me. They were barely watching, their eyes tired and bored. Shielding my hands from their view, I tucked the sea glass into a sock then shoved it into the bag. Though it was not against the rules to have this small present, I felt a strange urge to keep it a secret. I wanted it to be only mine. For it to be all to myself. I stuff the remaining sock on top, then pushed my thinned notebook into the bag and cinched it shut.

That was all I had.

A small bundle of clothing, a piece of sea glass, and the

notebook. I slipped the bag over my shoulder then turned to face the waiting officers.

"Would you like a moment to say goodbye?" he asked, motioning to my sleeping parents.

I looked down at them. My father's breathing was uneven, his eyes quivering slightly. I knew he was awake. "No," I said simply.

"Very well," the officer said. He moved out of the cell, motioning for me to follow. I tore my eyes away from my parents. As I walked out of the cell, I heard my father softly hush my mother. I didn't look back. As soon as I stepped out in the dark walkway the cell door slid back closed behind me, locking shut.

I followed the officers down the walk, out into the Commons, and finally down a dark hallway. We paused at a sealed door long enough for them to scan my metal bracelet, then each of their badges. The door slid open, and we passed through before it locked itself back closed.

The first officer clicked off his flashlight. The room we had stepped into was bright. The lights hurt my eyes. As I adjusted to the new lighting, I took in the room. The walls were painted white, framed images and flyers hanging neatly on their clean surface.

We walked through the strange white room quickly and passed through another door. This time there were more chairs, a small television set in one corner. Its screen glowed blue, still waiting to be turned off for the night. I could see magazines scattered across the surface of the many side tables.

The officers made me sit as they walked over to a desk and started to type on a buzzing computer. I gripped the bag in my hands, trying to calm the strange nervous shaking that kept crawling up my legs and into my hands.

A sign hanging on the wall across from me caught my attention.

Visiting hours: 9 AM to 7 PM
Please leave all personal belongings
in the provided lockers.
Photo ID required.
No items may be passed to inmates.
All visits are monitored and recorded.

This was a waiting room. A waiting room for visits.

No one inside had ever mentioned receiving visitors. I had always assumed that once you were locked away, that was it. The world disappeared from you. And you from it. I couldn't pull my eyes off of the sign. It seemed odd to me, that this waiting room still sat here. It was empty, the magazines looking brand new, the layer of dust hiding on top of the TV a sign that it this room was rarely used.

"942B, come with us."

I stood numbly, following the voice. The two officers were holding open a door across the room. The door opened to a glassed-in room, a white bench screwed along all four walls the only thing inside.

"You will wait in here until discharge."

"In here?" I asked, shocked. The lights were blazing bright, the benches solid wood. I knew I stood no chance of sleeping tonight.

The officer tightened his lips, obviously not wanting to repeat himself. I moved past him, avoiding eye contact as I entered the glassed-in room. Sitting down, I let the bag rest on the ground by my feet. The officer watched me until I had settled, then shut the door. I could hear the click of the lock as it sealed me in.

I waited.

Occasionally I could see an officer walk past. No one paused to check in on me. I would see their eyes flit to look in my direction, then quickly look away as they continued their uninterrupted walk. I felt invisible. Forgotten. My butt hurt and my back was stiff from leaning against the low wall. I could feel my eyes burning.

Hours passed. I could feel time ticking away.

My head finally drooped, my eyes too heavy to stay open any longer. In the darkness behind my closed eyelids I could see my father, his hand bleeding, his eyes lowered. He went to work, lining up along the other assembly line workers. Nobody seemed to notice the blood dripping from his hand as he set to work, silently clicking sharp metal sheets together into something I couldn't recognize. I tried to see what he was making, but could only see the gash on his hand, blood dripping in a stream like a dying waterfall.

My father disappeared. In his place stood my mother. She was frozen. Alone. The room she stood in was empty, no windows, not even a door. I could see her face, still as stone. Only her eyes moved. They darted back and forth, searching every corner in sheer fright. Then I finally saw it. Her arms were bound tightly around her, her legs tied tight together. She couldn't move if she wanted.

I thought about stepping forward to help her. Just as my hand reached out, she started to scream. Her body thrashed in seizure-like jerks, her lips distorted and twisted. Spit flew from her mouth as she bared her teeth, her eyes manic. I didn't know this woman. She was a wild animal. I backed against the solid wall, trying to get away from her as her scream died into a low chuckle.

Just as fast as her attack started, it ended. She went back to her frozen stance, twigs and dirt falling from her hair, her lips slightly quivering as she whispered over and over, "My baby. My baby."

Everything went dark. Through my lids, I could see the faint glow of the white room that surrounded me. But here, hidden behind my closed eyelids, it was dark. I sighed a breath of relief, my head nodding down slightly as I welcomed the solitude.

Then I saw his face. It slowly appeared in the dark, barely

visible. Shards of light hit his cheekbones, his furrowed brow, his straight nose. As he moved forward, my breath froze in my screaming lungs. His grin spread menacingly on his hungry face.

I snapped my eyes open. Gasping in a painful breath, I looked up to the ceiling. My heart beat hard in my chest, threatening to burst out. Breathing in deep again, I felt it finally slow. I was exhausted. But the need for sleep had been chased away by the fear of my dreams.

Lowering my eyes, I saw I wasn't alone in the room any more. A woman sat across from me, her hands cuffed tightly behind her back. The reek of beer stained her dirty clothing. Her hair was long and blonde, muddy at the tips with something dark. I watched her, her eyes glazed as she stared past me into the window behind my back.

"In or out?"

The sound of her slightly slurred voice jarred me. "What?" I asked.

"Going in or coming out?" she asked, her glazed eyes focusing onto me.

"Oh, uh, going out."

She scanned me with her eyes, a small hiccup escaping her chapped lips. "First release, huh?"

"How did you know?"

She laughed, her arms struggling a moment against the metal cuffs. "You scream it, hon. Just you wait. Prison Nation will chew you up and spit you right back out. It don't care."

That was the second time I had heard it called Prison Nation in the last day. It was a name I had never heard before. Everyone always reverently, respectfully called it The Nation. It was the great Nation. The good, the strong. This new name made no sense to me.

"Why did you call it that?" I asked. I stopped myself, surprised that I had asked this woman, who I had never met before, a question like that. Biting my lip, I nervously watched her.

"You kidding me?" She scanned me again, her lips curling in humor. "Well, 'course you ain't. You don't know. You're a Jail Baby huh? Born and raised in this great institution. Proud of this Nation with its correcting, righteous ways." She let out a rough laugh, the end of it breaking into a cough. "Let me tell you something, hon. Whether you are in these walls, or out of them, you are still in this prison. Get it? They got you. They got all of us. And we ain't going nowhere."

The woman let out a chuckle, low and angry. Something else hinted it though. Something light, barely there. As the angry chuckle died out, I could hear the hint of desperation on every breath she gasped in.

I watched her. She squirmed in her seat, her head lolling back a moment. I didn't know if I could believe a single word she was saying. It was obvious she was under more influence than just the alcohol whose stink had infiltrated the once clean air in this room. Her body was too skinny, bones sticking out where her bulky coat and baggy jeans didn't cover. She began to shake.

In a soft voice, distant as if talking to someone long gone, the woman whispered, "At least in here I can sleep."

The door swung open.

"942B." A new officer, a woman this time, stood at the door. Her bulky body fit tightly into her uniform, showing off her pudgy rolls. I stood up, grabbing my pack in a shaky hand. "Come on then." She glanced over at the handcuffed woman, then ushered me out and slammed the door. I could hear the woman chuckle lightly as the door clicked shut.

The officer led me to a new room, filled only with a bench and a small desk. A woman sat behind the desk, her clothing neatly pressed and clean. I took in her deep purple shirt, squirming in my own worn white t-shirt. It seemed to scratch me even more, reminding me that it would never be as smooth or soft as that woman's top. The officer led me to the bench, motioning for me to sit.

The woman at the desk looked up and offered me a small smile. "First off, let me congratulate you on your coming release into our great Nation." She glanced again at the screen of the computer that sat on her desk. "Millicent. Quite a name. Is there a story behind it?"

No one ever called me Millicent except when they looked at my paper work. I hated that name. It felt ugly on my tongue. I had no idea why my mother chose that name, but in the last few days I had come to realize she probably didn't have any reason. She didn't need one.

"My mother is crazy. She probably was told she needed a name and picked the first lame one that came to mind." I bit my lip. I didn't know why I kept saying things like that. I never had before. Looking at the woman, I saw her chuckle to herself.

"I'm a name buff myself. Every name has a meaning, did you know that?" She smiled at me. I could feel the tension as she tried to keep up the casual conversation. "Your name means 'mild strength.' Maybe your mother was trying to bless you."

I shrugged. I suddenly just wanted this woman in the deep purple shirt to stop trying. "Yeah. Maybe." I muttered.

The woman cleared her throat, glancing down at my paperwork. When she looked back up, I could see the attempted warmth had fizzled in her eyes. "Do you prefer Millicent or Millie?" she carefully asked.

"Millie," I answered softly.

"Very well. Your official ID will now read Millie 942B." A machine buzzed behind her. Something heavy dropped into a small tray. Without looking, she reached behind her and picked it up. Holding it out, she waited for the guard to come grab it from her. The guard looked at it a moment, then handed it to me.

It was small plastic card, my black and white photo printed on its surface. My face stared blankly back at me. Next to my photo was my name, printed in plain block letters. Under that was my birthday, eye color, and height. The only other thing on the card was a barcode.

The woman was typing. I could hear her fingers picking out the letters quickly, obviously well practiced at whatever she was doing. As she typed, she casually spoke to me. "That is your ID. Do not lose it. If you do, you will be charged for a reprint. You must have it on you at all times. You will not be paid if you do not have it. You cannot purchase food or other items if you do not have it." She stopped a moment and smiled at me. "So don't lose it, okay?"

I nodded.

Something in her smile made me want to apologize for my brashness before. I couldn't form the words. Instead, I just watched her.

The woman glanced at the computer screen. "According to your records, you have enough points for a total of two hundred dollars, after we have deducted your discharge fees. Would you like that in credit or cash?"

I had never held money in my life. I had heard others talk about it, but in prison, currency wasn't needed. Out of sheer curiosity, I answered, "Cash, please."

"Very well," she said. She nodded to the officer, who disappeared out the door. A moment later she returned, carrying an envelope and a small box. Handing the two items to me, she backed away again to her silent post.

"Inside the envelope is your cash," the woman continued, still typing. "The box contains one extra change of clothes, a razor, a bar of soap, a towel, and one box of sanitary napkins." I peeked inside the box while she spoke, pushing around the contents. The envelope sat fat in my hand. I felt myself strangely afraid to lose it and gripped my fingers tighter around its thin paper. Maybe I should have asked for it in credit.

"Do you have any questions?"

I shook my head.

"Very good." The woman looked at the screen again. "You have been assigned your probationary job. The Nation looks forward to your steady and loyal work. Your employer is waiting outside to pick you up and bring you to your new residence until your probationary month is over." Leaning back, she looked at me again. Her eyes flitted down to the metal bracelet on my wrist. "The ID bracelet will remain on until the month is over. If there are no more questions, then this is it." The woman stood, flattening her black pencil skirt against her toned legs. She smiled and held out a hand.

I stood, slinging the pack over my shoulder and tucking the envelope and box under one arm. I took a step toward her, my hand shaking as I held it out to her. She firmly gripped it a moment, watching me before offering one last warm smile. "Welcome to the Nation, citizen."

The officer placed a hand on my back, softly pushing me toward the door at the other end of the room. My feet stumbled underneath me as I made my way over to it. The officer pulled the small hand held device out of her pocket, scanned my wrist, and waited for the beep. As soon as the small beep sounded, she swiped a card across a panel near the door.

The door buzzed once, then swung open.

Sunlight spilled in, crisp with the fresh morning air. I squinted as we stepped out, taking in the pale blue sky dotted with drifting white clouds. In front of me stretched a parking lot. No razor wire topped fences. No guards patrolling. Just a normal parking lot with a few scattered cars resting in the morning light.

The guard walked me around the corner. Beds of neatly trimmed flowers lined the walk, their buds opening with dew. I could almost taste the dew on my tongue, full of the morning sun. We walked until we got to a small covered area. The guard stopped, motioning to someone in the distance.

I could hear the rumble of an engine. Looking around, I saw an old truck making its way toward us. Its paint was chipped, rust splattered across its once bright yellow surface. I could see a large dent on one side, bending the metal in at a strange, striking angle.

The truck pulled in under the covered waiting area. Without a word, the officer pulled open the passenger door, nodding once at me. I tightened my grip on my small bag and took a step forward. Still squinting from the bright light, I looked into the cab.

There, sitting behind the wheel, fist held tightly to lips, was Oscar Ramos.

▌▌▌12

I had never been in a vehicle before. My fingers gripped the worn handle on the door, nails digging into the soft plastic. My whole body bounced up and down as the truck pulled out of the lot and onto the worn road beyond.

The outside world was amazing. I had stood outside before, as near to the fence as I dared. I would stand and look at the world outside the fence, trying to forget the men up on the walks who always watched with guns held tight, making sure I didn't attempt an escape. Beyond the prison's fence, there was nothing else. Just a rolling expanse of tall grass. It would sway in the light breeze, always dried and crisp in the ever heated air. For miles I could see the waves of grass, only interrupted occasionally by a lone, shriveled tree.

As we drove down the road, the grass rising on either side, I felt sick. I turned my head, looking out the dusty window to my right. The prison was huge. I had always known it was large, but seeing it now from the outside took my breath away. It stretched away on either side, disappearing with the grass into the horizon. Spokane had no beginning, and no end.

I felt strange, knowing that hidden somewhere inside those dark rising walls and razor wire topped fences were the people I had known my entire life. They were at work, or sleeping in cells, or standing alone in the yard watching the grass bend and sway. My eyes suddenly stung, unexpected tears trying hard to find their way out.

I pulled my eyes away from the prison, turning in my seat to face forward again.

Oscar glanced over to me, both of his hands firmly gripping the steering wheel. "Buckle up," he said, his accent so strong I could barely understand his words.

"What?" I asked, confused.

"Buckle up. Uh, there." He pointed to a strap hanging at my right, then to a small metal buckle down by my left hip. I reached and grabbed the strap, pulling it across my body and toward the buckle. Glancing up at him, I raised my eyebrows in question. Oscar nodded.

I pushed the buckles together until they let out a light click. The strap tightened against me, pulling me firmly against the seat. I stared at the buckle a moment. I didn't like the feel of the strap confining me, pulling me tight into the worn seat. My lap was full with my box, bag, and envelope carefully balanced on top and I struggled to keep it all together as the truck bounced down the road. Glancing over to Oscar, I shoved the envelope of money into the bag, cinched it tightly shut then wrapped one arm securely around the small pile.

The car rumbled loudly down the road. Small buildings started to appear. Paint chipped off of their wooden walls, the windows boarded tightly shut against the empty air. Soon they grew closer together, their worn paint becoming nicer looking and their windows gradually opening. Glass panes shone in the sunlight, curtains on the inside masking whatever lay beyond. I saw people walking down the street along a thin concrete walk, casually talking or glancing into shops.

My eyes burned as I refused to blink. I felt the fear of the rumbling truck disappear with amazement at the life that now appeared before my eyes. Small children gripped parent's hands, tugging and laughing. A store passed, toys propped carefully in its clean window. An old man sitting on a wooden chair outside a shop raised his hand and waved.

Oscar nodded to him, passing without a pause. We soon were out of the small strip of buildings, turning onto a dirt road. The truck bounced haphazardly as it hit the deep potholes that were scattered everywhere. I felt my stomach churning with nausea. Focusing my eyes out of the dusty windshield, I worked hard to bite it back as I dug my nails harder into the plastic handle.

Ahead of us rose a tall building. In the distance, just beyond the building, were perfectly matching smaller buildings, neatly lined and carefully painted. Oscar pulled up in front of the large building and turned the truck off. Its engine sputtered once, then went silent. He glanced at me a moment, then pushed open his door and climbed out.

I figured he wanted me to do the same. My legs shook as I climbed out. I threw the pack over my shoulder, then wrapped my arms tightly around the small box and hurried to catch up to Oscar, who was already making his way down a cobble lined path.

We passed the large building. I gazed up at it, taking in its tall white walls and neatly cleaned windows lined with white lace curtains. The front door was a bright red, an apple neatly carved into its wooden surface.

Oscar made his way to the smaller buildings around back. People ambled by, their clothing dusty but neat. A few sat in the entrances to the buildings, casually talking as they ate food or whittled at pieces of wood. Oscar nodded to people as they passed, occasionally mumbling something I couldn't understand.

We finally reached one of the small buildings. Oscar stopped, pulled out a paper from his shirt pocket and glanced at it. Nodding to himself, he looked back at me and motioned me forward.

I stepped up to the small building. "This is your… uh… living space," Oscar said, obviously searching for words in his thick accent.

A woman walked out. Her skin was the same golden tone as Oscar's, her dark hair pulled into a single loose braid that hung down her back. She seemed to be only a few years older than me, her face still young and vibrant. Seeing Oscar, she let a bright white smile spread on her suntanned face.

"Hola Oscar," she said, leaning against the open doorway.

"Hola Maria," he answered quickly. "Este es Millie. La chica nueva." Maria looked over at me, then nodded and smiled at Oscar again.

"Hola Millie," she said, still smiling. Her teeth seemed to sparkle in the sunlight.

"Um. Hi." I knew that they were speaking Spanish. There were gangs of inmates who only spoke Spanish in the prison. I had always avoided them. They would watch me with slitted eyes every time I had to pass, murmuring even more strange words in their language I could never understand. Standing here now, in front of Maria and Oscar, I found myself wishing they would speak English. Not knowing what they were saying as they stood watching me sent my stomach into knots.

"¿Dónde este Reed?" Oscar asked Maria.

Maria shrugged. Oscar sighed, glancing over at me again. I

could tell he wanted to pass me on to someone else and be done with the job of my escort. His hands clenched into fists, one twitching as he fought it from rising to his lips.

"¿Te da miedo la bonita chica nueva?" Maria asked, her lips curling into a smile at the corners.

Oscar glanced at me, his fingers twitching again as they fought to rub against to his lips. "Uh, Maria... No sé..."

Maria sighed and took a step forward.

"Go on Oscar. I got her." Oscar glanced to Maria, then back to me. Maria shooed at him with her hands. "Si, Oscar. Ándale."

Oscar nodded, letting out a relieved sigh. Turning to me, he nodded again, then took off to the large building. Maria motioned me forward. Wrapping my arms tighter around my small box, I stepped up the small building, following her inside. She carelessly swished her hips as she walked down the narrow hall, her tight shirt showing off her figure underneath.

"Don't mind Oscar," she called behind her. Her voice was hinted with the same accent, though not nearly as thick as Oscar's. "He is always nervous when new ones move in. We have had trouble, in the past you know. But you won't be trouble, I can tell." She stopped and smiled at me, tapping her head. "I can see you are a good girl."

I nodded. Something about Maria made me like her. I didn't know if it was her smile, or the how she so comfortably spoke to me. There was something there though.

"Okay, this is your room."

She pushed open a curtain. Inside rested a small bed, blankets folded neatly on its padded mattress. It barely stood off the ground, propped up on a few thick boards. A small table with a single drawer sat wedged in next to the bed, an old lamp sitting on its rough surface. At the other end of the bed stood a small set of drawers.

Aside from that, the room was empty. Everything was crowded close together, the only remaining floor space barely big enough to spin on. Everything in the room seemed to be embraced in the deep brown of the wooden walls.

"It isn't much," Maria said, watching me take in the room. "But hey, it is home, sí?"

Maria couldn't see the relief that was flowing through me. I scanned the room again, taking in the one thing that made a smile finally creep across my face. There was no bunk. No other bed. I had never slept in a room all to myself in my life. It seemed too good to be true.

Walking in, I set my box and bag on the bed. "No, it's perfect," I said softly.

"Okay. Well, unpack then come ouside. Sí?"

I nodded.

Maria turned to leave. Before she could duck through the curtain, I stopped her. "What did you ask him? Oscar." Maria turned and looked at me, a smile still on her full lips. "Out there... I was just curious."

"Don't know much Español, huh?" Maria leaned against the doorway, her smile easy and welcoming. "I asked him if he was afraid of the pretty new girl."

"Oh." I looked away, staring at her feet instead of her laughing smile. "Is he?"

Maria laughed. "Millie, don't worry. Oscar is afraid of everything. Even his own shadow." I glanced back up at her. She winked playfully, pushing her body away from the door frame. "Just relax. Everyone is loco at first. We get used to it though. Most of the time. See you outside, chica."

Maria watched a moment longer, then turned and left. As soon as she disappeared through the curtain, I dumped out the contents of my small bag onto the bed and set to work sifting through them. Picking up the sock that held my sea glass, I paused a moment. I could feel the lump of the glass in the toe. I wanted to look at it again. To roll it between my fingers and try to hear the soft waves that had created it years before.

Sighing, I grabbed the envelope of cash and pushed it into the sock on top of the glass. Rolling the top of the sock shut tightly, I gathered my used clothes and walked over to the small dresser. I carefully laid out my clothing in the first drawer, making sure it was folded neatly and organized.

I walked back to my bed and ripped the top of the box open, then pulled out the new set of clothing. The shirt was a dark blue, the pants a light khaki covered in pockets. I stared at them a moment, my fingers trailing over the new fabric that almost seemed to crunch under my touch, then carefully folded them and laid them in their place in the open dresser drawer. I gathered up the extra socks and underwear and toiletries and tucked them all away too, then pushed the drawer shut.

All that was left on the bed now was my notebook and the empty cardboard box. I fiddled with the box a moment, then finally found a way to collapse it. Not knowing what to do with it, I kicked it under my bed. The cardboard scraped across the wood floor, then fell silent as it found its place in the shadows and dust.

I walked over to the head of the bed and finally let myself sit. The springs in the bed bounced back at me. I could feel them under my body, jabbing and poking, but it didn't matter. The bed felt like complete luxury. I took in a deep breath, letting my eyes scan the tiny room once more.

My room.

Without pausing to flip through the ratty pages, I slipped my notebook into the drawer on the bedside table, then rose and walked out of the room. The hallway was narrow, barely big enough for two people to stand side by side. I could see Maria leaning in the doorway, and made my way to her.

As I drew closer I could hear her talking to someone. Maria was laughing, her shoulders rising and falling happily. I reached her, unsure of whether I should wait or let her know I was there. I ended up standing awkwardly in the shadows, shifting my weight from foot to foot like a nervous child. I could hear the rumble of a man talking to her, his voice light and joking.

Maria laughed again. "Señor Reed, really. You will be kicked out of here faster than you know if you keep that up."

"Keep what up?" he asked, his voice pure and innocent. Maria chuckled again. "Um, you have someone. There. Behind you," Reed added, his voice still soft.

Maria looked over her shoulder, smiling at me. "Come on out, Millie. Come on. Rapído."

Stepping down out of the doorway, she motioned with her hands for me to follow. I took a step out, blinking in the bright sunlight. It took me a moment to adjust. I wasn't used to being out in the sun this much in one day.

I finally stopped blinking. A young man stood in front of me, leaning against the wall of my living quarters. He was tall, his body lean and his skin tanned a rich brown. Dark brown hair hung slightly shaggy on his smooth forehead. He smiled at me, his deep brown eyes light and happy.

"Hey there," he said. Taking a step forward, he held out a hand and waited. I watched him a moment, then I held out my hand and let him take a hold of it, gently shaking. "I'm Reed. Looks like I get you."

"Get me?" I asked, alarmed.

Reed furrowed his brows together a moment, then suddenly shot his eyes open in realization. "Oh, no. No, not like that." He laughed softly to himself, shaking his head as he kept his eyes on me. They had lost a bit of their humor, now studying me closely instead. "No, I get to show you the ropes. You know, the job."

I lowered my eyes, my cheeks suddenly burning. "Oh," I said simply.

Reed said a few more words to Maria, but I didn't bother to listen. I felt young and naïve. As if I shouldn't be there at all. Everyone seemed so relaxed and comfortable as they joked and walked past in the warm sunlight. Meanwhile I stood there, waiting for a fight to break out at any moment and for the thump of heavy boots as guards ran in from the shadows to break up the chaos.

"Hey?" I snapped out of my thoughts, seeing Reed watching me. His brows were still slightly furrowed, barely wrinkling his smooth forehead. "Ready?" He must have asked me already. The tone of his voice sounded repeated, almost exhausted.

"I am. I'm sorry."

"Hey, don't be sorry. You're new here. You're allowed to get lost in the fog a bit."

I paused again, staring at him. I had never told anyone about the fog that clouded my mind and memories. My mouth hung open, my thoughts racing to think of what to say. It was probably coincidence, that Reed had mentioned fog. But the way he looked back into my eyes didn't settle my suddenly racing heart.

Reed smiled, then started to walk away down the dirt path. I hurried to follow. We passed the small buildings, most empty now as the other workers made their way to their jobs. I found myself curious about what I would be doing for the next month, if not longer, of my life.

We finally left the gathering of small houses. Ahead of us stretched an orchard. Trees, full of bright green leaves, stretched up to the sky, casting shifting shadows on the grass below. As we got closer I saw that the branches of the trees were heavy with dark red apples.

Apples. I sighed. Of course it was apples.

Reed bent and picked up two baskets from a stack near the entrance to the orchard. Handing me one, he continued to walk, ducking under a few low hanging branches. I tucked the basket under my arm and hurried to keep up.

A few workers nearby called greetings to Reed as we passed, then went back to their work. They stood tiptoe on step ladders, reaching into the branches to pluck the apples and drop them into their baskets. A few were high in the branches, the only sign of their existence being a random flash of arms and legs as the leaves moved in the breeze.

Reed grabbed a step-ladder and leaned it up against a tree trunk. Slinging a strap from the basket around his shoulders, he jumped up into the tree, disappearing into the branches. I watched him climb up, my mouth slightly gaping in awe at how fearless he seemed as he scaled the tree.

I carefully stepped up on the ladder, feeling it wobble beneath my feet. Placing my hand against the tree trunk, I waited for the shaking to calm. The bark was cool under my hand. I caressed my fingers along its rough divots, feeling the bumps and curves of the wood press back against my skin. My fingers inched along the bark. They carefully explored the dips and rough edges, a small smile spreading on my face as the sun-warmed bark snagged on my fingertips. I had never touched a tree before.

"The tree feels loved."

I jumped. Looking up, I could barely see Reed's face through the branches. He smiled at me. The thump of apples echoed down to me as he dropped them into his basket.

My cheeks burned again in embarrassment.

I stepped up to the top step. Reaching up, I plucked an apple from a low hanging branch and tossed it into my basket. It rolled around, finally coming to a stop as it settled. I picked another one, throwing it in to begin its circle of rolling.

My stomach growled. I hadn't eaten since breakfast the day before. I could feel my head swim as my mouth started to water. I plucked another apple, then leaned against the trunk to look at its red surface. It shone in the sun light. The apple seemed to taunt me, daring me to bite into its red flesh. I thought of the mealy apples the prison always served, the dry taste on my tongue as the browned meat crunched in my mouth. I hated apples.

My stomach growled again.

Gritting my teeth, I lifted the apple to my mouth.

Before I could take a bite, a hand clamped down on my wrist. I looked up. Reed was hanging in front of me, his body wrapped around the branches to keep from falling. One hand gripped my wrist, his eyes bearing into me in alarm as his grasp tightened.

"What are you doing?" he asked, his voice strangely scared.

"I'm... I'm hungry. I was just going to eat an apple."

Reed jumped down from his perch, landing with a thump on the grassy ground. He reached up and took the apple from my hand, letting it drop into my nearly empty basket. Leaning in close to me, he looked around once before bearing his eyes into mine.

"You can't do that, Millie," he said, his voice soft and low. "These apples are property of whoever is buying them. They are owned. There are tons of contracts wrapped around these apples. None of which are signed by you."

"So?" I asked. "It's an apple. There are hundreds in the tree." I looked up as if to reassure myself. The tree seemed to answer me by shaking in the breeze, its branches hung heavy with the red apples.

"Theft. Have you heard of that?" Reed leaned closer, his voice low. "Well, that's what you will get slapped with if you decide to eat these apples. Along with whatever else they decide to add to the charge. This is serious, Millie. Take some notes, got it?"

I looked down in the basket. "But..."

Reed rubbed a hand across his face. "You grew up in the prison. How many people in there did you hear claim they were not guilty? That what they did wasn't wrong?" He raised his eyebrows to me. I parted my lips to answer, but no words came out. Reed motioned to the basket of apples. "Those are owned. By someone. I don't know who but I know it's not you or me. All we are supposed to do is pick the apples and put them in these baskets. Eat one, and you will go right back to Spokane."

I couldn't believe what I heard. Eating an apple wasn't a crime. The trees were full with the apples, waiting to be plucked and sold and eaten by others with growling stomachs. The dead cool seriousness of Reed's face let me know he was telling the truth.

I had almost broken the law. A law I never even knew existed.

Reed climbed back into the tree. I could feel him occasionally glancing at me, and I tried to focus on my apple picking as if I couldn't feel his eyes checking in on my every move. I knew he was just worried, but I wished he would stop checking. I wasn't going to eat an apple, at all. All his constant checking only set me further on edge. Reaching up, I plucked forbidden apple after apple, dropping them into my basket.

People in nearby trees casually talked and laughed. It was strange to see how relaxed they all were, sitting in trees in the sunshine and filling baskets as if they never had a fear or care in the world. I could hear the rhythmic thumping of the apples as Reed tossed them into his basket high above me. Letting out a breath, I leaned against the tree, one hand mindlessly stroking the bark as I watched the sunlight trickle down through the leaves.

"Well now, Reed. It looks like our tree is needing a room of its own with this new young lady here." Someone walked around the tree, leaning casually against it. He smiled at me, then winked. "Pity. Wouldn't mind a room of our own." I suddenly felt my throat tighten as Carl's face flashed before my eyes.

"With her, or the tree?" Reed called from the branches, his voice light with laughter.

"The tree, of course!" The new man winked at me again. "I like them sturdy."

Reed jumped down from the tree, landing heavily on his feet. He stumbled forward a step, his hands reaching forward to brace himself. The man jumped forward and caught Reed just before he face planted.

"Whoa there man. Don't wanna push the Insurance." The man said, laughing as he hauled Reed to his feet. He stood a few inches taller than Reed, his bright red hair a startling contrast to Reed's deep brown. He was slim like Reed, but his shoulders and chest were broader, thick with muscles. The man slapped a hand on Reed's back.

Reed slapped him back, chuckling. "Thanks Eddie." He paused, glancing at me, then back to Eddie. "Eddie, this is Millie."

Eddie looked at me, an amused smile creeping across his lips. "Millie." He leaned forward, his voice suddenly coming out in a loud, mocking whisper. "Need some alone time?" Eddie flitted his eyes back to the apple tree, then winked at me.

I could feel my cheeks burning. Opening my mouth to answer, I suddenly felt tongue-tied, unsure of how to answer his remark. Reed looked at my face a moment, then slapped his friend upside the head.

"Eddie, come on man. Millie is a recent Out."

"Really?" Eddie took a step forward, his eyes wide as he took me in.

"Yeah. Give her a break, okay? Probably the first time she has seen a real tree."

Eddie's eyes widened even more, if that was possible. "Is that true?"

I glanced at Reed. He was shaking his head at Eddie, his eyes rolling in mock annoyance. Meeting eyes with me, Reed shook his head and shrugged in apology. "Well, no. I've seen them," I answered. "I've just never... touched one."

My cheeks still burned. I was in awe of a tree, as everyone else around me walked past through the Orchard without a second glance. How much more obviously different could I get? Eddie opened his mouth to say something else, but Reed suddenly smacked him again, hard enough this time to cause Eddie to let out a choked cough. Reed smiled at me, then shot a look to Eddie. Sighing, Eddie rolled his eyes and slumped against the tree.

"It's alright, Millie," Reed said, taking a step closer to me. I could smell his light sweat on his body and something like peppermint every time he opened his mouth. "We get Outs here pretty often. They all do what you are doing. It's normal." Reed offered me a smile, lifting a hand to softly touch my arm. I tried to smile back, but only managed a weak grin.

"I feel so out of place," I admitted, shocked at the words as they tumbled from my lips.

"Don't feel that way," Reed said. "You belong here."

"Yeah you do." Eddie stepped up to us, a smile on his freckled face. Reed lowered his hand from my arm, the spot he had touched still warm as he took a step back. "And the tree knows it!"

"Eddie, honestly man." Reed couldn't help but laugh. I watched as his shoulders shook up and down, his white teeth flashing in honest laughter. A small chuckle escaped my lips. Reed reached over and playfully smacked Eddie on the arm again.

"So, Millie, care to have chow with us?" Eddie casually asked, rubbing at his shoulder where Reed had hit him. He folded his thick arms across his chest. "I hear it's gonna be the oh-so-delicious usual of veggie stew and baked rolls."

My mouth started to water, my stomach growling in anxious agreement. Hoping that Reed and Eddie hadn't heard, I quickly picked up my basket and held it tight against my demanding stomach. "Sure," I said, the smile still on my lips.

"Awesome," Eddie said, winking his eye at me again before jumping up and clamping a hand on Reed's shoulder. "Shall we?"

◻ ◻ ◻

The flames of the fire rose and licked the air, dancing as they grew and shrank in the light breeze. I couldn't stop staring. The countless nights of sitting huddled on the cold prison floor in front of the barely glowing light dimmed in my memory as I stared into the dancing flames. It was mesmerizing. Others around me casually lounged on the ground or on stools. I could hear the clink of spoons against metal bowls, and my stomach growled again.

"Here you go," Reed said as he sat beside me.

He held a small metal bowl, full to the brim with soup. I could see chunks of potatoes and carrots floating in the thick broth. Gratefully taking it from his hand, I held it in my lap, feeling the warmth from the bowl throb in my chilled hands. It had become cold very fast as soon as the sun began to set.

Eddie plopped down next to Reed. In one hand he had his bowl, in the other a plate piled high with rolls. I could smell their fresh baked dough drifting through the air. Steam still rose off of their golden crusts.

Seeing me eye the rolls, Reed picked one up and offered it to me. I smiled at him, taking it carefully from his hand and setting it on my lap. I was almost afraid to eat the food. It seemed too good. Too warm and delicious smelling.

"Don't get used to it," Eddie said, his mouth already full. "Da rolls are usually cold." He shoved another roll in his mouth, an audible groan of happiness escaping his lips as he shut his eyes and loudly chewed. I couldn't help but smile.

"And the carrots aren't always available," Reed added. "It's been a good season on the other farms."

I nodded. I looked at the soup again. Stirring my spoon slowly, I watched the carrots and potatoes spin. "At least it isn't apples."

Both of the men laughed. "What, not an apple fan?" Eddie asked.

I shook my head and shrugged. "I never have been. Something about their texture. Or something."

"Bad luck," Eddie said, obviously amused. Reed shot him a look, then let a chuckle escape his own lips as Eddie innocently batted his eyelashes in mock apology.

"So Reed, any news on the new buyer?" Eddie asked.

Reed shook his head. "Not much. Just some huge company or something. At least we have a buyer." Reed scooped up a spoonful of soup, blowing on it for a moment. "I hear other farms are losing business. Being shut down. They are giving more of the work to the prisons now."

Reed and Eddie both glanced at me. I just looked back at them, unsure of what to say. Reed ate the spoonful of soup, thinking for a moment as he carefully swallowed. "Maria said she heard that the inmates are being assigned more jobs. Working longer hours for the same low pay. Soon, the only work most of us will be able to find will be behind those walls."

"Awesome," Eddie sarcastically said, biting into another roll as he stared into the fire. "Before we know it, we will all be out of work."

"Or out of a country," Reed quietly mumbled. He glanced at me and I quickly looked back to the fire. I could feel him watch a moment before he too looked away. Reed fell silent as Eddie started to jammer on about something random. Drifting out of the conversation, I looked down at the warm bowl in my hands.

Lifting my spoon, I finally took a sip of the soup. It was thick and full of flavor, the warmth spreading over my tongue and down my dry throat. Shutting my eyes, I relished it, spooning in another mouthful. I could still feel the hot roll on my lap, but wanted to save it for later. After some time, I realized that Reed and Eddie had fallen quiet.

Opening my eyes, I glanced in their direction. Reed was watching me, his face soft, his lips in a calm smile. I could see the firelight twinkle in his eyes. Beyond him Eddie had a huge grin on his freckled face, his red head nodding and his eye winking at me in exaggerated happiness.

"Good isn't it?" Eddie asked in a cheery voice.

I couldn't help it. I laughed. It felt good to feel the laugh explode from my chest, my stomach tightening in the laughter that fell out of me in a gush. Reed's smile grew. He took a bite of his roll, watching me a moment longer, then turned to face the fire.

"Can I ask you something?" I asked, not sure which of the two I was questioning.

Reed turned back to me. "Of course." Eddie didn't answer, oblivious to the two of us as he tore into another roll hungrily.

"Why do people call this Prison Nation?"

I could see the muscles in Reed's jaw clench for a moment. He took in a deep breath, then looked back at the fire. "It must be hard for you. I mean, I saw the way you were looking at that tree. Just a tree. Was life hard? In there?"

"I don't know. I mean, it was... life."

Reed nodded. "You know that life. Life out here, it's different. I'm pretty sure you went to school in there." He glanced at me. I nodded. "Well, you will come to find out that what the Nation teaches is... missing some things."

"Missing?"

Reed picked at the remains of his rolls, staring back into the fire. "There used to be a quote, an unwritten law that people followed before the Nation took over. 'Guilty until proven innocent.' It's long gone now. We all live in the knowledge that most everything we do is now illegal, and wait for the day that someone decides to push that fact and throw us into the prison."

"But you get your trial. You can fight any charge. Not everyone goes to prison," I insisted.

Reed took in another deep breath. "You can fight all you want, Millie. But once they get it in their heads that you are guilty, that is it. It's all just words after that. We are all already guilty." Reed looked back at the fire. "That's why people call it Prison Nation. We are all already locked up."

He picked more at his roll, tossing the bits into the fire. It sputtered as the crumbs burned, casting up small sparks that danced in the night sky. He finally glanced down, realizing he had thrown all that had been left of his roll into the fire. I could see his lips tighten.

I looked at my roll, then held it out to him. Reed looked at it a moment, then shook his head. "No," he said. "You haven't even tried it yet. You should. They aren't nearly this good cold."

"I'm full." Reed raised his eyebrows at me, obviously not believing my lie. "Really. That was a lot of soup. In Spokane we were rarely given that much."

"There wasn't much in that bowl," Reed glanced at the bowl in my lap. "You still have some."

I followed his gaze. I hadn't realized I still had soup to finish. My stomach growled again, followed by a pang of pain from being stretched. "Meals in the prison have been getting smaller. I didn't even realize it, until recently. I guess my stomach just shrank, or something." I looked back at Reed and shrugged.

Reed pressed his lips together in thought. Reaching out, he softly took the roll from me. I could feel his fingertips brush mine gently. Gripping the roll in his hands, he tore it in half, then passed one half back to me.

"You still need to try it. It's good." With that, he took a bite of his half. His knees were drawn up to his chest, his free arm wrapped around them as he leaned forward against his legs.

I took a bite of the roll. It almost seemed to melt in my mouth, the light hint of butter teasing my tongue. It really was good. I chewed slowly, trying to not show how badly I wanted to devour the half of roll in my hands. From the way Reed watched me, I knew he would give the other half back if I let on how good it really was.

"Did you leave anyone, Millie?"

I stared into the fire, swallowing the last bit of roll. "My mother. And father."

"Any friends?"

I thought of Orrin. My mind drifted to the small piece of sea glass that was nestled safely in my drawer. Then I thought of Jude, his smile through the slit at the bottom of the door, the music that he would let me fall asleep to echoing in my mind. I looked at Reed and nodded.

"Do you miss them?" he asked softly.

"I don't know."

"How can you not know?" Reed asked.

I sighed, lowering my eyes to the trampled grass under my feet. "You try to not make too strong of ties, in there. People are always coming and going. Most of the time, you never know who they truly are. Some are murderers, some druggies, some petty thieves. You end up making friendships just long enough to make it to the next day, you know?"

"But do you miss them?"

"I don't know," I said softly. I thought for a moment, remembering the few people I had left behind. "I guess I do."

Reed watched me a moment, then softly asked, "And your parents?"

I stared at the grass, trying to bore holes into the earth with my eyes. "I don't think I will miss them." The sudden hardness of my voice caused Reed to stare back at the fire. I felt bad for how it had come out. But it was true.

We sat in silence. Eddie had disappeared at some point during our conversation. I could hear his laughter echoing in the night. "What about your parents?" I finally asked into the silence.

Reed didn't look at me. "They're gone," he said, barely audible above the hiss of the fire and the chatter of the other diners.

I shivered. Though the fire was warm against my feet, the rest of my body had grown cold in the night chill. Reed looked over at me. He watched a moment, thoughts crossing his eyes. Then he sighed and offered me a gentle smile.

"You look cold," he said. "And pretty tired. I bet it's been a long day for you. Come on, I'll take you to your quarters."

He stood and offered me his hand. I took it, letting him pull me to my feet. We left the gathering, the heat of the fire disappearing as we stepped into the cold of the night. I started to shiver more. Reed offered me another smile, then put an arm casually around me. I could feel the warmth of his body press against me.

The memory of Carl's body pressing hard against mine made me suddenly stumble. Reed held out a hand, grabbing my arm to brace me. I could feel Carl's grip on my arm, tight and lethal. I tore my arm away in sudden defense.

Reed pulled his arms away from me, holding them palm out near his head. I felt horrible. He was just trying to be kind, and I had literally just pushed him away. I stared at him a moment, then turned and started walking again, my pace quicker than before. We walked the rest of the way in silence. I wanted to apologize, to explain to him why I had suddenly treated him as if his touch had burned me. But the thought of explaining Carl to him sealed my lips shut.

We stopped in front of my quarters. Reed turned to face me, his hands shoved into the pockets of his jeans. My mind raced, trying to think of something to say. The hurt on his face that he was trying to mask drove me crazy. Our eyes met, watching each other in the near dark a moment before I tore mine away to look at the door.

"Thanks," I said simply.

I could hear Reed shuffle his feet. "Yeah, no problem."

I stepped up to the door, cracking it open. "Hey Millie?" Reed asked. I turned back to look at him. Reed was looking up at me. I could barely see his face, but I knew his eyes were searching for mine.

"Yeah?" I asked, my voice barely cracking out.

I could hear his mouth open, then shut again. "Sleep well."

With that, he turned and walked away. I could hear his footsteps as he disappeared in the night, heading back to the fire glowing in the distance. Biting my lip, I tried to focus on him, but he was gone. With a sigh, I pushed open the door and ducked inside.

◌ ◌ ◌

The bed was soft. I didn't mind that springs poked at my back and legs and that certain spots sagged into hidden holes. Every time I turned or moved the bed would creak loudly. Then I would have to spend time finding a comfortable spot again amidst the springs. None of that bothered me. The fact that I couldn't feel hard concrete flat against my body was all that mattered.

Regardless of the new bed, I couldn't sleep. I lay flat on my back, the blankets pulled tight around me, and stared out the small window above my bed. I had tried to open it earlier, wanting to breathe in the cool night air. Regardless of how hard I pushed, the thick layers of paint gluing the window shut didn't even crack.

I could see a small square of sky. Stars twinkled in the black. I couldn't take my eyes off of them. In my life I had only seen the stars a small handful of times. Each time consisted of mandatory searches and emergency drills that marched us out into the exercise yard to wait in the night. I never had a chance to stop and stare. Tonight, I couldn't take my eyes off of them.

Three small, blinking lights passed across the stars. I knew it was an airplane. I had read about them, heard other inmates talk about them. Watching the lights, I couldn't bring myself to believe there were people, miles above the surface, flying past. I could barely handle the ride in Oscar's truck.

Tears stung my eyes. I didn't know they were falling until I felt the warm streak trailing down my cheek. I felt so out of place. So confused. Everything around me was normal to the people who still sat outside around the warm fire. They didn't even look twice at the trees or the fire, or the stars.

I had seen how they had watched me out of the corners of their eyes. They were unsure of me. I was the strange new worker, just released from prison. Even though I had never committed a crime, I felt dirty. I felt less than them.

Reed didn't look at me that way though. I don't know why, but he had gone out of his way to make me feel normal. I felt oddly safe with him. Every time he left my side during the day, I felt cold and insecure until he reappeared and offered me his easy smile. It was a feeling I wasn't used to. A feeling I wasn't sure I wanted.

The horrible memory of the flash of pain in Reed's eyes as I shoved him away made my stomach knot up. I hated how I had caused that look. More than that though, I hated Carl. The memories of him still hung at the edges of my mind, the pain in my arms and back flaring as the memories fought to take me over. I angrily wiped at the tears that had started to trickle down my cheek. Fog teased my vision.

"I think he likes you."

Startled, I sat up and looked over at the doorway. Maria leaned against it, her arms folded across her as she leaned against the old wood.

"What? Who..."

Maria smiled. "Can I?" She nodded to the bed.

I nodded, tucking my legs under me. Maria stepped over to the bed and sat down, the old springs squeaking as she settled into her spot.

"Reed. I think he likes you. You can tell, with how he hovers." Maria leaned back against the wall, smiling at how my eyebrows knitted together. "It's a good thing, Millie. He is a good guy. Muy bien, sí?" With a light laugh she patted my leg.

"Where are you from?" I quickly asked, suddenly wanting to change the topic away from Reed. I could still see his hurt eyes.

"Me? Mexico. Mazatlan, but I was born in Guatemala."

"Mexico? But how did you —"

"How am I in el Nation Grande?" Maria sighed, the smile never leaving her face. I found myself wondering if this woman knew how to frown. "Once or twice a year, the Nation just so happens to have security gaps along the Mexican wall. They say it is an accident, but during those times Transplants cross and find work inside the Nation, no problemo."

"Transplants?"

"Sí. Refugees. Immigrants. Illegal aliens. You know?" Maria glanced at me, and I nodded. I still didn't get it, but didn't say anything. "We are Transplants. The Nation needs us workers to keep it going. With so many locked away the farms were dying out. And in my country... living is almost impossible. Since the Wall went up, Mexico has gone loco."

"So, you are illegal?"

"Who isn't?" Maria chuckled, patting my leg again lightly. "Sí, I am. Oscar too. And most every other Latino you see. The Nation will go around soon and gather a group up and send them back. As if they are sending a message. But a few weeks after that happens, there is always a lapse on the border and more are let back in. I have a brother and my parents still in Mazatlan. Last I heard, they are hoping to Transplant soon too." Maria paused, as if she was about to say something else, then sighed and offered me a smile instead.

It didn't seem right to me. The Nation wouldn't break its own laws. I fiddled with a loose string on my blanket, unsure of what to say.

Maria's voice came out soft. "When a body is dying, when it needs to be fixed but can't fix itself, sometimes it needs a transplant to keep it going. We are the Transplants." The room was quiet. I could hear Maria breathing, feel her eyes on me, but didn't look up. Maria let out a light laugh, breaking the silence. "Muy loco, sí?"

I nodded. "Yeah. Loco."

Maria patted my leg again, then stood and walked to the doorway. The curtain parted as she ducked out, leaning just her head back in. I looked up to see her smiling warmly at me. "Get some sleep, Millie. Buenos noche."

The curtain fell back into place, Maria's smile disappearing into the shadows beyond. I laid my head back down on my pillow, my eyes searching the stars outside my small window. My mind felt thick and slow, full of too many new facts that I couldn't process, that I didn't want to accept.

The fog rolled in. My mind welcomed it. It wrapped its arms around me, asking why I had chased it away. I embraced the release from my feelings as it clouded me and let me float away into silent dreams of beating hearts and sun-kissed apples.

14

Two weeks went by in a blur. When every day is the same, it becomes harder to keep track of time. Every morning I woke up to the hustle of the other women in my quarters throwing on their clothing and hurrying out the door, eager to pick their perch for the day of picking. To my dismay, I realized that most wore the same dark blue shirt and khaki pants that sat tucked away in my dresser drawer.

Breakfast was always fast, usually a stuffed roll or a random fruit. Water jugs waited, lined carefully along benches and filled to the brim with cool hose water. Hands would snatch up the food and water, rarely pausing as they made their way to the Orchard.

They never gave us apples.

Then we would enter to Orchards, the paths between trees still masked in the leaves' shadows as the morning sun struggled to rise on the distant horizon. The workers would find a basket, pick a tree, and spend the next few hours plucking apples. The Orchard fell into a rhythm of dropping apples, touched with the chime of casual chatter and hinted with the rustle of leaves always moving in the light breeze. As the day drew to a close, people would gather their baskets in tired arms and trudge back to the campfires, ready to eat amidst laughter and fall dead asleep on their worn beds.

Reed and Eddie always found me. No matter what tree I chose, they would come wandering over, then proceed to pick the waiting apples and joke the entire day. I found myself looking forward to their company. They made me feel special. They made me feel welcome. Even though Eddie's constant jabber and joke cracking could get old by the end of the day, I always found myself smiling when he winked or cracked his big toothy smile.

Then there was Reed. After the night where I had pushed him away, he had made sure to keep a slight distance between us, physically. Regardless of the forced physical distance, Reed still found a way to stay close to me during the day hours. His arm would almost graze my arm, his fingers almost meet mine when handing me my basket. It would never get further than almost. He seemed magnetized to me, always finding me, and never leaving until it was time for bed.

Back in Spokane, I would have been scared. Worried that he had a hidden agenda or plan behind his soft smile. Spokane wasn't completely full of horrible people. There were those who were gently doing their time and genuinely decent. That didn't matter much. The majority were out for themselves and nothing else. And those who were assigned to safe-guard us only yawned and ignored.

Or became Carl.

The thought of Carl would send my skin prickling and I would always find myself looking over my shoulder. It was pointless, I knew that. Carl was in Spokane, patrolling the walk. The walk my parents and Orrin lived on. The walk that Jude once patrolled. I was far away from Carl and his smirk and iron grip, even if they were not. Realizing that even a guard, a protector from the Nation, could send this fear down my spine, reminded me that anyone could hide their true intentions. Or desires.

When I thought of Reed, when I saw his face in my mind, I somehow knew that couldn't be true for him.

Those feelings were what scared me the most.

People don't stay. That was one thing I had for sure learned in my life. Everything was temporary, and you had to always be prepared for the change. I always knew that I would leave behind everything I had ever known. The people in the cells were constantly changing, the children coming and going. My parents were lies and Orrin a distant phantom in the night. And someday, I would leave them behind.

During those two weeks at the Orchard, I realized that the prison wasn't the only place people disappeared. The happy, familiar faces I would see throughout the day in the trees kept changing. Occasionally one would go missing, and would never reappear.

The happy red head, her hair always in two thick braids and whose voice carried too loud into the Orchard paths.

The short, squat Hispanic man who had to hold baskets on the ground for other pickers because he was too short to reach into the branches, even with a ladder.

The quiet brunette who would hide away in the taller trees to read her books.

They disappeared. Just... gone. And no one ever mentioned them again.

I found I had grown dreadfully terrified that one morning I would show up to work and smiling Eddie would never show. That I would wait by the tree to start the day and would never see Reed's easy walk towards me, his face already smiling before our eyes met.

My heart would almost go dead in my chest at thought of Reed disappearing.

I forced a painful distance between us. Though I still laughed and talked during work, as soon as dinner came I would quickly eat then excuse myself to bed. I had already started to become too attached. Too close. I had become too happy.

🔲 🔲 🔲

I sat on the thick branch, my legs wrapped tightly around it as I reached for an apple. I had become more daring, leaving behind the stepladder and venturing higher into the tree every day. I wasn't nearly as nimble in the branches as Reed. I was content with sitting on the thicker branches instead of teetering in the sun near the top. Every day I ventured one limb higher, one foot further from the ground. My breath always caught in my throat. My hands trembled and my heart pounded. Then I would calm and look around, viewing the world around me each day as if it were the first time I had ever seen it. The freedom of climbing was amazing, always facing the risk of falling frighteningly exhilarating.

I let out a sigh and leaned back against the trunk of the tree. I could hear Eddie lumbering around in the lower branches. He was like a bulldozer in the tree, always snapping branches and knocking down loose apples. I shook my head, lightly laughing, and reached for another apple. Something rustled above me. Looking up, I could barely see Reed leaning back against the trunk.

"Millie, can I ask you something?" he asked, his voice drifting softly through the leaves.

My stomach knotted, but I quickly sucked in a deep breath, forcing away the strange feeling. "Yeah, sure."

"Who hurt you?"

My mind seemed to run into a solid wall, shattering into a million pieces in an instant. His question was completely not what I had expected. I had thought he would ask why I kept him at a distance. Why I disappeared every night as soon as I could. Instead, he dove straight in and found the hidden question that I thought I had safe guarded against.

"What…" My tongue had gone thick, unable to form any words.

"You are always looking over your shoulder. Always… keeping your distance."

I didn't say anything. I just stared at the bottom of his foot, barely visible in the thick branches.

"I'm sorry," he said, his voice obviously mad at himself. "That was way too personal. Forget it."

"No, no it's okay." I took in a deep breath, feeling a lump form in my throat. "It was a guard." I could hear the sharp intake of Reed's breath, sucking in through his clenched teeth. "Reed, it wasn't like that. He just… he wanted me to stay there. I guess he had come to like me, in some way. One day he decided to tell me with a little more force than needed." My voice trailed off. I clenched my eyes a moment, my nails digging into the bark as I tried to force away the memory.

It shouldn't have bothered me that much. It had shaken me, yes, but the fact that it haunted me every time I was near another man, especially Reed, drove deep into my core.

I was happy that I couldn't see Reed. I didn't want to have to look into his eyes and see his sorrow for what I had gone through. It would only have made it worse. I could hear him breathing above me. Looking up, I could only see his feet, frozen mid swing, his hands gripping the branch he sat on. His knuckles were white.

"A guard," he said, his voice carefully low. "A guard should never do that. Even if it wasn't... wasn't..." He sighed. "They are supposed to protect us." He spat out the last words, the anger almost tangible in the air.

The branches above me rustled. Reed dropped down in front of me, grabbing onto the branch and righting his body in one quick swing. He sat a foot away, staring into my eyes.

"Millie, I will never hurt you. Never." He stared into my eyes, his own swimming with emotions I couldn't even fathom. "I promise."

I found myself staring back, never wanting to look away. "I believe you."

Time could have frozen there and I would have been content. Even perched high up in the tree, teetering slightly every time a breeze blew past, I had never felt safer in my life.

All of my resolve to stay distant, to safe-guard against this potential threat, dwindled as I looked back into Reed's eyes. I tried to grasp it. I tried to make it stay. Everyone had a potential of being bad, of betraying, of hurting. I couldn't risk letting Reed do that to me. But I couldn't fight this pull. Inside I twisted in confusion as I finally loosened on the self-imposed distance I had been holding so tight. Reed parted his lips to say something.

"Hey, you two!" I jumped, looking down wide-eyed at Eddie who stood on the ground now, gazing up into the branches. "I am way done with apple plucking for the day. How's about we get into town?"

I looked back at Reed. His lips were still parted, his eyes watching me as if he still wanted to say more. Then he glanced down to Eddie and nodded. "Yeah, coming down."

Reed swung down, landing on his feet neatly. I carefully climbed down after him, not daring to jump until I had reached the last branch. As I landed on the ground, I saw Reed holding a hand out, ready to catch me if I fell. I straightened myself, watching him tuck his hand self-consciously into his jeans pocket.

We started to walk back, our baskets held tightly in our arms. Reaching the end of the Orchard, we set the baskets down carefully, then made our way down the dirt path toward the cluster of buildings.

"Been in town yet, Millie?" Eddie asked, waving at a group of girls as we passed. The girls watched him a moment, then huddled in a circle and started to whisper to each other. I saw one girl glance back up, giggling and watching Eddie as we walked away.

"Um, no. I didn't know we could go."

Eddie laughed, smacking me lightly on the back. "Millie, you're not in prison anymore, remember? You can go to the town if you wanna go to the town."

I could see Reed watching Eddie, his lips suddenly tight. Whatever thought had taken hold of him passed and he let out a sigh. "Eddie, Millie is on her month long parole. She needs to check out."

"I need to what?" I was suddenly aware of how little I had found out about my parole rules. I should have known more, should have asked for more details on the rules.

"Don't worry, Millie," Reed said, moving to walk closer to me. "You just have to sign out. I'll show you where."

Eddie clapped his hands together. "Alright! You two get Mills permission to hit the town, and I will snag the outing goodies. Meet you by the gate." With that, Eddie bounded off, disappearing into a nearby house.

Reed just shook his head, a small laugh escaping his lips. "Eddie. What would we do without Eddie?" I felt myself laughing with him. We walked along the path, barely noticing that our shoulders were brushing as we laughed.

The large house rose ahead of us. I had yet to step foot inside of it. In fact, since I had arrived two weeks ago, I hadn't even walked near this large white house with perfect windows. I stared at it as we approached. It seemed almost too clean and perfect to be surrounded by the smaller, more run-down living quarters.

Reed walked up to a side door, not even pausing as he pulled it open and walked inside. I stayed close behind. The entryway was well lit, the walls just as white inside as they were outside. He turned down a hallway to the left and walked through another doorway, the white door propped open.

Inside the small room stood a desk, its surface covered in papers, plastic wrappers, and other loose ends. Every inch of the wall was covered in framed photographs. I slowed, taking in the images. Most were of the Orchard over the years, the first few so old that the black and white had faded to almost nothing. By the time I reached the end of the wall, I noticed that most of the images had Oscar standing off to one side, his hands nervously tucked at his side.

Noticing my eyes glued to the photographs, Reed stepped closer. Our shoulders barely brushed. Lifting a finger, he pointed at Oscar. "That's Oscar Ramos."

"I know," I said. "He was on my parole board."

Reed looked at me a moment, then nodded. "Makes sense. I have heard of them doing that before."

"So, who is Oscar?" I asked.

"He runs this farm. Not the owner mind you, but has been hired to make sure it keeps going." Reed looked at Oscar in one of the photos, then turned to me and smiled. "He's a good guy. Probably scared the crap out of him to have to sit in that prison."

Reed caught himself, his face suddenly full of apology. I hadn't even realized what he said until he looked at me with his eyes wide. "It's fine," I said softly. "I can't blame him. For being scared."

He started to walk toward a back room I hadn't noticed before.

I followed him, glancing once more at the photograph of Oscar before turning away. Reed spoke to me over his shoulder. "Oscar is a Transplant. So his English is a bit rough. And he prefers to still speak in his foreign tongue, which is cool and all, unless you have no idea what he is saying."

Pausing, Reed turned to me, his face slightly embarrassed. "Transplant. I bet you have no idea what Transplant is."

"No, it's alright," I interrupted, watching his face lighten a bit at my intrusion to his apology. "Maria told me about them. She's one too."

Reed smiled. "Maria." The way he said her name, his lips curled still into that smile, suddenly made my face heat. Reed looked at me a moment, the smile softening. "Maria is a good person. Did you know she has a husband?"

"She does?" I asked. Reed nodded. "Where is he? In Mexico still?"

His lips clenched tight for a moment before he turned and continued to the back room again, shaking his head. "He's in prison."

I hurried after him, wanting suddenly to hold his arm, to reassure him that Maria's husband was alright. That he was safe. I couldn't get myself to actually lift my hand to comfort him. I couldn't form the words. A few weeks ago I would have said them without pause. Now, I found myself newly wondering how true they would be once they passed my lips.

Reed rapped his knuckles on the open door's frame.

"Hey Lou," Reed said casually.

The man, Lou, nodded at Reed. "What can I do you for, Reed? Haven't had to see you in here for some time now."

"Yeah, I know." Reed motioned to me. Taking his cue, I walked forward and stood in front of Lou. "This is Millie. She was released two weeks ago. Eddie and I were hoping to take her into town today. Can you sign her out?"

Lou spun in his chair and opened a cabinet behind him. I watched as he flipped through some folders before finally finding the one he wanted. As he flopped it open, I saw my black and white photo plastered onto the first page. Did everyone have a file on me?

Lou read through a few pages, glancing at me occasionally, then leaned back and nodded. "Good marks. Looks like you passed with flying colors."

"Uh, yeah," I answered.

"You just have to sign here." Lou slid a clipboard to me, a paper stuck on it with columns carefully drawn out. I signed my name where he pointed. Lou turned to Reed. "You're taking responsibility for her then?" Reed nodded. Lou slid the board to him and Reed signed next to my name. "Got your ID card on you, Millie?"

I reached into my pocket, grabbed the small plastic card and handed it over to Lou. He glanced at it a moment, his eyes quickly flicking up to take in my face once, then handed it back to me.

"One more thing." Lou stood and reached into a cupboard above his head. I watched as he pulled down the small device that every guard in the prison carried. "New procedures. I guess they want to keep a better watch on their releases."

Out of reflex, I held out my wrist, twisting my hand so the carved code on my bracelet was easy for him to scan. Reed watched me, his brows knotted together. Lou quickly scanned the bracelet, waited for the device to beep, then nodded again.

"Alright, that's it. Have fun in town."

Reed thanked him quickly then motioned for me to head out of the room. He walked close behind me, causing me to hurry as we headed out the door.

"I'm sorry," he said under his breath.

"For what?" I had no idea what he would need to apologize for.

"I didn't know they would have to scan you."

"Reed, really, it's fine. I have had my wrist scanned pretty much daily for my entire life."

Reed shook his head, hands shoved into pockets as we made our way to the gate. "No, it's not fine. You aren't in there anymore. They shouldn't make you feel like you are."

"I don't –"

"You didn't see your face, Millie. You looked so… you looked like a prisoner waiting for your rations."

I didn't know what to say. Reed seemed genuinely angry. I couldn't tell if it was more at himself, or at the Prison. Either way, he had clammed up, keeping his mouth shut as he stared into the distance. I leaned against the post of the gate, watching him.

The sound of Eddie's heavy footsteps bounding towards us relieved the tension that hung in the air like thick smoke. I smiled at him, welcoming his playful wink. Eddie didn't seem to notice the mood Reed had fallen into. He playfully slapped his friend on the back, then made his way through the gate.

"Well, come on then!" Eddie said happily. "Let's get away from this apple picking prison already."

▌▌▌15

The town was just as I remembered it. People ambled down the walk, couples held hands, children laughed as they skipped and jumped in dizzy circles. Two weeks ago, the drive from the small town to the Orchard had been long and bumpy as I sat next to silent Oscar. Walking with always talking Eddie made time fly. Even with Reed still in his oddly quiet mood, I barely noticed the walk until we arrived at the first building.

We slowed as we passed. I turned to look in the windows, gazing in awe at the clothing that draped across display racks behind the clear glass. It was so colorful. Vibrant. Alive. Though I had on the dark blue shirt that had been given to me in my release box, I still wore the white t-shirt much too often for my liking. Peeking through the shop's shining window, I couldn't see a white shirt anywhere.

I reluctantly kept walking, my eyes still trailing the shop window.

In the reflection I caught Reed watching me, a soft smile spreading on his face. I warmed inside. It was good to see that smile again. As his smile grew, I could see the humor that tinged his lips, amusement as he watched me, and I felt my cheeks flush with heat.

Eddie took his place walking in front of us, hands tucked loosely in his pockets of his jacket, back straight as he coolly glanced around. I realized for the first time that he had grabbed a backpack, which now hung from one shoulder, swinging back and forth as he ambled down the sidewalk.

We passed other shops, some showing food, some posters for travel or houses for sale. I couldn't get enough. The sun kissed my face, the stirred dirt of the road tickled my nose. I took in a deep breath, tasting life.

Eddie steered to the left and twisted the shiny handle of a clear glass door. The door swung open smoothly. Eddie flashed me a cheesy smile, his chin held strangely high as he ushered Reed and me through the waiting doorway. I glanced at Reed. He was smiling, his head shaking slightly in humor at his friend.

Walking into the open entry, I was hit with the warm, amazing aromas of cooking food. The mixed smells of meat, baked bread, and fresh vegetables mixed to completely intoxicate the air. I had eaten more in the last two weeks than I could remember, and yet I still felt hungry. Eddie pushed ahead of me, hurrying to merge into a line that waited in front of a low counter.

We had just joined the line when a couple entered and moved to cut in front of us. They were young, most likely our age. Judging from the crispness of their clothing and sparkle of their jewelry, they did not work at the Orchard. Or anywhere remotely similar.

"Hey," Eddie said, his voice low and menacing. "Get in line like the rest of us have to."

The man turned to look at Eddie. He took his time to scan

Eddie, his lips pursed, jagged lines radiating out in an angry sun. Instantly an image of Dr. Eriks flooded my mind, her perfect spray of lines oddly detailed and focused. I didn't like thinking of her. I hadn't since my release. Instantly I knew I didn't like this man who looked down at Eddie from his much too perfect nose, even though Eddie towered over him.

The man chuckled. "Calm down, Ginger. You will get your grub."

The man reached out and roughly patted Eddie on the arm. I could see Eddie's shoulders suddenly bunch up, his fists tightening at his sides. Taking a step forward, Eddie seemed to grow even taller as he glowered down at the man.

"What are you going to do, apple picker?" the man asked. His voice sounded like it had been greased with oil, smooth and reeking of money. Eddie took another step forward, his hands rising at his sides into tight fists.

"Get. In. Line." Eddie growled. His face turned a deep red.

The man chuckled, his voice sounding slightly worried as he let his eyes flick down to Eddie's fists. "Hit me, Ginger, and I will see to it that this is the last hot meal you get. I hear the Prison needs more workers." He laughed again, his confidence regaining as his arrogance took over. "I bet you are just the type they would kill for."

Eddie growled, unable to make words as he pushed his body up against the man. The man's date took a step back, tightening her grasp on her small purse as her wide, heavily made-up eyes stared at Eddie.

Reed glanced at me a moment, then stepped forward and rested a hand firmly on Eddie's back. The woman laughed nervously. Reaching up, she rubbed her date's shoulder seductively before turning her back to us. She glanced over her shoulder once more at Eddie before coolly smiling, her eyes still alive with fear. Her hips swayed just enough under her tight skirt to distract her date. The man looked back to Eddie then over to Reed, whose hand still rested firmly on Eddie's back. Without another word, he smirked then turned away.

I could hear Reed speaking in a low voice, leaning in close to Eddie's ear. "Cool it man," he said, his other hand moving to hold Eddie's flexed arm. "You don't wanna get killed, do you? Or worse?"

Eddie took in a few heavy breaths, his hands still clenched in tight balls. Then he nodded, letting his shoulders relax, slightly. He remained on edge, constantly staring into the back of the man's head. I waited for a hole to appear at any moment in the man's finely smoothed hair.

The line moved forward, the couple finally being ushered off to find a table. I was happy to see them leave. I hated the way the woman stroked the man's back. The way the man kept leaning in to whisper dripping words into her ear made my skin crawl. As they walked away, the man glanced behind him at Eddie, winking with a sly grin before disappearing around the corner.

"Stupid pricks," Eddie muttered. His arms were folded across his chest, his chin tucked down angrily.

I felt strange on my feet. My mind kept trying to fog over and I fought it madly. I didn't want to disappear right now. It licked at the corners of my mind. It begged to embrace me and carry me away into my escape from reality. The man's sly smile as he passed out of sight sent the fog into a frenzy. I felt my body sway.

Reed moved closer. Carefully, so lightly I barely noticed, he laid his hand on the small of my back. I gratefully leaned against it. I could hear him breathing next to me, his eyes watching me as I let him support my weight. The fog backed away, barely visible now in the corner of my vision.

We moved forward. Reed kept his hand on my back, guiding me to a table sitting next to a large window. I sat down. I hadn't realized how tired my legs were. Reed waited until he saw me settle, then took the seat next to me. Eddie plopped down across from me, still glowering.

A car rolled by outside on the road, its wheels crunching on the paved road. We all paused and looked out the window. I could feel as we collectively held out breaths, watching the dusty police car creep past. The driver, a star pinned to his armored vest, looked through the glass back at us and nodded a short greeting before rolling on. Eddie watched the car a moment longer before letting a smile take over his darkened face.

"Well, like the prick said, time to get our grub on," Eddie said lightly. He opened a menu and started scanning the lists of food.

I had no money on me. I hadn't planned on coming into town, most likely ever, and when we had randomly decided to make the trip I had completely forgotten to grab any cash. In Spokane, we never used money, at all. I hadn't even thought to grab any before we headed into town. Resting my hand on top of the menu, I stared at the down, wanting desperately to order one of the delicious smelling foods that wafted through the air. But with no money, I knew I couldn't.

"What's wrong?" Reed asked, glancing over to me. My hand still rested on the closed menu.

"I forgot my money," I said, feeling stupid. My eyes tried to fog over, and I blinked it away angrily.

"Don't worry. I got it." Reed smiled at me. Reaching over, he picked up the menu, sliding it out from under my hand, and opened it. "You need to eat. I don't like how you were swaying back there."

"Reed…"

"It's just a few bucks. No problem." He smiled again and

tapped the menu, encouraging me to choose something.

I scanned the menu, trying to find something cheap. I felt horrible for making Reed pay. He smiled easily at me, still trying to reassure me that it was alright. I finally settled on a bowl of pumpkin soup, its description hinted with spices and warm French bread causing my stomach to growl. I had never had pumpkin before.

It didn't take long for the food to arrive. The soup smelled amazing, and before I knew it I was spooning it into my mouth, letting it envelope my tongue in its sweet silky flavor. Eddie pounded down a burger, topped with almost every option listed. I had no idea how he could eat so much, but somehow wasn't surprised when he called the waitress back to order a second burger.

Reed carefully ate his sandwich. He joined in Eddie's playful banter, but something obviously still nagged at his mind.

The meal went fast. The waitress came by once more, slipping a black folder onto the table.

"Here you go, handsome," she said, winking shamelessly at Eddie.

Eddie beamed a toothy smile, running his fingers through his red hair. "Why thank you, ma'am. Might I say, those burgers were delicious."

"Oh hon, they aren't the only delicious things here," the waitress replied, her voice dripping. The waitress glanced over at Reed and me. "Looks like the restaurant is full of delicious today." She winked at Reed.

Reed politely smiled back to the waitress, then reached into his pocket for some money, averting his eyes from her overly made-up ones. "Don't mind him," Eddie said, chuckling. "He's on a first date, and I'm just intruding."

"First... Eddie, honestly." Reed shook his head, forcing a nervous laugh. I could see him glance out of the corner of his eye in my direction, his cheeks looking more red than usual. I could feel my own cheeks reflecting his heat.

The waitress smiled at Eddie again, then turned and walked away. "See you later, Eddie," she called over her shoulder.

"Bye Rhonda," Eddie called back to her, pretending to blow a kiss to her back.

Reed raised an eyebrow at Eddie, his fingers counting out a few bills from his wallet.

"What?" Eddie asked innocently. "We went on a date. Once. I think." A bashful smile crept across his face as he ran his fingers through his hair again. "She said she liked my red curls."

The boys both chuckled, slipping their money into the black folder before standing. Eddie snatched a handful of fries from his almost empty plate, stuffing some into his mouth as he took a step away from the table. I glanced at the folder. Leaving it there on the table, full of money, did not seem like a good idea.

"It's okay," Reed said, leaning toward me. "They got it." He pointed to the waitress, who waited politely a few tables away. She nodded at me, flashing a brilliant smile before wiggling her fingers at Eddie.

Reed placed his hand on my back. I melted against his hand's gentle pressure. It felt strange to relish the touch of him. I no longer recoiled or pushed him away. Instead, against all my thoughts and will, I found myself looking forward to his next touch.

It confused me like nothing else.

We walked back out onto the sidewalk. Across the street there was an office that I hadn't noticed before, its windows blocked with thick white paper. On a board hung above the closed door, painted in fading black, it read: Records.

"What's that?" I asked, pointed at the office.

Reed's eyes followed the direction of my finger. "Records? It's a place where you can find out about the records of any newspaper, arrest, court sessions, sentencings… you know. All of that. Right in there." Reed clenched his jaw, nodding toward the office.

"Why would you want to do that?" I asked, shocked.

"Some people like to know the truth. Looking up records seems to be the only way to dig some of it up."

The truth. Everyone lately seemed to be more and more obsessed with that. Being a criminal, committing crimes, and being punished for them, that was the truth. I couldn't see what else they could look for.

Reed was watching my face, his own deep in thought. As if reading my mind, he leaned in closer, his voice soft. "There is a gray zone in life, Millie. People say everything is black and white. But sometimes… sometimes there is more to the story than what he said or she said. There is always some sort of gray zone."

Eddie stepped up beside me. He was munching on the fries he had snatched up from his plate, casually wiping his greasy hand on his jeans. "So Millie, what got your folks locked up?" he asked through the mouthful of fries.

I felt the knot rise in my throat. "Murder," I said, barely audible.

"Murder? Really?" Eddie laughed, choking on his fries as he tried to swallow the mouthful. "How awesome is that!" He moved to slap me on the back, but Reed suddenly intersected his hand, pushing it away sharply.

"Eddie. Really?"

Eddie stopped, lowering his hand to his side. He looked back and forth between us before a smile hinted at the corners of his mouth. "You know, I think I'm going to go mingle. Meet back up in an hour?"

Reed nodded. Eddie winked at me then wandered off down the sidewalk, his backpack swinging with his loose swagger.

"Sorry. About Eddie." Reed put his hands in his pockets, shifting his weight from foot to foot. "What he said in the restaurant, about it being a date, I didn't mean for it to seem like it was a —"

"It's fine," I interrupted, offering Reed a soft smile. "I didn't mind. I really don't."

Reed returned my smile. Together, we turned and looked at the Records office in silence. The sign swung slightly in the growing breeze, its hinges creaking. I read the sign over and over, my eyes tracing each letter as if searching for what truth the sign might hold.

"Have you ever thought of looking them up?" Reed asked.

"My parents?" I stopped, thinking. I had honestly never thought about it. Up until that moment, I had never even known that it was possible. "No, I guess not."

"You are mad at them, aren't you?"

I turned to Reed. "Wouldn't you be? If you were me, wouldn't you be mad?" I asked, my voice slicing through the air. I hung in mid breath, almost begging for his answer.

Reed lightly shrugged. "They would still be my parents," he said softly.

"They murdered people, Reed." My voice hissed, but I didn't care to stop it. I felt desperate, like I was suddenly drowning and my words were the only thing that could save me. "And what's even worse, they told me they didn't regret it. They said the men deserved it. The men deserved to be killed because my parents 'didn't like them.' What kind of monsters —"

"Monsters. They do sound like monsters." Reed looked me in the eyes, watching me. He leaned in closer, bending down to make sure I could see his face as he studied me. "But have you ever wondered if there could be more to the story?"

I felt my head nodding. I couldn't speak. Before my parents had told me their crime, I had always hoped there might be a loophole. Some sort of forgotten truth that would set them free. Some mistake that had happened that could prove they never deserved the life they had lived for the last eighteen years. Could it be possible that hope could still live?

"Maybe. Not right now though. I just..." I trailed out, letting my eyes drift back to the sign.

"Hey, no rush. That office isn't going anywhere."

Reed put his hand on my back again, guiding me down the sidewalk. We walked slowly, enjoying the still warm sun. It was nice to get away from the apple picking for the day. I hadn't realized how dull the routine at the Orchard had gotten until now. Walking down the side of the street, with nothing planned or expected turned out to be a welcome change.

I took a deep breath, the feeling of drowning disappearing with each step we took away from the office. The fog teased me, but I blinked it away.

"Reed," I asked, finally venturing into a question that had been on my mind. "You said your parents are gone... where are they?"

Reed stared ahead, his hand still light on my back. "Dead."

"Oh," I said, unable to think of a better response. "Do you know... who..."

"The Nation killed my parents." Out of the corner of my eye I saw Reed clench his eyes shut a moment, swallowing hard.

We stopped at a street corner. A few cars passed, followed by the same rolling police car. The man with the star pin, the Sheriff no doubt, drove slowly by. His eyes fastened on mine a moment before he looked away. I could barely see him through the tinted glass, talking into a small radio before driving on. Reed watched the car disappear around the corner. His eyes suddenly glittered, his breath coming quick as he grabbed my hand and held it tightly in his.

"Come on," he said. "I want to get you something."

He pulled me across the street, his mood suddenly light and happy. I tried to protest. I already felt strange that he had bought me food. I knew I would have to repay him. Now he wanted to get me something else. It didn't feel right. Reed shouldn't be spending anything on me. He barely knew me.

Reed ignored my silent protest. His hand, firmly holding mine, pulled me along behind him. I looked down to see his fingers wrapped around mine, tiny scars from working at the Orchard in the trees scattered across his tan knuckles. My hand looked so small and pale in his, but something that seemed right about their stark contrast.

I looked up in time to see he had pulled me to a stop in front of the clothing store we had first passed. The mannequins in the windows smiled at me, beckoning me in. I looked down at my dirty blue shirt, my used prison jeans. The loose seams, the dirt stains and tears made me very aware of Reed's other hand on my back, touching the worn-out shirt.

Reed opened the door and pulled me in. Inside it smelled of flowers and clean linen, light music playing from hidden speakers. I stopped for a moment, letting the music flow over me. Reed gently tugged on my hand, pulling me towards a stack on a clean white table

It seemed to hold a shirt in every color I could ever imagine, simple button downs made to fit snug against the body. I reached forward and touched one lightly. The fabric was soft, so soft.

"Well, pick one."

I glanced at Reed then looked back at the waiting shirts. I didn't know where to start. Slowly walking down the length of the rack, I took in every color. Then I saw it. A dark purple shirt, the same shade as the shirt of the woman who had released me, sat neatly folded at the edge of the rack.

I picked it up, running my fingers over it. The fabric felt so smooth under my touch, like warm summer water. I could barely imagine how it would feel wrapped around me. Reed smiled at me then pulled me to a small room at the back.

"Go in there and put it on," he said, opening the door for me.

I walked in, Reed shutting the door behind me, and quickly did as he told. Pulling off my blue shirt, I carefully put on the purple top, taking my time to button each button as delicately as I could. The fabric hugged tightly against my body, wrapping me in the silky smooth bliss.

Cracking the door open, I waited until I saw Reed's face smiling at me. "Well, do I get to see?" he asked, his eyebrows raised.

I stepped out tentatively. In front of me stretched a large mirror, my entire body reflecting back at me. I stared at the mirror, realizing I had never seen a clear reflection of myself before. My reflection had always been flits I saw in windows or the hammered metal mirrors, splashes in puddles of water, glimpses in the truck's side mirrors. This mirror was smooth and perfect, shining as my mirrored self stared back at me.

The top fit snug around my body, showing the curves of my hips and bust. Its vibrant purple made my skin seem to almost glow, my cheeks rosy above the crisp collar. I took a step closer, barely able to believe that the person staring back at me could actually be me. Even with the same jagged cropped hair, the same full lips and pale skin, I looked… different. It wasn't the light red always present on my cheeks from the long hours spent out in the sun. Or the always present layer of dirt under my short finger nails. There was something else, something new and very different, that I couldn't place.

In the reflection I could see Reed standing behind me. His hand slowly combed back through his dark hair. His eyes glittered, lips slightly parted as he took me in.

"Yup, that's a keeper," Reed said softly.

I turned to face him. He stood off to the side, arms folded loosely across his chest, smiling at me. His eyes were soft, his smile hiding something gentle. I wanted so bad to know the thoughts that caused that strange but oddly comforting look to grow on his face.

Reed took a step closer. He trailed a finger down my arm, taking in the smooth fabric. I could feel him breathing. Even with the space between us, I could feel the intake of breath, the slight pause, then the exhale as the air passed his parted lips. Reed let his eyes trail up to mine.

"You are beautiful, Millie. Do you know that?"

I couldn't answer. A small smile touched my lips.

Reed moved in closer. His eyes seemed to be searching mine for something. Hand still resting on my arm, he raised the other to tuck a loose strand of my still short hair behind my ear. He parted his lips to say something, then stopped. A moment later, he asked the question that hinted at his lips. "Do I know you?"

I felt myself laugh. "Of course you do, Reed."

Reed shook his head. "No, I mean. Have we met? Before?"

"How could you know me, before?" I could feel my brow wrinkle together.

"I don't know." Reed shook his head, his hand that had touched my hair just a moment ago now resting on my other arm. I heard him take a deep breath, the air rumbling in his chest. "You just seem familiar. There is something about you, something I can't place my finger on, that makes me swear I knew you before you came to the Orchard. I bet that sounds crazy, huh?"

I shook my head. "Doesn't sound crazy to me."

A smile spread on Reed's face. He seemed to glow. His hands tightened softly on my arms for a moment before he let go and took a step away. My arms felt cold without him.

"Come on, let's get it," he said. I moved to go and change out of the shirt, but Reed stopped me. "Nope. You are wearing that out. Millie, this is a new life. You are finally starting. It's about time to stop with the prison garb." He looked at me, his eyes still softened with that strange emotion. "You look beautiful."

My cheeks threatened to burn. I didn't say anything. How could I respond to that? I quickly snatched up my blue shirt and hurried to follow Reed. By the time I caught up to him, he was already handing a wrinkled bill to the woman standing behind the front counter. She smiled and nodded at him, wishing for him to have a good day.

Exiting out onto the sidewalk, I grew strangely self-conscience. My hands flattened the shirt over and over, trying in vain to smooth every wrinkle out of its purple fabric.

"Relax," Reed said in my ear, putting an arm around my waist. I was very aware of the way he was holding me closer, my body tingling at his touch. The strange distance between us still lingered, but he acted like nothing was wrong as he guided me back toward where we had split from Eddie.

I could feel eyes on me. People glanced at me as they walked past. Mostly men. Then the eyes got stronger. I could feel them bearing into me, watching my every move with hunger. Chills ran down my spine. I had felt that feeling before. In another life.

Stopping in my tracks, I spun around. Behind me, barely hidden around the corner of the building, I could see his blue eyes watching, the smirk plastered on his strong face.

"What is it?" Reed asked, his voice full of concern.

I glanced at Reed, my eyes wide. My breath had frozen in my chest, my bottom lip quivering as my stomach tightened into the old familiar knot. Fog teased at the corner of my vision. Turning my head back to where I had seen him, I found no one was there. A small child happily ran by, ducking around the corner to disappear after a rolling ball.

"Nothing." I smiled at Reed, forcing myself to turn away and walk again.

Reed nodded, pulling me back into stride. Behind me I could still feel the burn of Carl's hidden eyes on my stiff back.

▌▌▌16

I sat at the fire, the flames causing the shadows beyond to flicker in a dance that kept my skin prickling in goose bumps. I couldn't shake the feeling of eyes watching me. We had been back at the Orchard for hours now and I could still feel the penetrating gaze bearing into my back, no matter where I turned. I felt twitchy, constantly jerking to look behind me, so sure I would see Carl smirking at me, lunging for me. Even Reed's reassuring touch didn't calm the strange paranoia that had taken me over.

The fire glowed warm on my face. It felt good to sit around the flickering fire again, regardless of the distant shadows, Reed so close that I could feel his body heat hot against my chilled flesh. Every so often he would turn to talk to someone, his arm brushing mine. I felt tingles run up and down my body each time. As the night wore on, I found myself longing for more of those moments.

"Are you alright, Millie?" Reed asked. I had been sitting silent, knees tucked up to my chest, staring intensely into the fire for most of the evening. The feeling of eyes watching me bore into my soul, freezing me in fright. Staring into the fire was all I could manage to do.

Forcing a smile, I finally tore my eyes from the fire and looked into Reed's. "I'm fine. Tired. It was a long day."

Reed nodded. "Was it a good day?"

The smile became real on my lips.

"It was," I answered softly.

Reed smiled back. Inching closer, he carefully put an arm around me. I felt his hand mindlessly stroke the silky smoothness of my new shirt as he got lost in watching the flames. Occasionally a small group of men would wander by. Reed would glance up at them, watching as they whispered to each other and scanned me. I could see his face darken, his eyes bear into them until they finally moved on.

I had dealt with men like that my entire life. I knew they were there, I knew what was running through their minds when they cracked those sly smiles my way. But I couldn't seem to get myself to reassure Reed of this. I instead found myself melting into his protective arms, relishing the fact that, for once, I didn't have to be the only one on guard.

I wished he could make the eerie feeling of eyes watching my soul disappear.

I felt a shiver run down my spine. Shaking it away, I could feel Reed pull back enough to look at me. "Are you sure you are alright, Millie?"

"I'm tired," I said. It wasn't a lie. I could feel sleep tugging at my heavy eyes, my limbs heavy with needed rest. The exhaustion ran deeper than our busy day in town, but something about the fear in the pit of my stomach kept me from telling that to Reed. "I think I should get to bed."

Reed nodded, rising to his feet and helping me up. Without asking, he moved in closer, silently guarding me as we walked toward my quarters. He walked stiffly, constantly looking over his shoulder as the fire grew smaller behind us. I finally let out a heavy breath and turned my face to him.

"Reed, you can relax. I know they are watching me."

Reed glanced at me, then looked over his shoulder again. The group of men were watching, laughter boiling from their loose huddle. "You have no idea what those guys are like, Millie. They are trouble."

"I don't?" I asked, stopping in my tracks. "I really don't? Reed, those are the guys I have spent my entire life around. Rapists, pedophiles, thieves, murderers. Have you forgotten that little fact? I had to walk past those guys every single day. I have felt them watching me every time I dared to venture out of my cell."

Reed clenched his eyes shut, a hand reaching to rub the bridge of his nose. Something inside me flared. I took another step away from him. My breath shuddered as I sharply drew it in.

"Yes Reed, I lived in a cell. And do you know why? Because my parents are murderers. The Nation locked me in a cell for the first eighteen years of my life, because my parents decided to kill. That's the truth. It really happened. I am not some stupid little town girl who only wants to flirt and cuddle in your arms!" I could feel my face getting hot with anger. The words were spilling out of my mouth before I could stop them.

Reed slowly opened his eyes, his finger still gripping the bridge of his nose. He didn't move. He didn't even speak. He just stood there, his eyes watching me.

A moment ago I had been content in his arms. I relished his protection. Now I couldn't stand it. My body felt itchy, like my skin had grown too small for my bursting spirit. I didn't like how I kept snapping at Reed. He didn't deserve it. But I couldn't seem to stop myself. In some way, I didn't want to.

I let out another angry breath. My hands were clenching into fists at my side. "I have had to protect myself from those guys since the day I could remember." I pointed at the group of men, emphasizing who I was talking about. The men stopped their laughter as they saw me look their way. Without a word, they quickly moved off into the dark.

"The guards didn't protect me from them. My parents sure as hell didn't protect me from them. I did." My voice faltered. I could feel the lump rising in my throat.

I felt so angry. A helpless anger, aimed at no one in particular, and aimed at everyone in the world.

Reed lowered his hand from his face. I could see his body sway, as if wanting to move closer to me, then stopping itself before it had a chance to move an inch.

"I think your parents were protecting you more than you know, Millie," he said gently.

I couldn't speak. My lips refused to form words, my mind reeling at what he had said.

"Millie," he continued, his hands tucking into his pockets. "I know where you came from. But you aren't there anymore. I know you had to protect yourself your entire life. You might not need me, but it's about time you need someone. It's about time you let someone else do the protecting."

His eyes looked heavy. They searched mine a moment, almost begging for me to argue or consent, to say anything. When I didn't answer, he let his eyes blink, looking away back towards the fire. He nodded once, then started back down the path away from me. I wanted to stop him. I willed my voice to call his name. But nothing happened. I just watched as he disappeared into the night, then ran into my quarters.

§ § §

I pulled open the dresser drawer, shoving my clothes aside as I dug for the sock. My fingers finally brushed it and I snatched it up, slamming the drawer shut. I flopped onto the bed, feeling the springs bend around my body. The envelope of cash dumped out first. It landed on the mattress next to me, a few bills sliding out. I snatched up the sea glass, shoved the money back in, then pushed the sock aside.

I let the sea glass roll out into my palm. The light from the small lamp hit it, causing the green to glow slightly against my flesh. Rubbing a finger over it, I felt the small cracks and sandy rough spots, broken up by the wave-smoothed patches of time. The memory of Orrin crept into my mind.

For the first time since I had left the prison, I pulled open the drawer next to my bed and lifted out my notebook. Still clutching the glass in my hand, I cracked the book open and started to flip through the pages.

Every page held a different conversation. The scribbled words brought back memories. Some were angry, some goofy, some so boring I caught myself yawning as I turned past them. I flipped through the pages faster, working my way to the end of the stack.

Finally, I found what I was looking for. I pulled it out quickly, almost tearing the corner that I held too tightly between my fingers. Orrin's handwriting was perfect on the lined surface. I tucked up my knees, laying the page gently against them as I reread some of his final words.

You are who you are Millie. No one decides who you are but yourself. If you want to be mad like them, then be mad like them. But if you want to be different, please, be different.

... Dear, that is a question every child your age has asked since the dawn of time. Life is ahead of you. What this Nation is doing... they lock away the people and make them become the criminals they so fear. I do not know what you will become. But I pray to God that you don't allow them to decide your fate.

There is a lot you don't know yet Millie. There is a lot to learn. Remember everything your schooling has taught you. But remember: To every truth, there are a million untold truths.

I laid my head back, rolling the sea glass through my fingers. The stars twinkled in the sky outside my small window. I imagined Orrin sitting at the beach, watching the stars in their nightly guard. The waves crashed against the shore, the wind bent the grass in the night air. I found myself wondering if my parents ever laid under the same stars, taking in their beauty as they held hands in young love. Had life always been mad for them? Had it once been beautiful?

"Always a gray zone," I muttered to myself, my eyes searching the sky.

I wished Reed could meet Orrin. Deep inside of me, I knew they would somehow understand each other at a level most people never knew. They were so much alike. I felt a smile touch my lips at the thought of Reed, my hand brushing the purple shirt that I still wore. Then I remembered his final words that night, and the smile faltered.

Reed was right. There was always a gray zone. I sat up, shoving the notebook back into the drawer. A paper fell from it and I picked it. It was the entry I had written in one of my last meetings with Dr. Eriks. I read it, the same strange feeling that something about it was wrong rising in my stomach. My eyes traced the words, trying to place it.

It clicked. I finally realized what it was.

"Only a silent father and a state-proclaimed unstable mother. And it is because of them that I live in this cell," I read out loud, slowly pronouncing each word. "Because of them," I repeated, looking out the window again, the paper wrinkling in my tightened hand.

I had always thought the unease from that journal entry had been because I admitted my fear. I had thought it was because I somehow felt unworthy to be set free, unable to leave behind my criminal parents. But it had always been something deeper. Something hinted at in every conversation with Orrin, with Jude, even with Dr. Eriks.

I had been born into the Prison. I had been raised in the Prison. I had always assumed and been told that my condemned life was my parents' fault. And I had believed it. Now I sat, paper wrinkled in my shaking hand, tears stinging my eyes, and finally let the thought surface:

Was it?

▌▌▌

"I decided," I said aloud, sitting high in the tree. I could hear both guys pause at my words.

"What have you decided?" Reed asked, his voice strangely cautious.

"I want to know. I want to know the whole story of what my parents did." My voice softened. "I need to know."

I could hear Reed adjust himself on his branch, the plunk of an apple dropping into his basket echoing through our silence. "Are you sure, Millie?"

I nodded, knowing no one could see me. I needed to nod. I needed a physical reassurance that I did in fact want this. "I am."

Reed didn't answer. I could hear his apples dropping into his basket above me. Clenching my lips tight, I grabbed the branch above my head and pulled myself up. Reed balanced carefully on a branch just through the leaves. His legs were hanging limply around the limb, the basket nestled in a clustered of branches next to him.

His face was twisted up, as if in pain. His eyes were glued to an apple in his hand, staring intensely at it as his face tightened even more. The look of pure torment on his face stabbed my heart.

"Reed?" I asked softly.

His eyes snapped up from the apple. He let them waver unfocused a moment, then looked down at me. I reached up and grabbed another branch, pushing off with my feet and hauling myself up closer to him. He looked away from me, watching the apple again.

"Reed, about last night —"

"I don't even know how my parents died," he said, cutting me off. His voice sounded distant. "After they died, I was put into foster care. The Nation... it likes to keep children in their care. Every year, they make money off of the kids. They rip the child out of the home they had finally settled into and move them, then bill the family that had been assigned them for back pay. The family has to pay back everything the Nation had loaned them to take care of the foster child, plus interest. I was hated."

Reed spun the apple in his hand, watching its surface thoughtfully. "Eddie's family finally took me in and adopted me. Kind of. I had to keep my last name, and they had to pay the Nation a yearly fee for having me. But they did it."

"What happened to them?" I asked carefully.

"Eddie's family?" Reed spun the apple in his hand, a sigh

escaping his lips. "His older brother got arrested and thrown in prison for theft. Twenty years. Eddie's mom had a panic attack, which turned into a stroke that killed her. His father is still alive… somewhere. We don't know where he went."

I thought of Eddie, light-hearted happy Eddie. It was hard to believe that something like that had happened to his family. It was nearly impossible to believe anything bad had ever happened to Eddie.

"After that, Eddie and I came here. We had nowhere else to go. Being homeless wasn't an option. Becoming a GF was… We couldn't do that."

Reed finally looked over to me. His eyes were heavy, as if he hadn't slept at all. "When you said you didn't want to know the truth about your parents, I hated you, for that moment. I hated how you had your parents, had a chance to know the truth, and refused to take it. While I am here, wanting so badly to know and…" His voice trailed off. He stared at the apple again, then said roughly, "What if you find out more of the truth? Will you push me away, again? Will you close those doors in your mind and shut me out, expecting me to be here waiting once you feel like creaking them back open?" Reed let out a frustrated breath, staring up into the branches. "I can't… I am so sick of this."

I felt my body sway in the breeze and clutched the branch beneath me. "Sick of this?" I asked. I felt myself panic at the thought of what his answer would be.

Reed waved his hand around in the air, motioning to everything around him. "This. The Nation. The constant fear of breaking the law. The need to always work, never knowing what you are working for. Never being in control." He looked at me, his eyes heavy again. "Fearing that the goodbye you refused to say might have been your last."

I could only watch him, the memory of last night flowing in my mind.

Reed tossed the apple to me. I shot a hand out and caught it before it could fly past. Reed plucked another apple from the tree and stared at it a moment. The dark red skin shone in the bright daylight. Then, slowly, he took a huge bite. Juice sprayed from the apple, the meat bright white as he took a second bite into the crunchy surface.

"Reed..." I said, alarmed. My eyes scanned the ground beneath me, afraid someone passing would see what he had done. Reed wiped a stream of juice from his chin, carefully chewing and swallowing before looking back into my eyes.

"Millie, I am sick of not knowing who owns this delicious apple that I am never allowed to eat. I am sick of seeing the people I finally let myself grow close to disappear. I am sick of this fear that sticks to us every single day. There has to be more than this Nation. There has to be."

"Like what?" I asked.

"I don't know." He took another bite. I could hear him chewing the apple, his head leaned back against the trunk of the tree. I looked at the apple in my hand. Then looked back over at Reed.

"What are you going to do?" I asked, my voice barely audible.

Reed sighed and looked over at me. "I don't know, Millie. I don't know if I even can do anything." His eyes searched mine. "I don't want to risk losing the few things I do have. But there has to be something." He took another bite, watching me as he chewed. "First thing I know I am going to do. We are going to find out what really happened with your parents."

He looked at the remains of the apple in his hand, then let out a slow sigh. Leaning his head back again, I watched as he disappeared into his thoughts, his mouth mindlessly chewing the last bite he had taken of the apple.

"You were right. Last night." My voice was almost a whisper. I saw Reed's eyebrows slightly raise, his eyes watching me. "I do need you."

Reed slowly chewed the bite of apple. He let his eyes wander away from mine, deep breaths causing his chest to rise and fall in perfect rhythm.

"Reed, about last night —"

"Millie, stop" he said, cutting me short again. "This life we have been doomed to is much too short to hold grudges against friends."

I looked again at the apple in my hand then raised it to my lips. The skin was cool and smooth, smelling rich as it pressed against my teeth. I glanced up to Reed once more. Clenched my eyes shut. I took a bite. The apple was crisp, its juices spraying into my mouth and down my chin as I carefully chewed. I didn't feel myself cringe as I took another careful bite. This apple was different than the ones I had always known.

Maybe it was because it had been fresh picked off the tree that I sat in. It had never had the chance to soften and brown in its over-filled basket. Captivity and the end never loomed in front of it, stealing away its deep red and sweet juices. All it had ever known was the sun and the breeze and the song of the birds.

All it had ever known was freedom.

I leaned heavy against the trunk, finishing my apple alongside Reed. We didn't talk. We didn't need to. We knew without saying a word that something had just changed. Something deeper than eating an illegal apple. Something that was about to ignite a change that would landslide our entire lives.

17

"You sure?"

We stood in front of Records, the blocked windows menacing as they loomed in front of us. I stared at them a moment before slowly nodding. Reed reached out and gently took my hand, giving it a squeeze. I felt the spark jump into my body at his touch, his warmth racing up my arm to take me over. A moment later he let go. My hand felt cold and alone where he had just touched it. I folded my arms across my chest, trying to seal in the last spark of warmth from his touch.

Reed pulled the door open and stepped inside. A bell hanging on the door rang, cutting through the quiet air inside. I paused a moment, listening to its soft lilt in the air before following Reed inside. The door swung shut behind me. I jumped as it slammed back into place, killing the sound of the bell in one swift click.

Just a few feet away from the door stood a desk. We stepped

closer, watching the man behind it motion for us to wait. He was talking to someone on the phone, his voice lowering as we pulled to a stop in front of the desk. He wrinkled up his nose in thought, his dark brown skin stretching across his full cheeks. On his wide nose sat a thick-rimmed pair of glasses, the glass so thick it magnified his eyes to an almost comical size.

Waiting for his conversation to end, I let myself look around the room. A long table lined the wall to my right, its surface layered messily with old computers and loose papers. The other wall was solid window, all covered with the thick white paper. Nothing hung on the walls. No art, not even color. Just the solid white of a temporary life.

The white of the Prison.

The man clicked the phone back onto its base. "How can I help you?" He glanced up at us as he spoke, his words relaxed and easy.

Reed stepped closer. "I'm Reed Taylor. This is Millie 942B. We were hoping you could help us find records on a past crime?"

The man took us in slowly. Then he stood, pulling his pants up as his round belly tried to push them down. "Reed Taylor. I've heard your name around. Been here some time, eh?"

Reed nodded.

"Congrats on that," the man said. He looked over at me. "I'm figuring you're the one wanting to know the facts." He moved forward, a finger pushing his glasses up his nose. Holding out a hand, he waited for me to shake it. I held out my hand and he gripped it tightly, cranking it up and down. "Call me Rick. My mom named me Ricardo, which I always found stupid, being as Ricardo is a Mexi name and I'm a black man." He smiled at me, his teeth a startling white against his dark skin.

Moving away, Rick walked over to one of the computers and jammed a thumb down on the monitor button. The computer blinked to life. He motioned for us to sit in the plastic chairs on either side of him, then drummed his thick fingers on the computer keyboard.

"Crime date?" he asked.

"Crime date? I… uh… "

"Don't know it? Hmm, okay. Name of the victim or criminals?"

"Leann and Alan 942B." My mouth was fighting to go dry. "Criminals."

Rick glanced at me a moment, then turned and typed in the names. The computer buzzed indignantly, still waking from sleep mode. After a moment a list appeared on the screen. Rick muttered to himself as he read down cases on the list, finally clicking on one. Another list came up, small paragraphs appearing below each link. Rick opened the first and read it.

"Let's see. Leann Summers was charged with Murder 1 and Assault. Alan Summers with Murder 1 and Aiding. Both sentenced with Life. Looks like…" He clicked his tongue, scanning the text that rolled down the screen. "Two men were murdered, deadly intent. The third escaped and was able to retrieve authorities. The accused were appointed their representative, and finally entered a plea of guilty. The surviving man pushed for death penalty, but they were sentenced life with no parole." Rick paused a moment, thinking. "942B. The Life sentence walk. I thought so. Sound about right?"

I could only nod.

"Alright," Rick said, wiggling his fingers before bending over the keyboard again. "This is where the fun comes in. I don't do this for everyone, but being as I hear nothing but good about Mr. Taylor here, and you," he looked at me and smiled, "you just look like you need it, I won't charge you extra."

"How much?" Reed asked.

"One-fifty. That's the going rate." Reed started to reach into his pocket, but before he could grab his money I slammed the cash down on the table next to the keyboard. Reed lowered his hand, his eyes taking in the small pile of bills.

"It's alright, Reed," I said softly. "This is something I need to do."

Reed nodded at me, offering me a small smile before turning his face back to the screen. Rick shoved the money into his pocket then clicked on another link on the page.

"This is weird," he said, scanning the text.

I leaned in closer. Most of what appeared on the screen was strange legal wording. I had no idea what it actually said. "What is weird?" I asked.

"There's usually a recorded copy of the accused side of the story. Even if they settle, as these two did, there will still be a copy. It looks like they never even made one." He clicked on other links, his thick lips puckered up in thought as he read the files that popped up. "The copy is nowhere. That's just... weird."

"What's that mean?" Reed asked, his voice on edge.

"It means we get to talk to Lady Justice." Rick smiled again, his fingers already typing fast. Reed glanced at me. I raised my eyebrows at him in question but he just shrugged and shook his head, obviously having no idea what Rick was talking about.

A box popped up on the screen, asking for a password. Rick glanced at us, then leaned in over the keyboard and quickly began to type in a long password. I wondered if it was ever going to end. Finally hitting the send button, he leaned back and waited. A little clock appeared, its hands quickly spinning. Then the screen went black.

Rick didn't seem worried. A moment later, it came back to life, a bright white box popping up. A photo of a woman, her gown flowing over her curved body, a blindfold fastened tight over her eyes, stared back at us. In one hand she tightly gripped a sword. The other held out a set of hanging scales, perfectly balanced.

"That, my friends, is Lady Justice." Rick sat a moment, looking at the picture, then happily grunted to himself and started to type again. I had never seen her before. Yet there was something familiar about this woman, something that I knew I should know.

The computer buzzed.

Rick mumbled to himself, his fingers drumming on the desktop as he waited.

"Who is Lady Justice?" Reed finally asked.

"Lady Justice?" Rick perked up, his eyes focusing again on the black and white drawing on the computer screen. "She used to be a symbol for the justice system. You know: lawyers, judges, courts, all of that. It was the idea that justice is balanced. Those scales are truth and fairness, always balanced and always even." Rick pointed to the blindfold. "Justice is blind. It is objective." He pointed to the curved hips of the drawing, winking at Reed. "And man, this justice was hot."

Chuckling to himself, Rick leaned back and folded his chubby fingers across his round belly. "Naturally, when the Nation took over, Lady Justice was the first to go. There used to be statues and paintings of her in every courthouse, but now there are none. Pity.

"Anyway, a while back someone started printing a paper. She called herself Lady Justice. Made it her job to find out the truth about some of the court cases that seemed too simple. Then she would print it for everyone to read. The Nation has been trying to find her for years. Thing is, if you go by dates, this Lady Justice must be over one hundred years old now. Makes some think she is a phantom. Or a saint.

"When I can't find information on a case, such as yours, I pretty much know Lady here will have it." Rick eyed the image again, smiling wide. "Man, what I would give to meet her."

The machine finally stopped buzzing, a box popping up on the small screen.

An image of an old newspaper page had been scanned, framed now in the pop-up window. Across the top a smaller image of Lady Justice appeared, her name printed in block lettering next to her perfect form. Below it, in black and white, was a fading photograph of my parents.

I felt tears sting my eyes as I looked into their young faces. Though they were disheveled and strange looking, something still healthy clung to the young faces of Alan and Leann Summers. I felt a tear break free, running down my cheek.

"Whoa. Are you alright?" Rick asked, his eyes wide as he looked over to me.

I tried to nod, but couldn't move. I couldn't take my eyes off of my parents. "She's fine," Reed said in a soft voice. "Those are her parents."

Rick's eyes shot to the photograph then back to me. Realization slowly spread on his face, his eyes softening in understanding. "Oh. Okay." He licked his lips, scrolling the mouse down. "On we go. 942B, right?"

I nodded, my eyes never leaving the glowing screen.

Under the image was the same information Rick had already read to us. Their charges, their pleas, then their sentences. It all seemed so cold. As if they were just a number listed, a product waiting to be bought and used up.

Rick scrolled more. Another image appeared.

It seemed like a simple photograph of a pile of leaves. A tree trunk framed one side of the shot, a bush filling the other. The dirt had been kicked and turned, footsteps evident around the dried leaves. A number rested in the corner, propped up just like the numbers in the photographs Dr. Eriks had forced me to see before my release.

All three of us leaned closer. Something seemed strange. The leaves and dirt seemed staged, unnatural. They didn't flow with the rise and fall of the land. The leaves were pushed into a pile, lines left in the dirt from the fingers that had moved them carefully together.

We all saw it at once. Reed let out a groan. Rick gasped. I couldn't move. I couldn't blink. I desperately wanted to look away, to be anywhere but sitting there in that white office.

Barely visible to the uncaring eye, a little hand reached through the leaves, its young chubby fingers limply clutching the ripped remains of a dirty, torn blanket.

$$\square\ \square\ \square$$

Getting the pass to visit the prison turned out to be easier than I thought it would be. I didn't need to fill out any paper work. They already had everything about me on file, including a daily report of my work in the Orchard. It seemed strange that someone, somewhere, was filling out all of that information about me. At that moment though, I didn't have the time or energy to care.

While I sat with Lou and learned the rules about visiting, Reed hurried off to find Eddie and Oscar. My mind barely grasped anything Lou said to me. I nodded when I felt I needed to, answered with a word or two at other times. Inside I felt like a tornado had just torn me apart into pieces.

Lou finally held out a paper for me to sign. His face looked concerned, carefully watching me as I picked up the pen and signed my name along the dotted line. I forced a smile at him. He nodded once, then motioned that I could go. Picking up my copy of the signed paper, I quickly walked out of the house.

It wasn't until the door to the house closed behind me that I realized Lou hadn't scanned my bracelet. I turned back to the door, then stopped. He had been staring directly at it. Lou knew he hadn't scanned my bracelet. Glancing at the door one more time, I turned and hurried toward the front gate of the Orchard.

Reed stood next to Oscar's yellow truck, his hands shoved into his pockets. As soon as he saw me walk around the corner, he straightened. I walked closer and held out the paper. Without a word, he climbed into the driver seat and reached across to open the passenger door for me.

I climbed in and slammed it shut. Without pausing, I pulled the seat belt across my body and clicked it into place. Reed buckled himself in then cranked the key in the ignition. The engine turned over once then sputtered out.

"Stupid Dodge," he growled under his breath. Pumping the gas pedal, he cranked the key again. The engine roared to life, the entire truck rumbling.

I finally looked around. "No Eddie?"

Reed shook his head as he backed the truck out of the dirt drive way. "He thinks this is something you need to do. Said he will be waiting for us at dinner with extra rolls."

A smile tried to tug at the corners of my lips, but quickly died away. I looked down at the small stack of papers in my hand, my fingers nervously rubbing the top sheet. My legs were shaking, my heart racing nonstop. Nothing I did could calm me.

We rolled through the town. The same people as always ambled around. I saw them differently now though. Through their smiles and laughter, I could see their eyes watching each other warily. They glanced over their shoulders. The mothers always remained close to the carefree children. Every person wandering the sidewalks walked in the same path that they had the day before, just barely avoiding each other until they finally saw someone they could smile at and greet. It was all rehearsed, all well practiced and careful.

It was all fake.

We rolled by the Records office. Rick watched us from his door, his magnified eyes barely blinking as we passed. Locking eyes a moment, he nodded at me, his lips set in a tight line. Then we pulled out of the town and turned onto the road that led back to Spokane, leaving the town in our rumbling dust.

I tried to watch the countryside roll by. The swaying grass used to intrigue me. Now it just looked dead, left to become forgotten in this abyss of a land that led to nothing good. I tore my eyes away and stared at my shaking hands.

Reed's hand softly touched mine. His fingers stroked mine a moment then gently intertwined, locking our hands together. I stared at his hand holding mine. He gave me a soft squeeze, and I knew he was trying to offer me a smile, if I would just look back. I only seemed able to stare at his hand.

I didn't let go.

Before I expected it, Spokane rose up in front of us. I could have sworn the ride away from the Prison two weeks ago had been much longer than that. My legs were barely cramped, my back still not fully settled into the worn seat. I looked over to the dash and saw the speedometer ticking over the speed limit. Seeing that I had noticed, Reed offered me a small smile and slowed the truck down. Slightly.

Reed rolled past the entry gate and pulled to a stop in a marked parking spot. We were in the same parking lot Oscar had picked me up in when I had been released. I could see the covered area he had pulled into just a few weeks earlier. The flowers still grew perfectly groomed along the edge of the building, bright and fake like the people wandering in the distant town. It truly seemed like only yesterday when I had been passed off into Oscar's nervous hands.

The truck engine choked once then turned off. Reed moved to open the door, then stopped. He looked down at our hands, still clasped tightly together. My eyes were already glued to them. He squeezed my hand once more then reluctantly let go. Reed pulled the keys out of the ignition and shoved them into his pocket, then pushed his door open and climbed out. I followed, the sound of our doors slamming shut echoing in the near empty parking lot.

The same woman sat working at the desk as we entered. She wore the same purple shirt I had admired the first day we were there. I glanced down at my own purple shirt, the feeling of embarrassment trying to boil inside me, but I brushed it aside and stepped up to her desk.

The woman looked up at us, her eyes widening in surprise for a moment as she saw me. Blinking once, she composed herself and smiled. "How may I help you?"

"I am here for a visit," I said, my voice coming out strong regardless of the way my stomach churned in anxiety. I passed her the copy of the paper I had signed in Lou's office. The woman read it over, nodded, and turned to type on her computer.

She glanced at the small stack of papers held tightly in my hands. "I will need to see those before —"

"Why?" I asked. I shot her a look that froze her in her place. The woman glanced to my face then back at the papers. Something seemed to cross her mind and her face suddenly relaxed into what almost seemed like sympathy.

She pressed a button and a tag dropped out of a machine.

"Wear this at all times," she said, handing the tag to me.

Reed glanced at the tag, then back to the woman. I could see the question growing on his lips. Before he could ask, I turned to him, my hand coming to rest on his firm chest.

"You weren't approved for the visit," I said carefully. "Since I am their daughter, I am already on the approved list. I didn't have time to apply for you to be added. Anyway, I need to do this on my own."

Reed let out a slow breath, then nodded.

The woman sighed, obviously happy that I had handled this for her. "You may wait in the waiting room, sir." She turned her head to me. "The officer in the waiting room will let you through."

I nodded to her. Hitting a button on her desk, the door buzzed once then clicked open. I led the way, Reed close behind as we passed through into the waiting room I remembered from my release night.

I led Reed to a gathering of chairs. Without pausing, he sat down, his eyes watching me.

"Will you be alright?" he asked.

I nodded, my hands gripping the remaining papers. "I don't know how long it will be."

"That's fine," Reed said. He picked up a nearby magazine then motioned to the others scattered around the room. "I have lots of reading here."

A smile touched my lips for a moment. "Thank you Reed."

Reed looked at me again, his eyes soft. "Anytime."

"Ma'am?" The officer's voice behind me was soft, almost familiar. "Millie 942B?"

I took in a deep breath and slowly turned.

There, standing in crisp uniform, smile spreading on his young face, was Jude.

18

"Jude?"

"Hey there, Millie," he said, the smile growing on his face. He motioned for me to follow as he made his way to a locked door across the room. I glanced back at Reed. He was watching me, a question evident on his concerned face. I offered him a small smile, then turned away to follow Jude.

Jude stopped at the door and pulled out the small hand held device. Without hesitating, I lifted my wrist and let him quickly scan it. The device beeped once. Jude scanned the card that had been clipped to my shirt, waited for the device to beep once more, then opened the door and motioned me through.

We entered into a long hallway, the mortared cement blocks that made up the walls painted a solid white. I had almost forgotten how white these walls were. There were no doors or windows, just the long empty stretch of the wide hallway.

"Is this where they transferred you?" I asked as we started down the hall.

"Yep. I guess it beats trying to see by flashlight. But it sure can get boring." Jude smiled at me, then turned to watch ahead. "Not too many people visit the prison. Even if they have loved ones in here. It's almost as if people just don't care anymore. Once someone gets locked away, it's as if that person is now dead. Kind of sad if you ask me."

I nodded, watching the hallway ahead. Doors were starting to appear on either side. Solid metal doors, a window cut out of each one and covered in crisscrossed wire. We passed the first few without pause, then finally came to a stop in front of the door labeled with the number 5.

Jude turned to look at me. This was the first time I had ever seen him fully in the light, with no door between us. He was tall and thin, the gun hanging on his hip looking bulky and awkward. His tousled hair seemed longer than I remembered, brushing past his ears in waves. Jude stood straight, strong, his head held high and sure. His eyes watched me, concern flashing across them.

"Millie, are you sure about this?" His voice had lost its casual humor. He kept watching me carefully. "They have gone downhill since you left. I don't know how much you will get out of them."

"It hasn't even been a month," I said, my voice threatening to crack. "What happened?"

Jude glanced at the door then looked back to me. "It seems like your leaving did more damage than good to them. You're a hard one to let go." He let out a long breath. "I just need to make sure you are sure about this."

I looked down at the papers held tightly in my hands, then looked back into Jude's eyes. "Positive."

"Alright." He put a hand on the metal handle. "I will be the guard on duty right outside this door. The cameras... They have suddenly come down with some issues. It looks like, well…" He smiled at me, making an exaggerated innocent face. "It looks like this visit will accidentally fail to be recorded or fully monitored. Stupid technology." Jude winked at me then twisted the handle, the door swinging open a few inches. "It doesn't hurt to have privacy every so often. Especially with family. Have a good visit."

I took a deep breath, then stepped through the door. It closed silently behind me. In front of me I saw a metal stool, fastened firmly to the cement ground. A metal counter stretched from wall to wall, a sheet of glass firmly secured above it. The glass sandwiched a grid of thin metal wire inside.

I stepped closer. The icy coldness of the metal cut through my pants as I sat down. My hands, still clutching the papers, began to tremble. I could feel the pages bending and wrinkling in my nervous grip. I tried to lay them flat on the counter, but my fingers refused to let go of their tight grasp to the only thing remotely mine in this sterile room.

A door beyond the glass creaked open, two sets of unsteady footsteps drawing closer as the door clicked shut. I could hear the shuffle as they sat down. The gasp of breath.

I finally gathered the courage I had been searching desperately for and lifted my head. Staring back at me through the thick glass were my mother and father.

"Millie?" My father sounded confused. He looked somehow thinner, as if some piece of him had suddenly gone missing. His face was covered in scruff, his eyes heavy with dark bags. I could see a dirty bandage wrapped tightly around his hand.

"Hi Dad," I said.

I looked over at my mother. Her hair hung in a dirty mess off her head. Her face seemed even more tired, her body rocking back and forth slightly as she perched on her metal stool. Everything about her seemed distant and lost, a bird who had been caged too long and was unable to remember that it had wings. Except her eyes. Her eyes were watching me, not even blinking.

"Millie, how are you?" my father carefully asked.

"I'm sorry Dad." I took a deep breath, my hands finally stopping their nervous shaking. "I didn't come here to catch up. I need to know the truth."

My father looked at me, confusion evident on his exhausted face. I could still feel my mother's eyes bearing into me. Through the grating I could hear her whispering.

"My baby, my baby."

Her words gently cut through the air, over and over. I couldn't bring my eyes to look at her. Locking eyes with my father, I nodded slowly.

"It's time you both tell me the real story. I need to know... I need to know from you."

"Baby, my baby." My mother's voice rose.

Finally drifting my eyes over to her, I watched her a moment. She had started to rock back and forth harder, her fingers twitching as she sat limp on the metal counter. I could see that I was losing her. Her hidden world was engulfing her, faster than I had ever seen before.

I picked up the sheet of paper and slammed it against the glass. The image of the small pile of leaves pressed hard into the glass, my hand wrinkling the paper as I pushed. I stared into my mother's clouding vision.

"Who is Charlie?" I softly demanded.

My mother froze. Her mouth hung open, stopped in mid-word. I could see her eyes glued to the image, wide in sudden fear and memories. I watched her a moment longer, then turned slowly to my father. Tears were streaming down his face.

"Charlie," he whispered hoarsely.

"Dad, is it true. Is what this article says true?" I leaned closer. I wished so much that this glass wasn't there. I needed to feel connected to them. I needed this moment of truth to be fully real. But my parents were Lifers, and Lifers didn't get physical contact visits. "Please, Dad," I whispered, my lips close to the metal grating at the edge of the glass. "I need to know."

My father stared at the image a moment longer, then tore his glistening eyes away and looked at me. "We were traveling," he began, his voice coming out strange and distant, as if watching the past play before his eyes. "Your mother and I didn't have a car. So we had to walk. We were trying... we were trying to get out of the Nation before the Wall went up.

"Charlie was three. He was such a beautiful baby boy. Chubby and always happy, always wanting to wrestle and play. I loved him, so much." My father choked back a sob, fighting the urge to look again at the image. I slowly lowered it. As the paper crumpled into the counter, my father let his eyes trail to my face. He looked at me intensely, determination gritting his jaw tight. I had never seen this look in his eyes before.

"We had stopped to camp for the night near a small town. Your mother was making dinner, Charlie playing some cute make believe game a few feet away. Then the three men appeared. They told us that we were trespassing. I apologized and told your mother to gather our belongings, I told them we would leave. But they... they said it was too late." My father closed his eyes a moment, swallowing hard.

"I could see the way they were watching your mother. And how they watched Charlie. Charlie... he had no idea what was going on. Until one of the men grabbed him." My father suddenly slammed a fist down on the metal table, causing me to jump. "I tried to stop them," he sobbed. "The second one bashed me upside the head then followed the first as they dragged Charlie off. The third grabbed your mother. I couldn't move. I couldn't get my bearings.

"We listened as our baby cried. He cried so loud for us. Then... it was quiet."

My father let out a heart-wrenching sob. I couldn't blink. I could feel my lungs burning for air, but I couldn't breathe. He tried to form words, but every time he opened his mouth, another sob broke out.

"That's when I snapped," my mother said softly.

I looked over to her. She looked so calm. As if there had never been a care or worry in the world. Her eyes took me in, full of emotions I knew I would never fully understand. "When a momma's baby gets hurt, it's amazing what adrenaline will do to her. The man holding me said that according to the law, we were guilty. And that they could do with the guilty as 'justice' allowed. I snapped. I somehow threw the man to the ground. Then I hit him with a stone.

"The other two came back. They were monsters, Millie. They were the monsters. They were laughing. One grabbed me, saying things I could never repeat to you. Then he saw the man on the ground. He raised a hand to hit me, but I saw his knife and, and I took it. And stabbed."

My mother sucked in a shuddering breath. After a moment of silence, she continued, her voice slightly shaking. "With every stab I could hear Charlie's screams for his mommy less and less. With every stab I was pulled into the fog that took away this pain."

My mother gasped in another breath, her face cracking as a tear streamed down it. "That's when I saw your father drop the third man."

My father reached over and laid a hand on my mother's now

shaking fingers. They looked into each other's eyes, sharing a memory long since buried. Then my father turned to me. "Charlie was already gone when we got to him. They had just left him there, lying alone behind the bush. We buried him. We didn't want the other monsters of the world to find our baby.

"While we were doing that, the man your mother knocked out must have come to and ran off. He brought back the authorities, and told him we had jumped him and his 'pals' for no reason. That's when we were arrested."

I could feel the cold metal of the table digging into my stomach as I leaned as close as I could to the glass. Pulling away a few inches, I looked back and forth between the two of them. "But why didn't you tell them the truth?"

"I tried," my mother whispered. "I tried and tried. But they classified me as unstable. I was crazy." She took a deep breath. "Everything I said was thrown out on grounds of insanity."

My eyes darted to my father. "Why didn't you try?"

He looked at my mother a moment, then shook his head. "I couldn't."

"You couldn't?" I asked, my voice rising. "You couldn't? You couldn't defend your wife and murdered child? God, Dad! Really?" My fists slammed on the metal table, louder and harder than my father's had. My shadow of a father, who barely lifted a finger of any emotion, couldn't even defend his family at the worst of times. Anger flooded me, and I didn't try to calm it down.

"Millie," he said evenly. "Your mother needed me."

"You're right, Dad. She did. And you did nothing!"

"Nothing?" His voice cracked. I could see the pain flood his face as my words hit him. "I killed a man who had been intent on hurting her. I buried our little boy so that her last memory of touching him would be when he was warm and alive." He leaned in, tears flowing once again from his blood shot eyes. "I didn't tell the truth, Millie, because I was the only hope your mother had of staying with me and away from a mental house. If I stayed quiet, they let us stay together. I was told to keep her calm. If I did that, then we would stay together."

My mother turned her face to him, shock breaking through her own tears. "Alan..." By the haunted tone of her breaking voice, I realized she had never known what my father had just told me.

He reached over and gently stroked her wet cheek. "I couldn't let them do that you to you, Leann. They had taken away our baby, our future, our freedom... I couldn't let them take away our love."

I had never seen this affection between my parents. My father seemed so strong. My mother became tender in his outreached fingers, her face leaning against his protecting hand. This was the image I had always dreamed of my parents. Two people, madly in love. Two people who would do anything for each other. I had never realized they had already done everything for each other.

My father closed his eyes, his hand still holding my mother's face. "It was just after we were finally incarcerated here that we found out we were pregnant with you. They wanted us to abort you." He clenched his eyes shut tighter. "But one of our babies had already died. We couldn't let them kill you too."

My mother turned her face to me. The clarity in her eyes, the lack of any fog licking at her mind amazed me. "Charlie was my first baby. I see him sometimes, Millie. I see him as the baby he was, as the man he should be. I let myself fall into those fantasies of him. I know I shouldn't. But I can't control it. I need it. I know I look insane, that I haven't been the mother for you I should have been." She wiped the tears from her face and leaned to the glass. "But Millie, you are my baby too. You are my baby who saved me. Without you..." Her eyes became haunted. She blinked it away, but never finished the sentence.

I stared at them a moment. Then the words gently slipped from my lips. "I am so sorry."

I would have given anything right then for that glass to be gone. I needed my parents. I needed to feel their arms around me, holding me, protecting me from this dangerous world I thought I knew. I had thought I knew so much. Everything had been turned upside down though. I needed them, now, but the thick glass between us stood as a cold reminder that they were forever locked away from me.

"There has to be a way," I said, trying to let hope fill my choked voice. "There has to be a way to clear you. I will find it."

"No Millie," my father said forcefully.

"What? Why Dad? Do you really want to stay in there?" I couldn't believe my ears.

My father sighed. "This is our life now. In here, I can protect your mother. She gets the medicine she needs. We are... safe." He locked eyes with my mother a moment, then looked back to me. "We need to stay here."

"Mom..." I could feel my voice begging, searching for her to disagree with what my father had said.

"He's right, Millie." I could see her hand creep forward, reaching to me. Her fingers touched the glass. I could see her eyes cringe, her breath gasp as she let her fingers drop to the counter. "You need to stay free, Millie. For us. Please, there is so much you can do with your life. We will always be here. Don't let us hold you back."

I could see the pain killing her. My mother was saying goodbye to her baby. I was her only baby left, and she had to sit on the other side of glass and metal and say goodbye. It felt almost as bad as death. Ice cold and unforgiving. It held no love, no warmth, no final farewell. Just the taunt of the see-through wall.

I nodded, slowly.

Lifting a hand to the glass, I let its cold press against my palm. My fingers spread apart as I pressed harder. In my mind I could see my hand sinking through, reaching for my parents and holding them one last time. It didn't sink though. The glass pressed firmly back at me, denying me.

My mother lifted her hand. Her fingers shook as she slowly moved toward mine. She carefully laid her hand on mine, flattening her fingers on the icy glass. Her lips quivered as she looked at me, her eyes wide. I pressed harder, hoping that some warmth would find its way to her small palm

She stroked the glass, her eyes achingly full of pain and love. "My baby," she barely whispered.

Leaning in close, I spoke carefully through the grating. "Mom, I love you. Do you believe me?" She nodded, her head barely moving as if afraid she would lose eye contact with me at any moment. "I love you too, Dad." I glanced at him. He nodded to me, his eyes streaming still with the flood of tears. I looked back to my mother, locking my eyes to hers. "I will always love you Mom. Always. I will… I will always be your baby."

I could feel the sting of tears at my eyes. My mother let out a soft sob, her lips still quivering, and offered me a small smile. I watched my parents one last time. They were different now in my eyes. The monsters weren't sitting there across the glass. No, the monsters were waiting everywhere else in the outside world. I pressed my hand against the glass once more, then nodded and stood.

There were no more words.

We didn't need any more words.

I turned the handle, and walked out of the room.

Jude was waiting for me as I stepped back into the hall.

I knew he had heard every word. I could see it in his eyes, in the way he nervously reached for me, then lowered his hand before his fingers could brush my arm. I offered him a smile, lips quivering. A tear broke free and I quickly wiped it away with my fingertips.

"Millie… are you going to be alright?"

"I am," I said without hesitation. For a reason I could not understand, I knew that it was true. Something inside had clicked.

Jude smiled softly at me then motioned for me to walk down the hall. I took my place next to him and joined his slow pace as we headed to the waiting room door.

"How are things?" His voice sounded careful, as if trying to find the right question to ask.

I nodded. "They are good. Work is good. I like the trees." The smile on my face warmed.

"That's good. I was worried for a bit."

"Why?"

Jude stopped walking. I stopped beside him, just close enough to hear him take in a deep breath. "After you left," he said slowly, glancing toward the camera at the end of the hall. Its light was still dead. "Carl GF4 started to act strange. He tried to find a way to call you back. Said you shouldn't have been released. We all almost believed him. But I knew you deserved it. Your parents vouched for you. Another prisoner did too, named Orrin. Did you know him?"

At the sound of Orrin's name I felt my breath catch in my throat. I looked at Jude, my cheeks warming. "Um, yeah. We talked sometimes." Casting my eyes down, I added, "You know... Fishing."

Jude let out a laugh. "You fished? Oh, that's great." Jude shook his head, smiling.

The smile faltered as he went on. "They dismissed his petition. Carl made life hell around here. He started to overly discipline inmates. He became dark, moody... even other guards were scared. Your parents were forced to work longer hours by the staff, in hopes that Carl would leave them alone." Jude let out a clipped breath. "He was 'encouraged' to take some leave. Clear his head you know. Suddenly he was back to normal Carl. We all assumed the strange mood had passed. Guards... they get those moods sometimes. I don't know why."

Jude looked over to me, his eyes studying my face a moment, his lips tense. "I was worried, Millie. But if you say things are good, then I can stop worrying. That's great." Jude squinted his eyes a moment, thinking. "Why would he do that, Millie?"

I swallowed hard. "I don't know," I said. "I barely knew him."

"Strange."

Jude kept looking at me. I nervously shifted my weight, my eyes flitting to look back at the dead camera.

"You're different, Millie." He moved slightly closer. "You're not the Jail Baby that would lie on the floor late at night anymore. I don't know what it is, but something in you has changed."

"Oh." I couldn't think of anything better to say. I couldn't tell if he was upset, if he was happy. I knew his voice. I knew his laugh and his sigh. But seeing him there now, standing in front of me, seemed to change things. I couldn't read him.

"Remember what I told you about my family? Why I didn't go with them?" I nodded as he asked. "I think you were my reason. I knew there was something good I would need to do here. I think I waited for you."

Jude reached up and pulled a necklace out from under his uniform shirt. Lifting it over his head, he looked at it with a softly then held it out to me. It was a black leather cord. Something swung from it. Looking closer, I saw a small key, just big enough to fit in the palm of my hand, tied to the cord. Its smudged silver surface shone dully in the dim light.

I reached forward and took the key in my hand. It was very simple. No elaborate designs. Just the hole at one end with the leather tied through it, and the teeth on the other. The end of the teeth stopped abruptly, leaving the tip of the key flat and smooth. I ran my fingertip along the glassy tip. Smooth as ice.

"I don't know why my family was given access to the Wall. I guess we had high enough standing. That, or we had enough money." Jude started walking forward again and I followed, my eyes still fastened onto the small key. "My parents never used the key. They never let me set foot on the beach that I could hear day and night. I would see that key hanging around my father's neck, and wanted so badly to use it and escape to the ocean. When they left, he gave me the key. And now... I can't get myself to use it." He glanced at me, his eyes heavy with memories. "I want you to have it."

"Why are you giving me this?" I asked.

"I can see something in your eyes, Millie. You may not know it yet, but that key is what you need. The end has a small chip in it with my families DNA stored on file. The lock will only recognize that key, and that key alone. No one can pick it or fake it. Remember that."

I rolled the key between my fingers. Doubt tugged at my mind. I couldn't do anything else. I had found out the truth. Now I would return to the Orchard and finish my parole. Even with this key, the beach was just a distant dream, a hope I could never reach. My life had already been laid out for me. A tight knot formed in my throat.

Jude touched my arm. He carefully picked up the dangling leather cord and draped it around my neck. The key hung off of it, so light I could barely feel it until it bounced against my chest.

"Jude. I feel so lost." My voice was small.

Jude tucked a finger under my chin, lifting my face to look at him.

"Millie, I know you. You are the good, and the strong."

I nodded to him, tears stinging my eyes as a smile formed on my lips. Patting my arm, Jude started walking again.

We finally reached the door. Jude turned to me and offered his soft smile that had kept me awake and happy through to many lonely prison nights. "I'm going to miss you Millie. But I am happy I got to see you again. This one last time."

"Maybe... Maybe it won't be the last time."

Jude's smile didn't fade. "Maybe, maybe not. One thing life teaches you is that it is unpredictable. If we wait for something to happen, and it never happens, we will just waste our lives waiting. If I see you again Millie, I would love it. Believe me. But if I never see you again," he glanced at the camera. The red light suddenly flicked back on, glaring down at us. Jude lowered his eyes and looked at me once more. "Then I will be happy too."

Turning the handle, he motioned me through the door, then clicked it closed it behind me.

❚ ❚ ❚

Reed drove slowly. I could tell his mind was somewhere else. His brow furrowed, his jaw clenched and unclenched over and over. I reached over and gently touched his shoulder. Reed jumped, then let out a sigh and reached his hand up to hold mine. I could see his other hand tighten around the steering wheel.

"Reed, what's wrong?"

Reed stared at the road. Silence filled the small truck cab, and I started to think he didn't plan on responding.

"I can't do this anymore Millie," he said in a barely audible whisper. He glanced over to me, then focused his eyes back on the road. His voice came out stronger. "Being in there, knowing that there were all those people who were locked away just on the other side of those walls, knowing this Nation could so easily claim me, or you, I just... I need out."

"Out?"

"Millie, I need to leave the Nation." His voice suddenly came out rushed, as if afraid I would stop him at any moment. "I know Eddie will go with me. He has already talked about it. Every time we go into town he fills that bag of his with supplies. Food, maps, all that. We have everything we need." Reed pausing, sucking in a deep breath. "Millie, I need... I want you to come too."

I lowered my hand to the worn out seat, his fingers clinging to me as I let it go limp. "You want me to leave, leave the Nation, with you?"

Reed let out a heavy breath, glancing out the side window then looking back to me quickly. "When you know something Millie, you know it. I have spent my entire life not knowing too much. I don't know my parents. I don't know what happened to them. All I have is one name and some fading memories and those haven't gotten me anywhere." Reed wiped at his eyes, his fingers dragging along as if trying to pull out lost memories. Blinking once, he let his eyes trail to me. "But then I saw you. There was something familiar, and I had to know it more. I couldn't take my eyes off you, and not only because of how you look. You are... you are something I know."

Reed looked over to me. "I need you, Millie, because you make me feel needed."

His eyes stared into mine, his face soft. A fire burned in his eyes that begged for my answer, but my mouth couldn't move. I couldn't think. I could feel his fingers holding mine, but my body suddenly felt like it had lost gravity and was floating far away from me.

Reed pulled over to the side of the road. He pulled the brake, leaving the engine to rumble in the silent air. Unlocking his buckle, he moved closer to me. His hand rose to stroke my face, slowly cupping my cheek in a tender hold.

"I need you, Millie," he whispered. "I am falling in love with you, and I can't lose you now." He leaned in closer, his breath warm on my face. I closed my eyes, feeling his presence envelope me. Softly, gently, his lips pressed against mine.

Before I had time to react, he pulled back again. My lips were cold without his against them. I bit my lower lip, feeling the odd tingle that still ran over it. Reed looked me in the eyes, his face barely an inch from mine.

"Imagine living in happiness," he whispered, his forehead resting against mine. "Imagine eating all the apples you ever wanted, and knowing that at the end of the day, you would still be free. You would still be in my arms." He paused, swallowing hard. He pulled back just enough to look me in the eyes again. "Think about it."

I nodded.

Reed watched me, his face not moving. I found myself hoping he would lean in to press his lips against mine again. That we would share the same breath again, leaving my lips cold and tingling again. Instead, he let out a slow breath then backed away and buckled himself back in. Throwing the break, he steered the truck back onto the road.

I turned my eyes away from him, focusing on the road ahead. My mind felt strange. The fog had come back, tickling at the edges. It taunted me. It wanted to envelope me, to take away this tingle on my lips and decisions on my mind. So much had happened in just the last day. I felt myself tempted to give in and disappear.

The fog.

My mother had said the fog took her over. She said she let it take away her pain. My mind drifted back to the last visit I had just had with my parents. How could any pain I thought I felt compare to theirs? I had a brother. His name was Charlie. Disgusting monsters had killed him, and when my parents acted to protect what had been left of their lives, the Nation sided with the monsters.

What was right? My parents had killed two men. That was an undisputed fact. Men who had killed their baby, then were about to turn on them as well. The thoughts of what those men had running through their minds sent a sick shiver down my spine.

The Nation should have locked the remaining monster away.

Instead, it had sided with him.

I felt sick. The jostling of the truck didn't help at all. With every bounce and jerk, I could feel my stomach roll. I reached out and clenched my fingers around the handle on the door, hoping that it would make the world stop spinning. The fog laughed at me, readying itself to take me away from my reality. Looking over at Reed, I became suddenly afraid that I would never come back. I couldn't let it take me. I would not disappear.

Reed glanced over at me, his eyes growing wide as he took me in. We had just entered the town. Reed quickly pulled the truck into a parking spot along the road and killed the engine.

"Millie, you look sick."

I swallowed hard. "I feel sick. I... I need some air."

Reed nodded and climbed out of the car. Hurrying to my door, he pulled it open and let me out. I heard the door slam shut behind me, but didn't jump. I was numb.

I didn't want to make this decision. I didn't want to admit that the one thing I had always seen as my protection was, in truth, the enemy I had always feared. Reed had his hand on my back, directing me as we walked down the near empty sidewalk. I barely felt him there.

We finally got to a bench. It sat around the corner, hidden in a small alley against a brick building. A window sat open above it, the sound of a radio playing muffled music floating into the alley. Reed helped me sit down then sat himself down next to me, never taking a worried hand off of me.

"I am so sorry, Millie," he said, his voice almost sounding scared, "I shouldn't have —"

"It's okay, Reed." I said, forcing a thin smile. "It's just been a long day. I have... alot to process."

Someone screamed.

Jumping to his feet, Reed pushed me back into my seat when I tried to stand. The screaming grew louder. Frozen in our places, we waited. Down the street we saw a small group making its way toward us. As they neared, I felt my breath catch in my throat.

A tangle of men approached. Some I didn't recognize, but most were unmistakable. I could see the same sneering looks that they wore when they watched me at night around the fire now plastered on their scruffy faces. The men moved down the street, the screaming growing louder as they got closer.

I leaned forward, looking around Reed. In the center of their group, they were dragging someone. A few men broke away to jog ahead, disappearing into the building we were sitting against. As they left, I got a better look at the person being hauled.

Maria.

She screamed again, tears streaming down her face. The men held her arms tightly, dragging her as they walked. She fought against their grip, her feet searching for purchase but constantly being knocked out from under her. Another man jogged ahead into the building, and I finally got a full shot of her.

Her clothes were torn. As she flailed and fought, I could see the flaps of clothing swing around, showing her flesh underneath. I felt sudden embarrassment as I watched, her breasts flashing in the low sunlight before being covered again by a stray piece of her remaining shirt. Her skin was covered in bruises. Even from where I sat I could see the gashes that cut across her flesh, blood gushing to run in trails down her thin body.

The group pushed into the building. Without saying a word, Reed and I kneeled on the bench, peeking our eyes barely over the open windowsill. Inside, the music died with a click.

Along one wall stretched a row of metal bars. An officer stood and opened one of the cell doors. The group of men moved forward and threw Maria in. She landed hard on the ground, smacking her head before her hands were able to reach out and catch her fall. A sob broke free from her bleeding mouth. Maria scrambled into the corner furthest from the group of men, trying desperately to gather the shreds of the remaining clothing around her.

Standing near the window were the few men who had run ahead. They leaned against the wall, quietly speaking with a stiff police officer. I could see a star pinned to his chest, shining in the dusty air. He stood with his arms crossed against his proud chest, eyes occasionally flicking to Maria before returning to the men who stood in front of him.

"Tell me what happened again," he said, his voice husky.

One of the men let out an aggravated breath then shoved his hands into his pockets. I could see blood on his knuckles.

"I told you, Sheriff. This woman came across us when we were having our break. Offered herself to us. Well, we couldn't resist that, could we?" He flashed a smile at Maria. I could see her shoulders heave as she let out another sob. "Well, we were about done with the fun when the slut said we had to pay. We follow the law, Sheriff. And prostitution and pimping are major felonies. We had no idea that she had planned to trap us like that. I swear."

I recognized the man. Searching my thoughts, I finally placed his smug face. The man in the restaurant. The one who had taunted Eddie, who had draped the woman across him like a cheap accessory. I stared at him in shock as he leaned close to the Sheriff. The innocent look on his face made me want to scream. It was obviously forced, almost mocking as he watched Maria. I looked over to the Sheriff and saw him nodding in agreement.

The man went on. "Some of the fellows here had to detain her. She is a strong little whore. That's what's up with the..." He looked back at her a moment, his nose wrinkling up, "the revealing attire. We apologize for the way we brought her in, but the law is the law, right, Sheriff?"

The Sheriff, still nodding, cracked a smile at the man. "It is Paul. That it is."

Maria, crammed in the corner, started to shake. I could see her balled tight, her shoulders shuddering uncontrollably. Pure terror ran through her eyes. The Sheriff looked over to her again, then nodded at the officer who stood next to the cell. The officer nodded back and turned to Maria

"You have the right to remain silent. Anything you do say can and will be used against you —"

"No!" Maria cried. "Please, don't do this!"

Without pausing, the officer continued.

The man, Paul, leaned in to the Sheriff. "What are you going to book her on?"

"Oh, the standard," the Sheriff answered, ignoring the pleading of the bloodied woman. "Prostitution 1. Pimping. I bet there is some burglary or breaking and entering we can dig up."

Paul nodded, a disgusting smile spreading on his face. The other men in his group made their way out of the building. I could hear them chuckling and clapping each other on the back as they disappeared.

The Sheriff leaned closer, his hand resting casually on Paul's shoulder. I could see a splash of drying blood on the back of Paul's arm. I swallowed hard, forcing down the churning in my stomach. "A bit excessive on the force, don't you think Paul?"

Paul's shoulders shuddered as he let out a laugh. "I am proud of our oh-so-great Nation. I must do what I can, to prove that I am the good, the strong." His voice came out sharp, spitting the words as he laughed again.

The Sheriff shifted on his feet, smoothing his shirt as he made a point to avoid eye contact with Maria. "Any news on the apple contract?" he asked.

Paul shrugged. "Nothing has changed. We managed to get it signed and stamped, now it's processing. How ironic is it, that the apple pickers are sent to Spokane, then fed the very apples they picked? I'm telling you, that's justice."

The Sheriff chuckled lightly. "See you tonight Paul? Eight o'clock?"

"Yeah Dad, I wouldn't miss dinner for nothing."

The Sheriff clapped Paul on the shoulder, chuckling.

"Sheriff!" Maria cried. "Por favor. They... they raped me." Her voice broke, choking sobs sending her body in convulsions again. "Please believe me. They raped..."

The Sheriff let out a bored sigh, then followed Paul out the door as if Maria weren't there at all.

⫴ 20

"Okay," I choked out, my body slamming back down onto the wooden bench.

Reed stared into the window a moment longer, his lips so tight they were white. His breaths came in ragged gasps, uneven beats of loss and desperation. I could hear Maria sobbing, her voice carrying into the alley air where just moments ago there had been music. Her sobs mixed with Reed's gasps became a haunting duet that brought stinging tears to my eyes.

Reed turned and sank back onto the bench. He shut his eyes, his fingers rubbing over his clenched lids as if trying to smear out what we had just seen.

Lifting his head, he finally seemed to remember that I sat there next to him. "Okay?" he asked, his voice sounding lost and distant.

Maria's sobs finally quieted. Through the window I only heard a soft whimper, her begging quieted and long since forgotten.

"Reed, those men... that story they told the sheriff —"

"I know, Millie."

"They never even let Maria speak! Just looking at her, you can tell she was..." My voice caught in my throat. Fog tempted me. I shut my eyes, forcing it to clear. This was Maria. Happy, welcoming, gentle Maria. It could so easily have been me. "He believed his son. Without a question."

"Family," Reed's voice sounded choked. "They like to believe lies more than truth, when it comes to those they love. It would be too much to admit your son is a monster. It is so much easier to see him as a hero."

I opened my eyes and turned to Reed, searching his own pain filled eyes. "What will happen to her?"

Reed licked his lips, obviously trying to find a soft way to answer my searching question. "You already know, Millie. You grew up surrounded by women just like Maria."

"The women? They were prostitutes. They sold their own bodies for money, so they could buy drugs and who knows what else. They ruined the Nation."

Reed raised his eyebrows at me, his eyes almost begging. Could it be true? It was so easy to believe that they were all the criminals. Those women in the prison who strutted around, pushed themselves at the men, taunted the girls. I could see them now in my mind, walking in their tight groups, hands protectively holding each other, eyes always carefully watching every passing man even as their mouths said otherwise. Could they all be Marias, living to get by but always scared that their nightmare would just begin again?

Orrin's words crept into my mind. They lock away the people and make them become the criminals they so fear. Hearing Maria's lost sobs behind me, I finally understood what he meant.

"But, can't we... couldn't we just —"

"No," Reed said, stopping me. "We can't. The law has already decided what the truth is. We can't."

"In Prison Nation, the truth can't set you free," I muttered to myself. I thought back to my parents. To Orrin. To the workers who disappeared from the Orchard, the inmates who wandered lost and tear-streaked in Spokane. How many had a truth that would never be listened to?

I reached over and grabbed Reed's hand, my fingers lacing with his. "Okay," I said firmly. "Let's go."

"Go?" Reed asked cautiously.

"I will go with you, Reed. Away from here. From the Nation." I took a deep breath. "What just happened to Maria, that was a crime. And those men will do it over and over. How many more men are there in the Nation like that? And women? I thought... I thought the law protected me." I lowered my eyes a moment, then looked back at him. "I don't know if that's true anymore. I don't feel safe. And if you were to leave, I know I wouldn't be safe."

Reed lifted his hand, letting mine fall into my lap as he cupped my cheek. Leaning close, I could feel his breath on my skin. It sent tingles down my body. "If I had to live without you, Millie. If for some reason you were gone... I would never have to think twice. I would miss you with every fiber of who I am."

A tear broke free from my eye. It trailed down my cheek, stopping to rest on Reed's hand. In a soft flick, he wiped it away.

"I will never leave you, Millie," Reed said softly.

"I know. Because I am going with you."

Reed let a soft smile spread on his lips. Without another word, he pulled me to my feet and rushed back to the truck. I was more than eager to leave behind Maria's lost whimpers as she huddled locked and nearly naked in the cell behind us.

It seemed like the town had barely faded away when I saw the white house loom in front of us. Reed pulled the truck to a stop, dirt still flying behind it as he jumped out. I followed. We quickly made our way to my living quarters. I moved to step inside, when Reed grabbed my wrist.

He turned it and lifted my sleeve. My metal bracelet dropped down into sight.

"I forgot about this," he said, his voice tense.

"Can we take it off?" I asked.

Reed shook his head. "You have to have a certain machine to take it off. They only keep them at the prisons or under lock and key. We don't have time."

I stepped down off the step, peeling Reed's fingers off my wrist and lowering my sleeve to cover the bracelet again. "It's just an ID bracelet, Reed. It can stay on."

He opened his mouth to protest then stopped himself. "Okay," he said. "Get your stuff. Quickly. I will go get Eddie and our stuff. Meet back at the truck." I nodded to Reed then watched as he ran down the walk to his own living quarters. As soon as he disappeared inside, I turned and hurried down the hall.

My room was just as I had left it. For some reason I had expected it to be different. To be torn apart, to see a roommate waiting to take over my space. Something. It hadn't changed, yet things felt different. Something was missing. As I stepped inside, letting the curtain drape shut behind me, I could feel it.

Maria didn't lean against the door, welcoming me home with her English-Spanish mix. Maria, her entire presence, was suddenly gone from this room. It was gone from the building, from the Orchard. I felt a shudder go down my spine, realizing that she had just joined the horde of workers to disappear, never to be mentioned again.

Without another pause, I snatched up my bag and hurried to the dresser. I shoveled my clothes into the bag, not taking the time to pack them neatly. The sock, filled with my remaining money and the small piece of sea glass, fell out of the pile. It hit the ground, its contents spilling out. Setting the bag on my bed, I knelt down on the ground.

I had barely any money left. Even with my small pay I had received from the Orchard, the sock was nearly empty. After my discharge fees, and the research into my parent's case, I barely had one hundred. Folding the money, I shoved it into my back pocket of my jeans. The piece of glass peeked out of the sock, its soft green glowing in the dim light.

I let it drop into the palm of my hand. I didn't know what Reed's plan was. If he even had one. As I stared at the glass, I found myself hoping that we would somehow find our way to the beach. I wanted to see it. I wanted to feel what Orrin had felt that last time before his freedom had been taken away. That would never happen. The Wall was protected, built high and strong, the only ways through heavily guarded.

We were all locked in.

We were prisoners. This was Prison Nation.

A tear broke free from my eye, streaming down my cheek. Orrin. I would never see him again. He would never see freedom again. He was forever locked away, charged for a crime he didn't commit and knowing his family was slaughtered. The glass was all I had left.

I wiped the tear from my cheek. As I moved to tuck the glass back into the sock, I felt the cool key brush against my chest under my shirt. I pulled it out, laying it in my hand next to the glass. The key was barely larger than the glass. I sat there, staring at the two small pieces.

The fog crept in. It wanted to take over. It wanted to claim me.

Bending down, I ran my fingers under the bed, searching. They finally ran over a small piece of wire that had fallen free from the springs. I stood back up, the wire pinched in my fingers. The fog taunted me as I carefully wrapped the wire around Orrin's glass then fastened it to Jude's key. I stared at the necklace in my hand, the green glow of the glass now reflecting off of the rusted key, my only reminders I had left of the life I had lived.

I stared harder at the contents in my hand. Then something struck home.

The key.

I threw the necklace back around my neck and tucked it into my shirt, then quickly snatched up the last of my belongings. Ducking through the curtain, I left the small room without a second look. I didn't need to say goodbye. This wasn't home. It could never be home. It had been a temporary existence, a monitored life. This had been the second prison they had sentenced me to, and I was going to break free.

▮ ▮ ▮

Reed and Eddie were standing next to the truck, leaned in close together as they talked in hushed voices. I hurried towards them, watching as they glanced once more at each other before separating and smiling at me.

"Alright!" Eddie said, rubbing his hands together. "Let's get this adventure going!"

Reed grabbed the handle of the driver side door, pulling it open.

"Reed, what are you doing?" I asked. "This is Oscar's truck."

Reed glanced at Eddie, his hand flexing on the handle of the car. I could tell from the way they looked at each other that this is exactly what they had been discussing when I had hurried over.

"Reed," I stepped closer to him. "We can't take Oscar's truck."

Reed pushed the door shut, then fell against it. He leaned his head forward, running his fingers through his shaggy hair. "I know," he said. "I know, I know."

"Are you kidding me?" Eddie said, his voice coming out shockingly angry. "Really, Reed? Are you going to care about that right now?"

"Eddie, it's not ours!" Reed said back, his voice rising.

"Yeah. You're right. It's theft. Grand theft auto right? Punishable by up to thirty." He motioned to me, his eyes flared with anger. "And you want her to come with us? She is on probation! If she is caught, she goes right back to Spokane, no more chances! And what about us? We are bailing out on our work contracts. That is against the blasted law too, Reed! Are you really caring about that crap right now?"

Eddie's voice was getting too loud. Reed stood up, looking around with wide eyes. Luckily no one looked to be in earshot of us. Yet. "Eddie, calm down. We just need to…"

Eddie took a step toward Reed. I wanted to step in to stop him. I could see his fists clenching at his sides, his cheeks reddening with anger. I managed to utter a wimpy, "Eddie, please…"

Eddie didn't hear me. He was focused on Reed. "You come and get me, finally tell me we can get out of this Nation. And now you want us to what, walk? Hitch hike? Hell, why don't we just go kindly ask them to let us out?"

"Eddie! Will you shut up!" Reed yelled. I saw Eddie jump as the sudden boom of Reed's voice. My own body tensed in surprise. Reed ran a hand through his hair again then turned to me. "How much cash do you have?"

"One hundred. Barely."

"Okay." He fished into his pocket and pulled out a wad of bills. Flipping through it, he pulled out a good chunk and handed it to me.

"Add fifty to that." Without asking, I pulled out fifty from my pocket and added it to the stack. "Eddie, you too."

Eddie opened his mouth to protest.

"Eddie, just do it will you?" Reed shot at him before he could speak. Eddie huffed an angry breath, then pulled some money from his jacket pocket and slapped it onto the pile in my hands.

Reed pulled open the truck door and crawled inside. I could hear him shuffle things around before he backed out. He held out a wrinkled envelope, partly torn open and obviously stepped on. "Let me see that," he said, holding his hand out to me.

I handed him the stack. He shoved it into the envelope, then pulled a pen out of his jacket pocket. He quickly scribbled 'Oscar Ramos' on the front of it, scratching out the other writing that was jotted all over the envelope.

Mumbling something under his breath, Reed pushed past both of us and hurried to the house. He stopped by a door, its surface dirtier than the rest of the house. The doors around it looked new. This door was obviously used much more often. He stood for a moment, looking at it, then tucked the envelope under its stop and hurried back to us.

Reed looked at me, his eyebrows raised in question. I nodded to him, shifting my bag on my shoulder. Sighing, he opened the passenger door for me then hurried back to the driver side.

I climbed in, Eddie close behind me. Both men slammed the doors shut at the same time, the truck shaking as if afraid.

We sat for a moment, looking at the large house in front of us. "Why did you do that?" Eddie asked, his voice finally cooling.

"Oscar has been good to us, Eddie. The least we can do for taking his truck is leave him a little cash to find another one." Reed looked down at the key in his hand, staring at it a moment before pushing it into the ignition. "We aren't the criminals."

Eddie nodded.

Reed turned the key, the engine rumbling to life. We backed out of the driveway and turned onto the old road. Silence took over the cab, the air tense and apprehensive. The truck bounced down the dirt road, past the town, and finally turned onto the old paved highway. There was no one else on the road. Nothing but dirt, dead grass, and the occasional lonely bird.

"Hey man," Eddie muttered finally. "I'm sorry."

Reed grunted, his lips tight. "You really need to learn to cool it, Eddie. That temper is going to get you killed someday."

Eddie chuckled, then playfully elbowed me. "Blame it on the hair," he said, pointing to his messy red locks. "You know what they say. I have fire for hair, so must have fire for a temper. Stupid hair, huh?" I smiled at him, relieved to see the twinkle in his eyes. Eddie scared me when he lost his temper. He leaned past me, smacking Reed on the arm. "So, where to Captain?"

I could hear Reed let out a slow breath. "I'm not really sure."

"Awesome." Eddie slammed back against the seat again, turning to look out his window.

"By night they will know we are gone," Reed went on calmly. "They probably won't care too much about you and me. Just put a warrant on our records and call it good. Millie though... they seem more protective of their prison born. I don't know why."

"What does that mean?" I asked.

Reed glanced at me. Offering me a small smile, he reached down and held my hand gently. "It's just something some of us have noticed. Those like you, who were born in the Prison, the Nation seems more protective of. They keep a closer eye on you, even when the parole is over.

"You haven't been out long," Reed went on, his eyes focused back on the road. "For those of us who have always been out, we've noticed that most of the people convicted lately are the ones who are dirt born. Those born in the prison are staying free more."

Eddie turned away from the window. "Tell me, little Jail Baby, what the heck are they preaching to you in there?" He smiled as he asked, but I still cringed at the title.

I licked my lips. "The same things they teach in school for you. The history of the great Nation. Why it is important that the Nation keeps its criminals locked away." I lowered my eyes, letting them settle on Reed's hand as he held mine. "That the Nation needs the good and the strong."

Eddie snorted. Snapping my eyes up, I looked over at him. "Sounds like some grade-A brainwashing," Eddie said, his voice suppressing another laugh. "Or more like some grade-A —"

"Eddie, come on," Reed interrupted. I could hear the hint of laughter on his voice.

"Hey man, we are in a truck heading somewhere we don't even know. I don't think there is any Big Brother in here."

"Big brother?" I asked.

Eddie looked at me, his mouth curled at the corners. "Yeah, you know. 1984."

I shook my head.

"Aw, come on! They preach to you about being all good and strong for the Nation, but they don't even let you read classics like that?"

"I read my school books. They let me read other books, sometimes... but that had been a treat. We were taught that we needed to learn the truth. That the criminals believed in lies because they were taught lies. The Nation was the strong, and those of us who learned the truth became the good. Didn't they teach you —"

Reed shook his head. "You learn something different, Millie, when you're living the truth." His face turned thoughtful for a moment. "Makes sense though."

"What does?" I asked.

"Why they lock us up, the ones born on the outside. They don't want us being out here. They want you."

"Me?"

"Jail Babies. The ones who actually believe in the Nation. The ones who love it."

"It's a Jail Baby apocalypse!" Eddie said, waving his hands in the air as he laughed.

I looked over to Reed. He smiled, lifted my hand and kissed my fingers. His lips were warm and soft, pressing gently for a second then lifting just enough that I could barely feel his skin brushing mine. I could feel his breath on my fingers, moist in the cool air. Reed held my hand there a moment, then let it drop into my lap as he gripped the steering wheel with both hands. The smile still rested lightly on his lips.

Eddie leaned in toward me again. "And for the record: we were home schooled. We learned useful things. Like the square root of x." Eddie laughed and moved to look back out his window at the passing land.

We let the truck settle into a calm quiet. The engine rumbled, the sound of the tires rolling down the road becoming a constant hum. I let my mind drift to the sounds. Leaning my head against Reed's shoulder, I closed my eyes. My fingers lightly played with my metal bracelet, spinning it around and around.

It was cold against my wrist. I could feel the etching of my name under my fingertips as it spun. The image of the small devices used to scan the bracelets trickled into my mind. I had never even bothered to learn what it was called. My entire life my bracelet had been scanned, and I didn't even know how. I felt something stir in my thoughts. There was something I should know, but no matter how hard I tried to grasp it, it escaped me. There had been so much I had never asked.

I finally gave up. Sighing, I let my bracelet drop to hang heavy against my wrist as I lifted my hand to touch the key through my thin shirt. I could feel the sea glass tied to it, a small lump under my shirt. My fingers carefully pushed it against my chest. I hadn't mentioned the key yet. I found myself wishing I could keep it to myself, keep it safe and perfect, the memories of Orrin and Jude secured safely near my heart.

Reed mumbled to himself, reading the road signs as they passed. A few times he slowed, almost taking an exit, then shook his head and sped past. He didn't have a plan. He wanted to be free, but didn't know which direction freedom waited. My heart ached, pressing the key harder against my skin. Sitting up, I glanced at Eddie who snored lightly next to me, then looked over to Reed.

"I know."

Reed glanced at me, his brow furrowed in question. "What?"

I could hear Eddie lift his head drowsily. "What do you know, Mills?"

I focused my eyes ahead of us. The road was still empty. Shadows stretched long and lonely as the sun began to set in the distance. I carefully pulled the key out from under my shirt, holding it out in my open palm so the glass glowed in the warm sunlight.

"I know how we can escape."

Reed didn't want to stop for the night. After I had told him about the door in the Wall, and the key Jude had given me, he insisted we needed to get there as soon as we could. The sky had darkened to a thick black, only a few hints of the sun's rays glowing faintly in the distance. Memories of the life we were leaving behind pushed us forward.

Eddie was asleep again. His head leaned against the cool glass of the window. Occasionally Reed would hit a bump in the road and I could hear the dull smack of Eddie's head as it bounced against the glass. A few times he woke up enough to mutter something angrily to Reed. Reed would just chuckle without responding, and Eddie would drift back to sleep.

I felt safe.

Sitting between Reed and Eddie, even as the truck barreled down the deserted highway, I finally felt like I could breathe. Reed's hand had found its way to my knee, his fingers mindlessly tapping and rubbing as he drove in silence. His touch felt good.

Ever since I had told them about Jude and the key, Reed had sunk into his thoughts. The decision to head to Cannon Beach had been easy. I knew he wasn't worrying about that. Something else ate at his mind.

"Millie?" His voice was quiet, his eyes glancing to make sure Eddie was still asleep. Eddie confirmed with a light snore. "Can I ask you something?"

"Yeah, of course."

Reed cleared his throat. I could barely see his silhouette in the darkness. The headlights cast a dim glow on his face, though not enough to make out any expressions he might have been making. "Jude. Were you two —"

"No!" I shook my head. This had been the thought eating at Reed the entire ride? "Jude was a guard."

"Was he..." Reed swallowed hard. "Was he the guard that —"

"No, Reed. No." I reached over and laid my hand on top of his. "Jude is... was a friend. The first time I ever even met him face to face in the light was at the prison today."

"I thought guards weren't supposed to be friends with the inmates." I didn't like the sound of Reed's voice. It sounded too much like he didn't believe me.

"You're right." I reached my hand up to his face, turning it enough to look at me. I couldn't see him, but I knew he watched me in the dark. "But I am telling the truth. Jude was a friend. Almost like a brother. He may have broken some rules by talking to me as much as he did, but there wasn't anything more. I promise."

I couldn't understand why Reed was acting so strange.

Reed squeezed my hand. "Okay," he sighed. "Okay. I'm sorry. I just... I can't shake what you had said, about that other guard. I hate the idea that he wanted to hurt you. That he... that he even did what he did. People get busted for a lot less than that every day. And he didn't even get a wrist slap. What kind of justice is that?"

"From what I have been learning," I said quietly, "it's the exact kind of justice the Nation wants."

Reed lifted my hand and kissed it again. "Try to sleep," he said, resting his hand back on my knee. I nodded, more to myself than to him. Leaning my head on his shoulder, I let my eyes shut and carry me off into sleep.

❚ ❚ ❚

I watched the Prison. Its dark stone walls rose high into the overcast sky. There was no one around. I stood alone, staring up at the menacing walls topped with razor wire. Something inside me made me want to run away, to get as far from the Prison as I possibly could. I tried to turn. I tried to run. Instead, I felt my body pulled towards the waiting door.

I didn't want to go in. The walls darkened, angry at me for rejecting them. The sky rolled with clouds. I held my breath. In the silence I faintly began to hear the rhythm of the life I had left. The heavy beat of the laundry room throbbed slow and deep, rumbling the earth with every throb. The faint shuffled feet of life inside. The perfectly timed angry shout, the dull thump of a fist making contact, the matching crescendo of guard's boots. The light sobs like a descant of a broken woman.

Tears stung my eyes as the music of the prison enveloped me. It called to me. It reminded me of where I had come from, of who I truly was. It beckoned the fog to return me to my coming insanity.

I tried to wipe the tears from my cold cheeks, but my hands wouldn't respond. They hung limply at my side, my fingertips tapping along with the music. My parents were in there. Orrin was in there. Maria. So many people, all were locked away inside those walls. Why did I deserve to be outside?

The music suddenly stopped. Silence suffocated me for a moment before the air was filled with the ear shattering alarm of lights out. It seemed to ring forever, filling the air around me in its engulfing vibrations.

As it died out, I heard someone move behind me. The feel of cold metal on my wrists froze my breath mid gasp. The cuffs locked into place, painfully pulling my arms behind my body.

He laughed. Stepping around me, I could see his face, smugly smiling.

"Welcome home," he said in a voice too smooth. He leaned in, his hot breath on my face. I felt tears sting my eyes. "I got you." His lips closed the gap, painfully crushing down on mine before I could scream.

The fog swallowed me alive.

▯ ▯ ▯

My eyes snapped open.

I could feel the sting of tears still in my tired eyes. Reaching up, I lightly wiped away the stray tear that had trickled down my cheek. My head still rested on Reed's shoulder, his hand still lightly holding my knee.

I covered the tears, pretending to rub sleep from my eyes. As I sat up, I could see the rays of sun that were rising over the earth. Carl was behind me. He was lost somewhere in his own insanity, without any idea that I was gone. Though he haunted my dreams, I knew I would never see him again. I still shook, regardless. The feel of his lips crushing against mine left a lingering sting.

I looked out the window. We were driving past a city, its tall buildings glittering in the dawn.

"Where are we?" I asked.

Reed glanced over to the city. A river ran past it, reflecting the sun and the truck's headlights in its slow moving surface. There were barely any lights on in the city. It looked fast asleep, as if it never planned to wake back up.

"Portland," he said, his voice distant.

"It's beautiful," I said.

"Yeah, it is. But we don't want to stop in it. The cities... most aren't safe now."

"What do you mean?" I asked. Of all places, the cities were supposed to be the safest. They were supposed to be filled with loyal citizens, patrols of the Nation's officers keeping the roads clean and safe as life continued and thrived. My stomach tightened at the words that had been hammered into my mind my entire life.

Reed lifted his hand from my leg and rubbed his eyes. He had been driving all night, with no break, and the exhaustion was obvious on his face. "The cities are where the people are. Too many people. Too many... enforcers."

"Too many arrests," Eddie muttered.

I turned and looked at him. His head leaned against the window, his eyes barely cracked open as they watched the passing city. He didn't say anything else.

We rumbled down the road, leaving Portland behind us. Cars would pass occasionally, always covered in rust and rumbling as if any moment they planned to give up and crumble. Every time one would pass, we held our breath. We shared the unspoken fear that one of the passing cars would turn on hidden flashing lights and pull us over. We didn't need to share the fear out loud. The cab would just fall silent until the passing car disappeared into the dark.

The truck started to sputter. Mumbling to himself, Reed glanced down at the gas gauge. It sat flat on the red line.

"We need some gas, and quick," he said. I could hear the rising nerves in his voice.

At that moment, as if called into existence, a gas station emerged from behind a thick gathering of trees. Eddie sat up, his eyes scanning the surroundings as Reed pulled the truck alongside the gas pump. With a single nod to each other, they both climbed out before the engine had even quieted. I followed Reed, staying close to his side as we all scanned the station.

A man stood inside at the cash register, carefully watching us. Trying to act casual, Eddie leaned against the hood as Reed started to pump gas into the old truck. Just as the gas pump clicked alive, the sound of tires crunching on pavement cut into the quiet air. We snapped our heads toward the source.

A police car had just pulled in to a parking space in front of the station. The officer stepped out, hand on gun as he made his way inside. Eddie looked over to Reed, his eyes alert. "Let's speed up that pumping a bit?"

Reed heaved a sigh. "It's going as fast as it will go, Eddie."

Eddie watched the pump a moment then looked back to the officer. He had walked out of the station, a soda held in one hand. The other hand still rested on his gun. He was about to turn to his car when he saw us and meandered in our direction instead.

"Everything good over here?" The officer's voice was low and clear.

I could see Reed's shoulders stiffen a moment before he let them relax, his easy gaze turning to the officer. "Just fine, Officer," he said, a smile on his lips. "Just getting a fill up."

The officer nodded, still watching us carefully. "Can you believe these prices? Nine dollars a gallon. Seems a bit high, ya think?"

Reed just shrugged. "Anything that betters the Nation betters us."

A thin smile spread on the Officers stubble covered face. His eyes wandered to Eddie. Recognition flashed across his eyes. Taking a step closer, he studied Eddie's reddening face. "Do I know you?"

Eddie shook his head. "Can't say you do. First time in these parts for me."

"I swear I have met you before."

"Well, you know us redheads. We all look alike." Eddie smiled and winked at the officer. I could see the forced lines of his smile. The lines seemed strange and foreign on Eddie's face. His smile had always come so easy to him.

The officer watched him a moment longer, then shrugged and turned his eyes to me. I could feel Reed tense beside me. The Officer just watched a moment, his eyes flicking down to the metal bracelet on my wrist. He smiled, tipping his head in my direction. "Well then, have a good day. Ma'am. Boys." With that, he wandered back to his car and drove away. I thought I saw him speaking into his small radio, but the sun shone into the tinted windows and blocked even his silhouette as he disappeared around the corner.

Eddie ran in to pay. Reed, his hand on the small of my back, led me back into the truck. The engine was already rumbling as Eddie climbed back in.

We drove in silence. Reed kept glancing at Eddie. Eddie's face had darkened, his eyes piercing as he stared out the window. "He knew me," Eddie finally said into the quiet.

"That's impossible, Eddie." Reed answered, his voice sounding like he already doubted what he said.

Eddie shook his head. "My mom always told me that my brother Bill and I looked like twins. Two years apart in age, twins in looks. Even in temper." Eddie sighed, his breath shuddering. "That officer knew Bill. So, he knew me."

I glanced at Reed before looking back to Eddie. "Bill. He is in prison now, right?" I asked carefully.

"My brother Bill was living in Portland when he got busted." Eddie answered. "He had sniped a pack of cigarettes. In the old days, he would have been slapped with a fine and maybe a few days in jail."

I remembered what Reed had told me. Eddie's brother had been sentenced to twenty years. Eddie finally looked away from the window, rubbing his eyes. I thought I saw the glitter of a tear, but it vanished before I could look again.

"I guess there had been some prostituting on the nearby street corner. The cop that busted Bill reported that he had seen Bill interacting with the prostitutes. Turns out the group had just stolen a whole lot more than a pack of smokes. And Bill had had the luck of passing the group when they got caught. So he got locked away for twenty.

"I wouldn't be surprised if that cop back there was the one who busted Bill. Wouldn't be able to tell anyway. They all are the same." Eddie tore his eyes from the city. "I hate cities."

"Stupid Po," Reed said, smiling to Eddie.

"Stupid Po," Eddie answered, a smile cracking on his face. A quiet moment passed, they both chuckled. "Let's get away from this place. How much longer, sir Captain?"

"I don't know," Reed said. "Guess we just stay on this road. That's what the signs say at least."

Eddie nodded, leaning his head back. "Want me to take a turn at the wheel?"

"Are you kidding?" Reed laughed. "I've seen how you drive. We won't even make it a few miles before you crash."

Eddie snorted, then leaned his head back against the torn headrest. The last glimmer of the city disappeared behind us.

◻ ◻ ◻

I found myself getting lost in watching the tall green trees that grew thick around the road. I had never seen trees like this before. Eddie told me they were evergreens. Their branches were full of deep green needles, heavy and dropping over the worn road. I could smell them as we passed. Their musky aroma filled the truck's cab. It was intoxicating.

I wanted to wander through the dense trees. The bark of the trunks looked rough and thick, small bushes and grasses rising high around the roots. I imagined what it would be like, to sit in the shade of these towering giants, completely covered by their shadows. To hear the birds lightly singing, the breeze rustling the pine needles as the drip of last night's rain fell to the forest floor.

I wanted to hear the music of the free world.

My thoughts carried me away. I lost track of time. The smell of the trees, the rumble of the old truck, and Reed's warm hand on my knee wrapped around and pulled me away into a sweet, safe world of my own.

The trees disappeared. Buildings appeared, old and falling apart. We turned on a small two-lane road, and slowed as we made our way into the town. Everything looked dead. I felt a chill as the ghosts of the town covered it in a strange forgotten dust. Windows on the buildings were boarded over, a few which hadn't been covered now shattered into jagged shards. The entire town had a cold, gray tinge to it. A memory long abandoned, and long forgotten.

Ahead, in the distance just past the town, was the Wall.

It rose high, reaching the tips of the few evergreens that still managed to grow. Razor wire was twisted along its top, casting a web-like shadow down to the dirt below. Eddie rolled his window down. Muffled behind the Wall, we could hear the rolling crash of water.

"Shit," Reed suddenly hissed, hitting the breaks hard. The truck jerked to a stop, throwing all three of us forward as its wheels dug into the asphalt.

Parked in the road, blocking our passing, were three cars. Their lights flashed, illuminating the three police officers that stood, aiming their guns in our direction.

"Get out of the truck, slowly, with your hands up!" one of the offers yelled.

I looked at Reed. His eyes bore into me, heavy with sorrow. I swallowed, my throat dry, then reached down and squeezed his hand.

"We tried," I said.

"No," Reed said in a low voice, his lips barely moving. "This is not it. This is not how it is going to end."

"Damn right!" Eddie yelled. Before we could stop him, he swung open the door and jumped out.

"I said slowly with your hands up!" the officer called again, his gun now aimed at Eddie.

Reed pushed his door open and climbed out. He lifted his hands above his head, his eyes glued to the second officer who carefully watched him. Motioning for me to follow, Reed stepped away from the truck. I climbed out after him, my hands shaking in the air.

Keeping my face forward, I searched with my eyes for Eddie. He stood on the other side of the truck, his hands clenched into fists at his side. The first officer had his gun locked on Eddie's chest.

"I will not say it again. Put your hands. In the air. Now."

Eddie suddenly barreled forward. The officer shot a hand down to his hip, pulled out a smaller gun and aimed it at Eddie's chest. As

Eddie ran towards him, the officer pulled the trigger. Eddie jerked and fell to the ground, his body twitching. I could see two small metal claws dig into his chest, a long wire attaching them to the gun held in the officer's hand.

The officer watched Eddie twitch on the ground, then took a step towards us. My eyes focused on the officer, watching out of the corner of my eyes as Eddie's jerking finally stopped.

"Millie 942B, you are in violation of your probationary period. You are now hereby under arrest." He turned his face to Reed. "Reed Taylor, you have been charged for grand theft auto, breaking of Nation Contract, plotting against the Nation, and kidnapping. You are hereby under arrest."

The two remaining officers were slowly making their way toward us. I could hear the clink of their handcuffs as they pulled them off of their bulky utility belts. My mouth went dry, my eyes burned against growing tears. Had he just said kidnapping?

Reed moved closer to me. I could feel his raised arm press against mine. I knew he was trying to comfort me, but at that moment his touch only reminded me that somehow I had become responsible for his doom. Reed pressed his arm harder against mine. I could feel it tense.

Perplexed, I looked away from the officer's cold face. As my vision focused, I saw Eddie. He stood rigidly behind the three officers. Blood dripped down his chest where he had ripped out the metal prongs. His face contorted in rage.

Before I could even gasp, Eddie launched himself at the guards. He tackled both at once, his arms wrapping around their necks as he hauled them to the ground. Never giving them a chance to recover, he started slamming his fists into both of them, screaming in a coarse voice, "Reed, get out of here!"

Reed wrapped his arms around me, his fingers digging into my skin like iron clamps.

"Come on," he urged in my ear.

I couldn't move. My feet were cemented to the ground, my eyes glued to Eddie as he pummeled his fists into the two dazed officers. Reed managed to drag me back a few steps, then stopped.

The third officer had aimed his gun at Eddie, and fired. The air cracked with the echo of the bullet shooting out of the small metal barrel. Everything seemed silent for a moment before we heard the dull thud of Eddie dropping to the ground. He clutched at his chest, his shirt deepening in dark red at a sickening rate.

The two officers Eddie had been pummeling stood up, bracing each other as they rubbed their swelling and bruised faces. The one who had shot the gun stepped closer, his sidearm still carefully aimed at Eddie.

Eddie gasped for breath. He squeezed his eyes shut a moment, then turned his head enough to look at us. Cracking a painful smile, he raised a finger and pointed at his matted hair that gleamed like copper in the rising sun.

"S-Stupid... red hair..." he forced out. I could see blood covering his teeth. The officer stood over him now, glaring down at Eddie.

Without another pause, he spun his gun around and bashed the handle hard against Eddie's head. Eddie flailed once then went limp, his head rolling awkwardly to the side.

The feeling of ice-cold metal shook me from my daze. While we had watched Eddie die, the two battered officers had made their way behind us. My arms were pulled painfully behind me, the handcuffs locking together. I could heard Reed choke a sob next to me, his eyes still watching Eddie as if he hoped his best friend would suddenly sit back up and smile.

The officer who stood over Eddie wiped the butt of his gun off on his pant leg then turned to us. His eyes smoldered in anger, but a smug smile spread on his chubby face.

"You have the right to remain silent," he said, his voice booming out the dreaded words. "Anything you say can and will be used against you —"

"I will take it from here."

My body went ice cold. My eyes slowly turned toward the source of the voice that had just cut off the officer's memorized words.

He emerged from the shadows of a nearby building. His short blonde hair shone in the sunlight, his smile wide as he stepped closer.

"You three are excused," he said smoothly.

The officer's eyes widened. "But —"

"I am a Prison GF, officer. I outrank you. And 942B is under probation from my prison. Do I need to cite you on jurisdictional arguments?"

The officer shook his head.

"I will call if I need back-up." Carl shot the officer a dark look, his jaw clenching. The officer still hadn't moved. "I said, you three are excused."

The officer gritted his teeth together, then nodded and quickly headed back to his parked patrol car. The two behind us joined him. We watched as they pulled away down the road, their lights still flashing as they disappeared into the distance.

My eyes slowly moved back.

Carl was smiling at me.

"Hello, Millie," he said in a mockingly sweet voice.

Carl walked up to us, hands resting lightly on his utility belt. His eyes trailed over to Reed, taking him in with a smirk. I could hear Reed suck in an angry breath. He knew. He knew this was the guard. There was no way he could doubt it.

Carl chuckled, then suddenly raised his gun and smacked the butt hard on Reed's head. A small groan escaped Reed's throat before he toppled down to the paved road.

"No!" I screamed. I fought against the cuffs, but they were holding my arms too tightly behind my back. "No, no, no!"

"Come on, Millie," Carl said, his fingers locking down on my tensed arm. "Let's go catch up."

22

The shadows of the alley loomed ahead.

Carl dragged me toward the alley where his white patrol car waited, my feet constantly stumbling and tripping beneath me. As we passed Eddie, my nose filled with the coppery smell of his blood. It stung my senses, bringing tears to my eyes. I watched him, hoping to see his fingers twitch or eyelids flutter. He didn't move.

The world had gone quiet. There was no laughter. No happy sighs. No soft voices. All that echoed now was the crunch of our feet on the littered street, Carl's lofty breath, my grunt as he shoved me into the car and slammed the door shut. Most patrol cars had some sort of barrier between the officers and the criminals. Carl's didn't. As he climbed into the driver seat, he reached back and patted my leg, smirking at me before revving the engine and backing out of the alley into the sun.

I felt my head try to turn to look behind us. I knew Eddie lay there, motionless and gone. That just beyond him, motionless in a crumpled mess on the ground, lay Reed. I couldn't turn my head to look. I couldn't bear the thought that he too wouldn't be moving, that he too may be gone to a place I couldn't free him. All I could do was stare ahead.

"Oh Millie, what trouble you have caused," Carl said, his voice casual and teasing. "There I was, keeping my eye on you as you picked those stupid apples and bought pretty new clothes, then suddenly you decide it wasn't good enough for you. You just had to try and leave. You really don't like to follow orders, do you."

It didn't sound like a question. His voice had turned hard and cold, the laughter slowly bleeding away. I didn't answer. Squirming in my seat, I tried to ease the pain in my shoulders from the cuffs that held my wrists tight behind me.

"If it wasn't for those inmates sticking up for you, and that stupid young night guard, you would be back where you belong and I would have my way. But no," Carl spat toward the empty passenger seat. "No, I was the one over-reacting. I was the one who 'needed a break.' Even that Dr. Eriks stopped helping me. She thinks I have lost it." An angry laugh rumbled from his lips, his shoulders barely shaking. "And there you are, picking apples and falling for the first dirt born brat you run across. It is disgusting."

The car rolled slowly down the old road, passing each boarded up building and hanging street sign without pausing. Carl stared straight ahead, his shoulders stiff. I could see his face in the small rearview mirror, his eyes intense as they stared at the road ahead of us.

"I get what I want," he continued, his voice growing more intense. "You can't run away in the night and expect that to change. I have my plans, Millie, and you will not mess them up. That piece of crap lying in the road back there sure as hell won't mess them up."

Carl finally glanced into the mirror, his eyes locking onto mine. "If only you knew what I have planned for him. Life in prison isn't good enough. No, I have great plans for your little love back there, Millie."

I didn't think. I didn't pause or question what I was doing. I lunged forward. My body flew over the seat, my shoulder slamming into Carl with all of my weight. Carl yelled out, his hands suddenly cranking the wheel to the right.

The car veered roughly. Our bodies slammed into each other again, my shoulder flaring in pain as it hit the front dash. I could hear the crash before I felt it. The unmistakable crunch of metal as it bent in, meeting with the concrete wall of the old building in front of us, followed by the slow hiss of leaking air.

The impact threw me back, my body slamming roughly into the worn seat. All of the air knocked out of me, leaving me to gasp in ragged breaths. I could hear the crunch as Carl's body slammed into the door. Chancing a look over, I saw his shoulder pushed up against the door at a bad angle, his head bleeding where it had hit the glass. Carl blinked, the blood dripping into his dazed eyes.

I turned my back to the door and anxiously felt for the metal handle. My fingers groped along the plastic, desperation building inside as I watched Carl blink harder. Finally my fingers slid along the handle's cool surface. I pulled. The door swung open and my body toppled out, landing painfully on the ground.

Struggling to my feet, I blinked the dirt out of my eyes and tried to get my bearings. My whole body ached. Nothing felt broken, but I could feel the pain of deep bruises along my arm and back. I finally cleared my vision and took a shaky step forward.

A hand clamped down on my bruised arm. I cried out in pain, my knees buckling underneath me as Carl dragged me backwards across the road. I tried to dig my heels into the ground to slow him.

It didn't help.

Carl pulled me up a few cement steps. He stopped long enough to kick in an old wooden door, then pushed me inside and slammed the broken door behind us. My eyes took a moment to adjust in the now dim light. The windows were all carefully boarded over, only letting thin streams of the sunlight to filter in.

To my left was a desk, its surface covered in dust and cracks. Behind it leaned a row of old metal filing cabinets. Everything was covered in the same thick dust. My eyes scanned the rest of the room, coming to a rest on the only remaining wall.

The opposite wall was lined with bars.

Carl turned a key in my handcuffs. They fell to the ground, clanging loudly. Without saying anything, he shoved me into the nearest open cell. I stumbled forward, barely catching myself as I fell to the ground. As I turned, I saw him wipe a stream of blood from his face, the open gash on his forehead still dripping. His chest heaved with angry gasps.

"Amazing little building, don't you think?" Carl hissed, standing in the small opening of the cell. "Once the Nation rose, they put these all over the place. Holding houses they called them. There was no need for small jails anymore. All those criminals were going to the same place." Carl ran a finger down the rusted bars. "All they needed were these holding houses, until prison transport could come and whisk away the evil doers."

I scooted myself back against the cold wall. An image of Maria, battered and almost naked as she huddled in the corner, flashed through my mind. I drew my knees up to my chest.

"Don't worry, Millie," Carl said. "I'm not going to hurt you." A thin smile spread on his face. He straightened his back, wincing in pain as he tried to roll his injured shoulder back. His arm hanged limply at his side, fingers barely moving.

"How did you find me?" I managed to ask.

Carl's smile widened. "I never lost you." He leaned on the bars, his arms crossing loosely over his armored chest. "You didn't think that that bracelet was just for looks, did you?"

I glanced down at the metal bracelet that hung loosely from my wrist. Carl pulled the small device from his belt, the same one all of the guards carried, and casually tossed it from hand to hand. "This is called an ELIS. Electronic Location and Identity Scanner. Your pretty little bracelet there has a chip in it with all of your information on it. This," he said, tapping the ELIS, "not only knows exactly who you are, but can find you too. You should have listened to your boyfriend when he said he didn't like it."

I felt like an idiot. I should have known there was more to this bracelet than my name scratched into its surface. All those years of it being scanned daily, and it had never registered in my mind.

I had given us away. We had been stopped because of me. Eddie had died, because of me. Reed... I shut my eyes tight, trying to breath.

Carl hit a button on the ELIS. A small orange light started to blink. "This will notify my back up. They will be here soon, to gather the criminal and his dead accomplice outside, and escort them to their sentences." He let out a low growl. "I cannot wait to be at that hearing."

Carl tucked the ELIS back into his belt.

"Now, Millie, we need to talk." He crossed his arms loosely across his chest, wincing again in pain. "I gave you some advice, and you didn't listen, did you."

I shook my head.

"Do you think that made me happy?" he asked.

I shook my head again.

"I like you, Millie. I like your spirit. Your brains. Your..." His eyes scanned me a moment. "I like your looks. And I have told you before: I get what I want."

Carl moved closer. "I like Prison Babies. The best citizens are those born afraid. And boy, are those babies afraid. They will do anything to be the good and the strong. Anything." He took another step. I could smell his sweat, tinged with hot blood. "So tell me, my little Jail Baby, are you scared?"

I clenched my eyes shut again, my body aching. I could feel his breath near me. The heat of his body was oppressing as it burned too close. I tried to scoot away, but the wall held me where I crouched. Carl chuckled in my ear.

"I believe in this Nation," he whispered. "I like this Nation. It gives the good what they deserve. And the scum what they have coming to them. Scum like your parents, Millie. And that stupid, stupid guard who tried to help you escape."

My eyes flicked open. Carl had knelt right next to me, his face only a few inches away from mine. I could smell the sweat on his skin.

"Oh, don't worry," he said, the smile spreading once again on his face. "He won't have any trouble from me. He's not worth my time. I know he gave you something. What was it?" I clenched my jaw, refusing to answer. Carl chuckled, his voice low and too close. "Doesn't matter. I will figure it out."

"What do you want?" I asked.

"What do I want?" Carl sat back in mock shock, his hand rising to cup my cheek. "I have already told you Millie. I want you."

"Why?" My voice shook, despite my effort to keep it even.

"Think of it as… an obsession. I just can't keep my eyes off of you." He leaned close again, barely brushing his lips against my cheek. "Just like my uncles and father just couldn't keep their eyes off your mother. So, so long ago."

"My…" The realization struck me, churning my stomach and freezing my breath.

Carl nodded slowly, his hand tightening around my cheek. Fire lit dangerously behind his blue eyes. "Your crazy mother killed my father. She killed him! And now she plays the part of the poor, insane criminal who was only defending herself. And your father…" Carl sighed, patting my cheek. "When I found out they were in Spokane, I had to transfer there. I had to find the scum that had killed my family. Little did I expect you."

Carl tightened his hand down around my chin. A gasp of pain escaped my lips. With a grunt, he lifted me up and slammed me against the bars of the small cell. Pain shot up my back as the bars dug into me. His hand tightly held my chin, keeping me standing on my toes.

"It is all so perfect," he hissed out. "Your stupid parents take away my family. And now, now I get to have theirs." Carl pushed close, his lips almost brushing my cheek again. "It helps that you are already such a catch as it is. Would have been a pity if you were ugly."

"Your… uncles…" I squeezed out, trying to bite back the pain that now shot through my entire body. "Your father. They were monsters. You don't even know what they —"

"Shut up!" Carl yelled. "Do you think I haven't heard those rumors? Do you really think I am that ignorant, Millie?" He pushed me against the bars again. I could feel tears sting my eyes. "Lies. Those are all lies. The Nation captured the criminals. Alan and Leann Summers. The criminals that gave birth to you."

He pushed me once more before backing away a step. I gasped for breath. My entire body shook. I could feel the bars still imprinted on my back, the spots where they had dug in now tender and throbbing. Carl swayed a moment, his hand reaching up to hold his forehead. New blood ran down his face, his anger boiling it to the surface in deep red gushes.

"I will have you," Carl hissed. "That boy out there won't. That stupid, naïve guard won't. No one else will. I own you! Do you understand?"

I felt my head beginning to nod.

I stopped.

Carl stepped close again. I could see the glitter of the handcuffs as he picked them up from the ground. He watched me intently, brutal desire flickering across his eyes. "I will enjoy it, so much, letting your parents know that you are now mine. I will relish the look on their faces. They are nothing," he spat. "Nothing. They are crazed, blood thirsty criminals and the great Nation must be rid of them. They are scum. And you…" Carl pressed against me again, his mouth finding mine. His lips pushed painfully against mine, crushing them hard against my teeth. I could feel him smiling against my lips. I couldn't breathe. My lips throbbed as he pulled away. "You are mine."

"No," I said softly.

Carl's eyebrows knitted darkly together. "What did you just say?"

Something surged inside me. I could feel it tingle as it coursed through my body, igniting a flame somewhere deep inside that I never knew existed. I straightened my back, standing up tall as my fists clenched at my side.

"No," I repeated.

"How. Dare. You." Carl spat. He lunged forward, swinging his fist at me. I felt myself jump to the side. It was as if someone else were controlling my body, directing me where to dive and jump as he swung again.

Carl screamed in rage and lunged into me. I dove to the side again, my body screaming in pain as I hit the ground. I could hear Carl slam into the bars above me. Looking up, I watched as he spun around, spitting blood from his mouth. I gritted my teeth, hoping the fire inside would keep burning as I lunged toward him. Without knowing why, I threw out my hand, grabbing his injured shoulder and shoving it back.

It ground under my hand, the injury popping hard as my hand forced further back. Carl screamed, his eyes shutting just long enough for me to reach forward with my other hand and slam the side of his head into the bars. His body went limp. I let go. Stepping back, I watched him slide to the ground, fresh blood pouring from his head. He blinked his eyes in a daze, his hands flailing to find me.

I bent down and picked up the handcuffs. Carl mumbled something, but I tuned it out as I grabbed his wrist and slapped the cuff around it. Stringing the cuffs through the bar above his head, I slapped the remaining one around his other hand. Before backing away, I pulled the ELIS from his belt and tucked it into my pocket. I paused for a moment, my hand resting over Carl's gun, then removed it from his belt, my fingers wrapped tightly around its handle.

I looked down at him. Carl shook his head, his eyes finally clearing. He jerked his arms hard against the bars, grunting in pain. The bars barely shook. He struggled harder. Finally giving up, he flopped back against the bars, heaving an angry breath.

"You idiot," he said coolly, his eyes shut. "You stupid, ignorant Jail Baby. You have no idea what you are doing."

I stood there, looking down at him. My body shook, the adrenaline that had just coursed through me fading fast. I could feel my head swimming, and clenched my fists harder in the effort to keep my balance. I couldn't look weak, not now.

Carl shook his head slowly, creeping his eyes open. They

hesitated a moment on his gun, now held tightly in my hand, before rising to meet mine. His eyes were full of nothing but hate. "Look at you. You were stupid Dr. Eriks' pride and joy. So good, so perfectly perfect. A perfect example for the future. She had it all planned... Now, look at you." He spat, blood splattering across the ground near my feet. "You are just like them. You are scum, just like them."

"No, I am not," I said, carefully and slowly. "I am no one but me. My parents didn't decide who I am. This Nation didn't decide who I am. And you, you sure as hell will never decide who I am." I bore my eyes into his, making sure he heard every word I said.

"I am free."

I turned and walked to the door. Carl started struggling against the cuffs again. I could hear him behind me, screaming so loud it vibrated the walls around me. I didn't look back. I didn't even pause. Opening the door, I stepped out and pulled it tightly shut behind me.

The door clicked shut, and Carl disappeared.

Part Three

‖‖‖HAPPINESS

23

I stood with my back against the door, the gun cool in my hand. I should have been shaking. Tears should have been streaming down my still sore cheeks. Instead, I stood tall, my body calm and still. For a moment, just a moment as I had stared into Carl's eyes, I had thought of pulling the trigger. I could feel the hunger for the satisfaction of the crack of ammunition, the shock on his face, the end of his hunt. Even now, standing outside with the ocean air in my lungs, I could taste that hunger.

I didn't pull the trigger. I didn't even aim. I was better than that. The gun remained cold in my hand, barely held by my steady fingers.

I breathed in deep, tasting the light salt in the air. In the distance, behind the menacing Wall, I could hear the crash of the waves on the hidden shore. It beat back and forth, life's rhythm writing a new song in my mind. My head felt clear. I felt like the only person left in this locked away world, mere steps away from the freedom I never thought could exist.

I knew I shouldn't be alone. I knew someone should be standing next to me, his hand protectively holding mind. Something was missing... My mind kicked into overdrive, suddenly remembering everything that had just taken place.

"Reed!" I yelled, pushing off from the door.

I turned down the street, running as fast as I could. The air was still crisp, stinging my lungs with the taunt of morning as I gasped in desperate breaths. My feet pounded the pavement, barely noticing the rocks and rubble that they stomped as I sped forward.

I ran forever. In my mind, I thought I would never stop running. I would forever be gasping in the chilling air, my legs and feet forever pounding the earth, and I would never reach Reed. I could feel panic burn in my mind, the urgency pushing my feet harder than before.

Ahead of me, I saw Oscar's yellow truck.

"Reed!" I screamed again, my voice raw from the desperate gasps of air. I could see him lying near the truck, still slumped to the ground where we had left him. He wasn't moving. "Reed! Reed, Reed, Reed!" I called his name over and over, my voice beating with the waves of the hidden ocean.

He groaned.

I skidded to a stop next to him, falling to my knees.

Reed stirred again, another groan escaping his lips. He blinked his eyes open, shooting a hand up to cradle his head. Scooping my arms around him, I pulled him into a sitting position. He leaned heavy against me, blinking his eyes over and over as if unable to believe that he was actually awake.

"Reed, are you alright?" I asked, running my hands over his head. I could feel a large lump where Carl's gun had made contact. As my fingers brushed it, Reed let out a sharp gasp.

"I'm… I'm okay," he answered.

He pushed himself away from me, just enough to spin and look at my face. I saw his eyes widen as he took me in. "Millie, what happened?" Reed tried to push himself to his feet, but as he started to rise he suddenly gripped his head again and fell back down. "What did he do to you?" he asked through clenched teeth.

I opened my mouth to answer, then stopped myself. I could only imagine how I looked. My entire body throbbed, the blood now coursing through me pounding at my bruises. I wanted to tell Reed everything that had just happened. But something deeper surfaced in my mind.

"He set me free."

"He… what?" Reed squinted his eyes at me. I could see his eyes focusing more. They weren't swimming around anymore, blinking for desperate focus.

A small smile spread on my lips. "I will explain it later."

Standing up, I pulled the ELIS from my pocket. I had never looked at one up close before. Smaller than a gun, the scanner consisted of a flat box with a small screen on top and a thin handle underneath. Around the screen were tiny black buttons. I stared at the buttons, hoping one would jump out and give me the answer I needed.

I finally saw it.

I held the scanner up to my metal bracelet then hit the button simply labeled 'Detach.' The machine stayed silent a moment before it let out one long beep. I could feel the bracelet vibrate, as if fighting the command. It clicked loudly, and fell to the ground.

I picked it up, tenderly holding it between my thumb and index finger. My name, etched in the metal surface, almost seemed to glitter in the sun. I had worn this bracelet my entire life. It had always been with me, had always been a part of who I was. Now I knew the truth: It wasn't a part of me. It was a part of the Nation.

With all my strength, I heaved the bracelet into the air. It soared over the rooftops, glittering in the sun once more before diving out of sight. I stood in silence, staring at the last spot I had seen it.

"Millie?" Reed had moved to stand closer to me, his hand still holding his head tenderly. He wobbled slightly on his feet, but seemed to have most of his bearings back. Rubbing his head, he looked down at the ground. His eyes stared at the gun I had dropped when I dove for him. "What's going on?"

I glanced at the ELIS. The light still blinked. Finding the button I had seen Carl push, I pressed it and watched as the light blinked once more then went dead. "We need to get out of here. Those cops will be back. Soon."

Reed gave me a single nod and hurried over to the truck. Reaching into the back, he pulled out our bags and hefted them over his shoulder. I bent down and picked up the gun. It suddenly felt heavier in my hands, foreign and deadly. I watched as Reed stared into the bed, then slowly reached in and pulled out Eddie's bag.

Eddie.

My eyes trailed over to Eddie. Deep inside, I had been hoping he would somehow be alright. That what I had seen earlier had been a nightmare. A messed-up memory. Anything. As my eyes settled on Eddie, I knew I wouldn't get that wish.

Reed lightly touched my shoulder as he passed. He had pulled a blanket from Eddie's bag and carefully laid it over his friend's now cold body. He knelt there, watching Eddie's face, his hands hovering above Eddie's still body as if they were afraid to touch him. Reed let out a sigh, the sound of a choked sob obvious in his tired voice, and pulled the blanket over Eddie's head.

Turning to me, he held out his hand. I saw the glint of tears in his eyes. "You shouldn't be holding that. I hate seeing it in your hands." I looked down at the gun, my own eyes blurred with tears. Reed stepped forward, gently taking it from me. "It's okay." His voice was soft. He lifted a hand and gently touched my face, running his fingers along my cheek and back through my hair as a stray tear escaped and trailed down his tan cheek. "It will be alright."

Looking down at Eddie's covered body, I felt my stomach knot. "We can't just leave him here," I said, my voice almost begging.

"We have to," Reed answered softly, tucking the gun into the back of his pants. "We don't have time to take him with us, or bury him." Reed glanced up at the sky a moment, then looked back to me and smiled. "Eddie would understand."

I nodded. Took Reed's hand. He squeezed my fingers gently, then pulled me to his side as we started down the deserted road.

❚ ❚ ❚

We walked for a good hour. The town had disappeared some time ago, turning slowly into houses that lined the road, covered in forgotten dust. I expected at any moment to hear the wail of police cars, the shots of guns as they found us. I glanced over my shoulder, anticipating the flash of the lights as they bore us down. Everything remained calm and quiet. No one was anywhere in sight except for Reed and me.

The whale on top of the house spun slightly in the breeze. Reed and I stopped at the open gate, staring up at the house. Though it didn't seem nearly as huge as the house back at the Orchard, it was still large. A porch wrapped around the entire house, the corners covered in spider webs and debris. All of the windows were tightly boarded over. Even the door had nails driven into its hinges. No one was going in.

I pictured Jude as a young boy, his smile huge on his face, as he jumped around on the open deck. I could almost see him as he laughed and sang, disappearing around the corner to run down to the beach. I imagined him standing in front of the huge Wall, his young eyes following it up to the sky, the sound of the waves on the other side singing to him.

Following the ghost of a memory, I stepped up onto the deck. The boards creaked under my feet. With Reed close at my side, I made my way around the corner. Every window we passed had been boarded tight some time ago. Though the outside of the house had been worn and damaged from weather, I knew that inside was a tomb of a life long since abandoned.

I reached forward and trailed my fingers along one of the boarded windows, paint chipping away under my touch. Memories of Jude flashed in my mind. He had been my friend. One of my only friends. I knew he was safe, his job and money protecting him in this dangerous world. Still, something inside ached strangely for his easy smile and musical voice.

"Hey Jude, don't make it bad. Take a sad song and make it better…" I softly sang the words to the song lost in my memory, my voice cracking with the paint that fell to the old porch below.

Reed softly laid his hand on my shoulder. I leaned into it, letting his warmth fill me. I stared at the window a moment longer. Then, nodding once, I let Reed lead me around the last corner of the house.

We stopped dead in our tracks. There, only a few steps from the back porch, rose the Wall. Bushes and over grown flower beds covered what remained of the yard, scattered with weeds and fallen leaves. A cobbled path wound away from the steps, leading straight to the Wall.

Reed carefully walked down the steps, his hand lowering to wrap around mine. I followed him, glad to let someone else lead. I felt as if I were in a trance. No fog taunted me. No angry noise filled my ears. Instead, everything seemed as if a window had finally been opened. The light glittered, the edges of every object now detailed and sharp.

We walked down the cobbled path, our eyes glued to the Wall. The path ended abruptly, disappearing into the Wall. There was nothing there. Just the solid wall, not a crack or dent in sight.

"Where's the door?" Reed asked, his voice low.

I pulled the key from my shirt and stared at it. The sea glass glowed in the morning light. "It has to be here."

Reed nodded. Adjusting the bags on his shoulders, he let go of my hand and pushed into the bushes to his left. I followed his lead, making my way to the right. I inched along, the branches and thorns stabbing at my back and legs. Letting my eyes shut, my fingers guided me, feeling the wall as I pushed further into the brush.

The tips of my fingers curled around an edge. Opening my eyes, I pushed forward to look. It was the doorway, the entry a few feet deep before ending at a locked door.

"Reed!" I shouted. "I found it!"

Branches snapped and crashed as Reed pushed himself through to find me. We stepped into the doorway together. The door was solid metal. It had no handle, just a slot barely big enough for the key.

I pulled the necklace over my head and moved closer to the door. Carefully, almost afraid it would suddenly shatter to dust, I pressed the key into the slot. The door hummed. Gears whizzed inside, occasionally joined with a beep or soft buzz.

Creaking against layers of rust and time, the door swung open.

I looked over at Reed. His eyes were wide, his lips clenched so tight they were white. He was staring at the door. He let his eyes slide away, locking onto me instead. His face softened, his lips relaxing as he took me in.

"I love you, Millie." His voice was a breath.

My heart fluttered. My body inched back toward him, wanting to feel his warmth. His safety. His love. "I love you too," I whispered back.

Reed wrapped his arms around me, pulling me tight against his body. I could feel his lips press against mine, softly at first then pressing harder as he melted against me. I pushed back, breathing him in. There truly was no one else in the world. There was only Reed, his arms holding me safe. I could have lived the rest of my life in that moment, and never looked back.

A wave crashing against the shore pulled us out of our kiss. We turned our heads towards the door. Another wave crashed, calling to us. Hand in hand, we pushed the door open and stepped through.

▯ ▯ ▯

It was beautiful.

We stepped down from the doorway, our eyes wide as the beach filled our vision. I pulled the key from the door as we walked away, the door swinging on its hinges as if unsure whether it should close or stay open to the salt air that breathed around us.

The sand sunk under our feet as we slowly made our way down to the water. We had to carefully step over large pieces of wood, their surfaces covered in dried sea foam and green algae. It seemed to take forever to get past the piles of driftwood. Then, as if a line had been drawn in the sandy shore, they suddenly disappeared.

The beach before us glittered. Waves rolled against the shore, catching the light and reflecting it in prisms that took my breath away. I couldn't see anything beyond the waves. They stretched on, disappearing into the distant horizon. Everything glowed green and blue and perfect.

Reed wasn't looking at the waves. He instead stared down at the sandy ground. Following his gaze, I looked down. Sea glass, scattered across the entire shore, shone in the dimming light. I lifted the key, letting the sun's rays shine through Orrin's sea glass. Its green glow mixed perfectly with the blues and whites and greens of the glass that covered the shore.

Reed glanced up to the key then lowered his eyes back to the shore. Letting out a slow breath, he sat down in the sand. He scooped up a handful of sea glass, sand pouring out through his fingers.

"It's just how he told me it would be," I said softly.

"Who?" Reed's voice sounded distant, his thoughts taking over.

"A friend. Back in Spokane. He gave me this piece of sea glass I have, as my birthday present." I sat down next to Reed. He glanced at me then looked away again, his fingers trailing over a small pile of sea glass in the sand. "He told me that the beach was beautiful. It really is."

Reed didn't respond. Looking over to him, I watched as he picked up a small piece of white glass, turning it between his fingers. His face had gone blank, only his eyes showing emotion as they stared at the glowing glass. "Reed, what's wrong?"

Reed, his eyes still fastened to the handful of glowing glass, let out another heavy sigh. "This is beautiful."

I nodded. "Yes, it is."

"When I was little, I think I lived near a beach. I can't really remember." Reed dropped the white piece of sea glass. It fell back into the sand, barely making a sound. "I can remember the sea glass though. There was never this much. It was a treasure hunt, just to find one piece."

Reed turned to me and softly smiled. "My mom loved this glass," he went on, lost in the memory. "My last memory, of my parents, of my family... I can remember being with my father and brother. We had been scouring the beach all day for some glass for my mother. We were so happy. I can still hear my father's booming laugh as he chased us down the beach. But... as hard as I try, I can't remember his face.

"We finally found a piece. Small. And green." Reed's eyes trailed down the key dangling from my hand. He reached forward and lightly touched the sea glass tied to it. "Just like that one you have, actually. We were so excited. But when we got back to the house, the police were waiting. They took away my father. And then the memory just stops. I can't remember anything else until I was put into my first foster home."

I couldn't breathe.

I swung the key into my hand. My fingers clutched Orrin's sea glass, the wire cutting into my flesh. I didn't feel it though. My mind had frozen at Reed's words, disbelief washing over me.

"Reed, you said once that you could remember a name." Reed nodded. I swallowed hard, my throat dry. "Was it your father's name?" As he opened his mouth to answer me, I slowly asked, "Is it Orrin?"

Reed dropped the piece of glass and turned to me. "How did you know that?" he demanded.

I held out the glass, gleaming against Jude's key. Reed's eyes trailed to it, then widened as he realized what I knew. Reed reached out, carefully, and took the key from my hand. He held it in his palm, his eyes searching the small piece of green glass.

"But... I was told he was gone," he whispered.

I swallowed hard. I could feel the sting of tears at my eyes. I didn't know why they were there, why I felt this choke inside. Looking at Reed, I could see the same shock mirrored on his own face.

Reed clenched the key in his hand. For a moment, I thought he would to throw it in to the crashing ocean. I saw his muscles tighten, his fingers whitening as they gripped it tightly. Then he sighed and opened his hand again. The key had pressed so hard into his palm that I could see a clear outline, bright red, imprinted on his flesh.

"I can't leave him," Reed said, his voice shaking.

24

"Reed, he is in Spokane. On a life sentence."

"He is innocent."

"How do you know? You can't remember anything about him."

Reed looked at me. His eyes looked strangely calm, a stark contrast to the waves that were now pounding on the shore. "I know because you trusted him."

My throat tightened again. I barely managed to nod.

Reed looked down the coastline. It wound away into the distance, curving around a small rocky cliff. I followed his gaze. Past that cliff, miles away, was our escape.

"Eddie died for this," I whispered.

Reed stood, brushing the sand from his pants. "Eddie..." Reed's voice choked off. He shut his eyes, swallowing hard. When he spoke again, his voice came out rough. "Eddie died for freedom." Offering me a hand, he waited until I reached up and let him pull me to my feet. He rested a finger under my chin, raising my face to look into his. "Your parents have chosen to stay locked away. But my father —"

"He wants to be free," I said, reassuring Reed.

I knew what he was thinking. I could feel it in the tenseness of his body, in the strong gaze of his eyes. I turned and looked back at the rocky cliff in the distance. A fog had rolled in, covering it in a thick white. The fog thickened, the cliff slowly disappearing behind it like a lost memory.

"This Nation," Reed said, his face now watching the crashing waves, "it needs to be stopped. It needs to be freed. We… we need to be freed."

"But what can we do? We barely made it, Reed. Eddie died. Carl…"

Reed stopped me. His hand held mine, his eyes sweeping out to the ocean. "We made it though, Millie. If all we can do is show others how to do that, than we have done something." Reed looked out to the waves, his eyes shimmering in the sun. "I can't leave him"

I moved in closer to Reed. He wrapped his arms around me, pulling me against his warm body. I watched the waves roll in the horizon. One wave grew, rising high before suddenly crashing to the shore. The water sprayed high. I heard the soft thud as new pieces of sea glass fell with the water spray, landing to join the others on the glittering beach.

The ocean had made clean and beautiful another once sharp piece of glass. It now rested with its brothers and sisters, glowing in the sun. Clean. Beautiful. Perfect.

Life as we knew it was over. Life, as we knew it, was brand new and promising. Everything was about to change. From the moment I had scribbled my final journal entry, what seemed like a century ago, life had changed. Now, as I stood on the abandoned beach,

Reed holding me, the wind teasing my hair, I did not dread life.

I welcomed it.

We turned and made our way back to the still swinging door. I could hear the waves crashing behind me, calling me back. They roared and rolled, reminding me that escape waited just over the horizon.

"Wait," I said.

I reached into my bag, pulling out my old journal. The edges were tattered, the pages loose and trying to fall free. I carefully pulled out the piece I wanted then shoved the notebook back into my bag.

It was wrinkled and worn, the penciled words barely readable now from the many times I had crumpled the page. I read the entry again, remembering the unsettled and unknown feelings that had made me afraid to leave the Prison. I remembered Dr. Eriks' sun sprays, the glares of the inmates. Carl's stare. The loving gaze of my mother.

Tearing up the page, I opened my fingers. A breeze, light off of the ocean, tickled my skin. It kissed my fingers, easing the throbbing in my body before it caught the torn pieces and carried them away into the distant fog.

I had thought that the freedom would be there in the waves. That it hid beyond the fog and diving birds, beyond the Nation's Wall. As we stepped into the dark doorway, I knew better now. I could feel the waves inside me, crashing against my soul.

I had always been free.

"My name is Millie Summers," I said, the words, sweet and true. "And I am free."

Closing my eyes, I let Reed pull me into the shadows of the doorway. The metal door swung once more, then slammed shut.

"Man is free at the moment he wishes to be."

— Voltaire

Acknowledgements

Thank you to **my amazing husband Shane**, for all the support, patience and love you show me every single day. You are so amazing. I love you, always. Sweet nothings.

My children, for remembering mommy loves you even when her make-believe worlds claim her. Your dreams can happen kiddos, remember that.

My parents, for always believing in me, no matter what.

Zach, for giving me the inspiration and strength to create this world.

Kimmel, for pushing me on and rooting for me every step of the crazy way. **Keary**, for all your advice, tips, and mutual crazy writer mama moments. I love you both.

My beta readers: Kimmel, Keary, Teri, Jessie, Nick, Megan and Kelsey. Thank you for reading this in all its rawness and still pushing me to finish. Honestly, I couldn't have done it without you.

Allie, for sharing your natural beauty with my cover.

Vince James Photography, for creating my first every author photo. You made this even more real for me!

NaNoWriMo, for finally giving me that incentive I needed to get this thing done. Thanks to you, I am no longer a "one day" novelist, but a true blue author. What a ride!

My blogging community, for following me along the way amidst all my rants and raves.

My friends and family, who never let me live my "I will be an author" boast down. You all keep me going.

My Heavenly Father, for giving me this priceless gift in my life.

And last but most definitely not least –
Thank YOU: For giving my book, and me, a chance.

Jenni Merritt was born and raised on a small island in the Puget Sound. From a young age she discovered and fell in love with the world of writing and has been happily obsessed ever since. She is now married to the love of her life, and has two crazy but amazing little boys. When not busying herself with being a stay-at-home mom, writing books, keeping her blog, and diving into photography, Jenni sometimes manages to snag some much needed sleep.

Prison Nation is Jenni's first finished novel.

To learn more about Jenni and her writing process, visit her blog at: **jennimerritt.blogspot.com**

16631565R00161

Made in the USA
Charleston, SC
03 January 2013